RECEIVED

SEP 19 2013

WASHOE COUNTY LIBRARY SYSTEM
RENO, NEVADA

THE HIDDEN DEEP

THRESHOLD SERIES

THE HIDDEN DEEP

BOOK TWO

CHRISTA KINDE

ZONDERVAN.com/
AUTHORTRACKER
follow your favorite authors

ZONDERKIDZ

The Hidden Deep
Copyright © 2013 by Christa Kinde

This title is also available as a Zondervan ebook.
Visit www.zondervan.com/ebooks.

Requests for information should be addressed to:

Zondervan, 5300 Patterson Ave SE, Grand Rapids, Michigan 49530

Library of Congress Cataloging-in-Publication Data

Kinde, Christa.
The hidden deep / by Christa Kinde.
p. cm. – (Threshold series ; bk. two)
ISBN 978-0-310-72489-6 (hardcover)
1. Angels—Juvenile fiction. 2. Demonology—Juvenile fiction. 3. Christian life—Juvenile fiction. 4. Families—Juvenile fiction. [1. Angels—Fiction. 2. Demonology—Fiction. 3. Christian life—Fiction. 4. Family life—Fiction. 5. Farm life—Fiction.] I. Title.
PZ7.K56584Hid 2013
813.6—dc23 2012044352

All Scripture quotations, unless otherwise indicated, are taken from The Holy Bible, *New International Version®, NIV®*. Copyright © 1973, 1978, 1984, 2011 by Biblica, Inc.™ Used by permission. All rights reserved worldwide.

Any Internet addresses (websites, blogs, etc.) and telephone numbers in this book are offered as a resource. They are not intended in any way to be or imply an endorsement by Zondervan, nor does Zondervan vouch for the content of these sites and numbers for the life of this book.

All rights reserved. No part of this publication may be reproduced, stored in a retrieval system, or transmitted in any form or by any means—electronic, mechanical, photocopy, recording, or any other—except for brief quotations in printed reviews, without the prior permission of the publisher.

Published in association with KLO Publishing Service, LLC.
(www.KLOPublishing.com)

Zonderkidz is a trademark of Zondervan.

Cover design: Cindy Davis
Editor: Kim Childress
Interior design and composition: Greg Johnson/Textbook Perfect

Printed in the United States of America

---

13 14 15 16 17 18 /DCI/ 20 19 18 17 16 15 14 13 12 11 10 9 8 7 6 5 4 3 2 1

For all those who forge families —
May yours know the sweetness of home.

TABLE OF CONTENTS

1

THE NAMING DEBACLE

Milo cut through the air, skimming across shifting beams of light with what *looked* like reckless abandon. However, this angel had learned caution. Though there was joy in his flight, he continuously scanned above and below for signs of danger. Just off his flank, a flare of dusky purple revealed the presence of his armor-clad companion. Taweel flew with sword in hand, ready to defend his teammate.

"Race you back!" Milo challenged, folding outstretched wings and streaking through a sky as blue as his eyes.

With a soft grunt that may have been amusement, the Guardian followed.

Just north of the small town of West Edinton, the Messenger banked into a steep spiral that ended with an expert flick and fold, then he climbed back into the driver's seat of his old, green car. Checking his reflection in the rear-view mirror, Milo ran his hand over short-cropped blond curls and buckled the seat belt across his mailman's uniform. As the engine rumbled to life, Taweel leaned down to peer through the open window.

"We'll try again after I finish my route," Milo promised. Then he put the car in gear and took off down the road, kicking up gravel and a small cloud of dust.

Prissie and her next-younger brother Beau climbed onto the white-painted plank fence that stood behind the twin mailboxes at the end of their long driveway. An oval sign showing an overflowing basket of apples proudly announced *Pomeroy Orchard*, and the block letters on the pair of red and white flags on either side of the gate let people know that the apple barn was open for business.

Throughout the summer months, afternoons had found Prissie right here, waiting for the mail, but today was different. Today, she was waiting for the school bus. Settling onto her perch, she crossed her ankles in a ladylike manner and smoothed the skirt of her pink and white sundress. "It shouldn't be much longer," she remarked, gazing off in the direction of the highway.

Beau nodded. He never said much. To be honest, Prissie was a little surprised the thirteen-year-old had volunteered to join her. He usually buried himself in a book or spent time on the computer after school. Their bus had dropped them off nearly an hour ago, but they were waiting on Zeke and Jude, who would be arriving on the elementary bus.

Six-year-old Jude was going to school "for real" this year.

According to him, kindergarten was just a warm-up, but he was finally following in the footsteps of his older siblings. At Momma's request, all of the Pomeroy kids were sticking around the house to have milk and cookies with the little guy to celebrate his milestone. Prissie and Beau listened closely for the telltale rumble of an engine, but the only sound was the lazy buzz of the bees that droned in the riot of purple coneflowers that Grandma Nell had planted around the mailboxes.

"You think the bus will beat Milo?" Beau asked.

Prissie favored her brother with a long look, trying to decide if he was teasing her. Milo Leggett was a long-time family friend, and her fondness for him was something of a sore spot. Everyone in town knew the young man, but Prissie always thought of him as *theirs*. He went to their church, taught Zeke's Sunday school class, and regularly dropped in to chat since their farm was the last stop on his route. Milo's visits had been a cause for excitement ever since she was a little girl because he was *special*. Of course, up until this last July, she hadn't realized just *how* special.

There was no sly glint in Beau's blue eyes, so Prissie resisted the urge to snip. "It'll probably be close. They might even get here at the same time."

"Jude would like that," he remarked thoughtfully.

Privately hoping Milo's timing was providential today, she replied, "It *would* be nice."

Another minute ticked by before Beau spoke again. "Say, Priss ... about Koji." He peeked at her out of the corner of his eye.

Prissie began to fiddle with the end of one honey-colored braid. Was *this* why Beau was here? In a house as crowded as theirs, it wasn't easy to hold a private conversation, and it was even harder to find a time when Prissie and Koji weren't together. The boy probably would have been with her now except that he'd begged Grandpa Pete to let him help out with the farm animals. Tad was showing Koji the ropes of his new responsibilities.

"Did he do okay at school today?"

"Of course!" she said defensively. "I made sure of it!"

Officially, Koji was an exchange student who was boarding with the Pomeroy family for the year. To everyone else, he seemed like an overly curious boy with exotic features — golden skin, almond-shaped eyes, and glossy, black, shoulder-length hair. Her whole family believed he was from a set of tiny islands in the middle of the Pacific.

Only Prissie knew the truth.

Meeting Koji had been an accident, or at least something that didn't happen very often. For reasons no one yet understood, Prissie had spotted the young angel watching her from a branch in one of her grandfather's apple trees. In the weeks after that first meeting, one thing led to another. Or maybe it was better to say that one angel led to another.

Prissie had discovered that angels were living as regular people in and around West Edinton. It had been hard learning that Milo was one of them. Their mailman was a Messenger, as was his mentor, Harken Mercer, who owned a used bookstore on Main Street. After getting over her initial shock, they'd introduced her to Baird and Kester, "Worshipers" who led music at the DeeVee, a church down in Harper.

Since then, she'd met or heard about other varieties of angels. Each had a special role. For instance, Koji was an apprentice Observer, and he was thrilled by his chance to live as a human instead of just watching them from afar. For the most part, Prissie didn't mind having him around. Koji's delight was contagious. He'd proven himself a good friend, but it was still difficult to reconcile everyday things with the fantastical ones she'd witnessed.

Beau stared up into the sky. "Koji can be strange."

"How do you mean?" Prissie asked carefully.

"Well, I know he's from another country and everything, but some of the questions he asks are way out there. It's almost like he's from another planet."

She rolled her eyes. "He's not an alien."

"I know, I know," Beau muttered. "But sometimes he takes foreign to a whole different level. Have you ever tried to explain sneezing to someone? And he'd never tasted bananas before."

"Maybe they don't have them where he comes from?"

"I checked online. That island where he's from has whole banana plantations."

"I'll tell him not to bug you with such weird questions."

"I don't mind," Beau quickly assured. "His questions make me think, and it's kind of interesting to try to answer them."

Prissie frowned. Beau didn't speak up unless he had something to say, and it felt as though he was still working up to it. "I think Koji looks at things differently than most people," she suggested.

"Do you know that he'd never used nail clippers before? He watched me trim mine, then asked me to do his, too."

"That was nice of you," she said nervously.

Beau shrugged. "It's kind of like having another little brother, except that he's older than me. *You're* his favorite, though. Does Margery know she's been displaced?"

Prissie's expression clouded. "I doubt she minds." She and her best friend Margery had drifted apart over the summer. Since Prissie needed to show Koji around, she'd barely said two words to her in school today. Not that Margery noticed. *She'd* been busy giving the grand tour to Elise Hanson — another newcomer to West Edinton.

Her brother took a deep breath. "You're not going to ditch Koji, are you?"

"*What*?" she exclaimed.

With a determined expression, Beau forged ahead. "I know you don't mind being his best friend around here, but how are you going to treat him when other people are around? You might get teased because he's different."

With flashing eyes and flaming cheeks, Prissie demanded, "You think I'd be that awful to someone?"

"Hope not," he muttered.

He dropped his gaze, but his back was straight, and that meant he was sticking by his question. She scowled. "There's no way! Koji's *ours* now, and I'm not letting *anyone* make fun of him!"

"Ours, huh?" Beau looked embarrassed and relieved at the same time, as if his almost-accusation had been as hard for him to say as it had been for her to hear. "So you really *are* okay with him and his weirdness?"

"Obviously."

"Good."

Although Beau let the subject drop, Prissie's conscience nagged at her. It was easy to overlook Koji's bizarre qualities because she knew he was an angel. If he'd been a regular boy, would she treat him the same way? Thankfully, she didn't have to answer that question. Just then, the school bus swung into view—right behind an old, green car. "Milo!" she cheered, immediately feeling better.

There were times when Prissie hated how crowded and noisy her house could get, but there were also times when she wouldn't trade the hubbub for the world. Today, she was glad to be part of a big family.

Momma herded everyone into the kitchen, where Grandma Nell lifted fresh cookies onto cooling racks, filling the room with the mouthwatering smell of melting chocolate. Grandpa Pete found an excuse to come in for a cup of coffee, but even with Milo and Koji added to the mix, there was no need to squeeze around the sturdy kitchen table. It had been built to serve a crowd.

Questions and answers flew through the air as notes were compared. Yes, Prissie's oft-rehearsed fears of alphabetical seating arrangements had been realized. No, Zeke's teacher hadn't fainted dead away at the sight of him. She'd taught Neil, after all. She was brave. Yes, the school bus driver still listened to country music while he drove. No, Beau hadn't forgotten his lunch box in his locker. He was turning over a new leaf now that he was out of elementary school.

Milo was right in the thick of things. He asked Tad if he'd still have time to work on the old truck he was rebuilding now that classes were back in session, and he checked with Neil to see if the football coach had finalized the roster for Friday's game. However, it didn't take long for Zeke and Jude to mob the mailman, eager to share their grade school adventures.

As the conversation took a turn to pencil sharpeners and dodgeball, Koji claimed a place at Prissie's side. "I *drove*!" he whispered eagerly.

"Tad let you drive the quad?" she asked, amused by his excitement. All the Pomeroys learned to drive as soon as their feet reached the pedals of the various mowers and tractors on the farm. One of the jobs Grandpa had given Koji was to help Tad feed and water the pigs, and since their shed was in the back forty, they used a four-wheeler to drive out there.

Koji nodded. "We took them apple mash from the cider press, and I tried to use the pump. It was difficult, but Tad is quite able."

"It sounds like you had fun, but it's a lot *less* fun if the weather's bad," Prissie warned.

"I will not neglect the task your grandfather entrusted to me," Koji promised.

When they turned their attention back to the group, her family was a sight to behold. Prissie shook her head at the level of ridiculousness on display, but with five brothers, she'd come to expect it. She knew from experience that it could get much, *much* worse.

"Beat this!" Neil gloated.

"Mine's better!" Zeke argued.

"Milo's dripping," said Jude with a giggle.

Koji gazed around the table in fascination, then leaned close to whisper, "What is the goal of this contest?"

"No point," Prissie said. "Just silliness."

Zeke crossed his eyes as he tried to catch a glimpse of his milk moustache, and Jude beamed up at Tad. "Come on, Prissie," coaxed Neil. "Don't be such a stick in the mud!"

Even Milo's smile wasn't enough to tempt her into joining in. "No thank you. I prefer to drink my milk, not wear it. Who started this, anyhow?"

Everyone immediately pointed to Milo, who sheepishly

reached for a napkin. Prissie looked at him with raised eyebrows. "Sorry, Miss Priscilla." Once she'd accepted his apology with a smile, he cheerfully changed the subject. "It sounds like everyone made it through their first day intact."

"Not me!" Beau replied with a groan. "Mr. Hawkins started roll call before I could tell him not to use my full name!"

"So it's out," Tad said sympathetically.

"Maybe no one noticed?" Prissie ventured, earning a flat look.

"It will take *months* to live this down," the thirteen-year-old grumbled.

Koji looked from one sibling to the next. "What are you talking about?"

"Names," Tad supplied.

"My name isn't *really* Beau," the middle brother explained. "That's my nickname. It's short for ... my full name."

Neil reached for another chocolate chip cookie, then shook it at Koji. "We who bear the name of Pomeroy share a tragic flaw, handed down to us by our parents." Glancing around the table, the sixteen-year-old asked, "Shall we let him in on our darkest secret?"

"Why not?" Tad replied with a friendly smile. "I think he'll keep quiet."

Koji's eyes widened. "Thank you for your trust."

"Okay, then," Neil agreed, picking up his tale. "It may interest you to know that Momma and Dad gave all of us Bible names."

The young angel looked from one sibling to the next, then glanced toward Mrs. Pomeroy, who stood on the other side of the kitchen. Naomi had obviously heard these grievances many times before, and her gray eyes were dancing. "I think they're fine names," Momma said, trading an amused glance with her mother-in-law.

"Very traditional," Grandma Nell agreed.

"And very unfortunate," countered Neil.

Tipping his head to one side, Koji said, "I do not recognize most of your names from Scripture."

"We shortened them," Beau said with a disapproving look in his mother's direction.

Tad took this as his cue, folding his hands on the table and fixing Koji with a serious gaze. "I don't like it to get around, but my full name is Thaddeus," he revealed. "I've been calling myself Tad since the first grade."

"Indeed," Koji replied before looking to the next brother. "Neil is short for...?"

"Cornelius," he replied with a grimace.

"I might have guessed that one," Koji replied. Gazing into Prissie's face he asked, "Are you unhappy with your name?"

She shook her head, but admitted, "I do usually introduce myself as Prissie, though."

"Aquilla and Priscilla were lovely people," Milo interjected.

Prissie blinked in surprise. It sounded like the Messenger had known them. Was it possible for Milo to be *that* old?

Koji's dark eyes sparkled with interest as he looked at eight-year-old Zeke. The boy's unruly mop of blond hair was a testament to his energetic nature. "Zeke must be short for Ezekiel?"

"Nope. Hezekiah," announced the boy.

"Is that worse?" inquired the young angel curiously.

"*Way* worse."

Turning to the humiliated teen, Koji asked, "What is Beau short for?" The teen put his hands over his face and mumbled his reply, but the young angel's ears were sharp. "Your name is Boaz?"

"The kinsman redeemer," Mrs. Pomeroy said with a dreamy sigh. "I just love his and Ruth's story! *So* romantic!"

One blue eye peeped out long enough to roll expressively. "Maybe so, but that doesn't mean you should inflict his name on a poor, unsuspecting baby."

"What is Jude short for?" Koji inquired, looking at the youngest family member. "Judah?"

Neil leaned forward. "Here's the thing. When Momma was expecting Jude, we ganged up and issued a formal protest. All of us are stuck with impossible handles, but we thought the new little twerp should be spared the indignity."

Tad nodded. "We begged our folks to come up with a name that wasn't embarrassing."

"Of course, Momma didn't want to settle on something *easy* like John or Mark," Neil continued. "She said those were too *boring*."

"Calling him Jude was a compromise," Mrs. Pomeroy said as she nibbled her own cookie. "Short, but different enough to be interesting.

"So we call him Judicious, just to be contrary," Tad concluded.

Koji smiled at the littlest brother, who was obviously proud of both his name and the story behind it.

Once the conversation moved on, the young Observer nudged Prissie with his elbow and confided, "Koji is my nickname, too."

"Really? What's your full name?"

"I cannot tell," he admitted. "It is a name only known to me and the One who gave it."

"Only God knows your real name?" she asked, mystified.

The angel searched her face, then nodded once. "It will be the same for you one day."

Prissie's brows rose. "Don't be ridiculous. Everyone already knows my name."

With a hint of a smile, Koji replied, "You will be given a new one. It is promised."

"Oh," she replied blankly. After some thought, she had to admit she was looking forward to finding out what her new name might be.

Later that evening, Prissie stood beside Grandma Nell at the stove, carefully stirring applesauce so it wouldn't scorch. During harvesttime, this was pretty much a daily chore, and the two of them had the routine down pat. The only difference this year was the addition of a new helper. While Grandma Nell ladled hot, cinnamon-spiked sauce into gleaming jars, Koji added the lids. When they were done, Prissie's grandmother tallied up the quarts. "Two more batches should do it, so report for duty again tomorrow night."

"Isn't this more than last year?" Prissie ventured as she lugged the big pot over to the sink to wash up.

"We have an extra mouth to feed this year," Grandma Nell countered, smiling Koji's way.

Once the kitchen was restored to order, Prissie's mind turned to homework and the reading she needed to do for the week, but Koji tapped her shoulder. "I am going outside to talk with the others for a while," he said quietly.

Prissie's heart sped up. "May I come along?"

The boy's face brightened. "I would like that."

Since the evenings were growing chilly, she slipped a sweater over her light dress and followed Koji onto the back porch. Stars were already out, and for several moments, the young angel stared up at them. "They will come to us," Koji announced.

Prissie often wondered how he knew where his teammates were, what they were doing, and sometimes even what kind of mood they were in. She guessed it was probably the same as her and Grandma making applesauce. He'd learned their routine and knew what to do. Either that, or he'd received a message. It was strange to think that Koji could *hear* God, and even stranger to think that God would pass along a time and place for a meeting.

Tansy offered a soft meow from the seat she'd claimed on the porch swing, and Prissie soon had a lapful of purring barn cat. Koji sat on the steps, his dark eyes fixed on a point in the distance. "What do you see?" she whispered, hoping she would get to visit with Omri again.

"Jedrick is coming!"

"Is that good or bad?" she asked nervously. Koji didn't have time to answer before there was a silent explosion of green light just beyond the garden. Though she'd only seen the phenomenon a few times before, Prissie vividly remembered the beautiful shifting patterns of light and color that made up an angel's wings.

"He is here," Koji announced unnecessarily.

A towering, armor-clad figure strode up the walk, and as he drew nearer, a second angel slipped out of the shadows just beyond the hydrangeas lining the porch. Prissie tried not to stare but failed miserably. Angelic warriors were huge, well-armed, and actually kind of scary, so it was hard to look away, especially once she realized that even without the porch light on, she could see them quite well. It was as if they brought their own light with them into the darkness. Could this be an angel's halo?

Rich green fell from Jedrick's shoulders, flowing almost like a cloak or cape as he strode forward on booted feet. "Are you well, Prissie Pomeroy?" inquired the stern-faced warrior. Jedrick was a Protector, and he was captain of the team of angels that Milo, Koji, and the rest belonged to. His light brown hair was cropped close around his head except for one long braid, which hung over his left shoulder; the jeweled pommel of the sword strapped to his back was visible over his right.

His inquiry was hard to answer. It felt like a trick question. Up until a few moments ago, Prissie had been just fine, but Jedrick's arrival brought back unsettling memories and made her wonder if there were invisible enemies prowling around in the dark. She hugged her cat close and shrugged.

Just behind him stood Tamaes, a Guardian whose long, brown hair only partially covered the jagged scar that marred his otherwise handsome face. He stepped forward. "Do not be afraid, little one," he said gently. "Jedrick is *not* here because of danger nearby."

Jedrick looked sharply at his companion, then his expression altered subtly. Though his face lost none of its fierce quality, the Protector's green eyes softened somewhat. "On the contrary, it is a quiet night."

Prissie glanced at Tamaes. It was irksome that he had known exactly what was on her mind, but she shouldn't have been surprised. Tamaes was her guardian angel. Since the moment her life began, he'd been watching over her. It made sense that he would understand how she felt. He looked as though he wanted to say more, but was too bashful to get it out. Instead, Tamaes gazed at her with undisguised fondness, and she was the one who glanced away.

Koji joined her on the porch swing and touched the back of her hand. When she met his earnest gaze, he said, "Prissie, I would not lead you into danger."

"There *are* things to be afraid of, though."

"Indeed," Koji said.

A war was being waged, and there were enemies so terrible, she'd been told to be grateful they were hidden from her eyes. But here and now, she was as safe as she could be. If only things could stay this way. "So why *are* you here?" she asked in a quiet voice.

"I am often here," Jedrick replied, looking amused. "My responsibilities keep me close."

"What are those?" she asked.

The captain folded his muscular arms and cocked his head to one side. "I protect those in my Flight, and we each have our role to fill. Some stand guard over that which is ours to keep. Some seek that which has been lost. Some can only watch and wait."

Prissie glanced at Koji, whose pensive face was once more turned skyward. "That which has been lost? Do you mean Ephron?" she asked carefully. Ephron was Koji's predecessor, an apprentice Observer who'd been taken by the enemy.

"I do," Jedrick confirmed. "Koji, I need to ask you to tell me more about your dream."

"He was somewhere close. Somewhere dark," the boy replied.

This was nothing new, but his captain nodded encouragingly. "Go on."

"He was hurt. Frightened." Koji's voice trembled. "And he said he would keep your trust no matter what else was taken."

Jedrick exchanged a long look with Tamaes before saying, "They *are* questioning him. It is as Abner feared."

Tamaes winced. "It is my fault."

"Do not think it," Jedrick said. "None of us can take the blame for those who chose to fall."

"What do they mean?" Prissie whispered to Koji.

He looked at her with sorrowful eyes. "Ephron came to visit Tamaes on the day he was taken. The enemy captured him *here*, in your family's orchard."

2

THE BUMPER CROP

Kester let himself into his mentor's apartment and eyed the walls with thinly veiled amusement. Baird's tastes were as understated as his personality. The red wall had a teal door, and the door on the turquoise wall was orange. Instead of proper furnishings, bright beanbag chairs were piled in one corner of the living area. Baird didn't bother with anything more since the room was mostly used for band rehearsals. At the moment, he was slouched in a purple beanbag with his guitar across his lap, fingers idly running through chords on the frets.

Kester noted that the other Worshiper looked more than a little lost. "Is something wrong?"

"Not sure."

"I brought the revised *Messiah* score," Kester said. "Would you like to go through it?"

"I don't feel like singing," Baird confessed in a weary voice.

The tall angel crossed to his mentor and knelt before him. "Sing with me."

The redhead lifted old eyes and shook his head. "I'm songed out."

"Impossible," Kester replied calmly. "Sing with me, and you will remember joy."

Baird smiled crookedly. "Promise?"

"Most assuredly."

The Pomeroys lived on an apple orchard, but farming wasn't the *only* family business. Jayce Pomeroy owned the bakery on Main Street. Loafing Around would be celebrating its twentieth year this coming spring, and Prissie's dad regularly hinted that he was cooking up something special for the anniversary. He often proposed crazy ideas at the dinner table, but his actual plans were veiled in secrecy.

"Apron," Auntie Lou said, handing Prissie one of her father's crisp white chef's aprons. While Prissie slipped it on and knotted the ties, the woman pulled open a drawer, counted out four forks, and set them beside the small stack of plates already waiting on the big work table in the center of the room. One of the secrets to the bakery's success was Louise Cook. She was a tiny woman in her late sixties who favored flowery aprons, and she was probably the only person in the world who could boss around Jayce in his own kitchen.

The back door swung open, and Prissie's father strolled through with Ransom close on his heels. Each of them carried a bushel basket of apples, which they added to the lineup on one of the side tables. "This is the last of them," Jayce announced brightly. "Are you ready to start, Princess?"

"*Dad,*" Prissie protested with a sidelong glance at the teenager who slouched over the sink, washing up.

With an unapologetic grin, Jayce pulled his daughter into a one-armed hug and stage whispered, "Sorry, my girl. Don't mind me."

They'd been up with the chickens and out the door before anyone else in the house was stirring — just the two of them. It was a big deal to have one-on-one time with Dad, and Prissie was beside herself with excitement over his plans for this morning. He'd been so impressed by the recipe she'd developed for the pie baking competition at their county fair that he wanted to add it to the short list of limited edition pies they sold during the fall. Today, Prissie was going to teach her dad and Auntie Lou how to make her Candy Apple Pie. The only downside was the fact that Ransom had horned in on the lesson.

Ransom Pavlos was in Prissie's class at school, and he was probably the most annoying person she knew. It had come as a big surprise when her dad announced that Ransom wanted to learn the baking trade. She'd tried to tell her dad what kind of a person the boy was, but all of her warnings had fallen on deaf ears. Jayce hired him anyhow. Prissie cast a mopey glance at her classmate, and he quirked a brow in return as he calmly fitted a hairnet over his bush of brown hair.

"We have two hours before I need to drive you two over to school," Jayce said, calling them to order. "Let's start with a sample, shall we?"

Prissie lifted her test pie out of its carrier and set it beside the plates and forks. It didn't look like much on the outside.

The plain crust was all lumpy and bumpy from the apples inside, and it was just an ordinary golden-brown. Since Auntie Lou's pies were real show-stoppers, Prissie was pretty embarrassed that her meager skills were getting so much attention. The woman smiled encouragingly as she handed Prissie a knife.

"You do the honors, dear."

Prissie was very conscious of Ransom's scrutiny as she lifted out the first piece and placed it on a plate. Mercifully, the pie didn't fall apart on her. "Pink!" he exclaimed with an odd smile on his face.

"Such a lovely shade," cooed Auntie Lou, who passed the slice to Jayce.

By the time Prissie took a bite, Ransom had already inhaled his piece and was poking through the bushel baskets. "Six kinds of apples?" he asked curiously. "Isn't that a little much?"

Jayce shook his head. "This pie is so good because it has depth ... complexity. Each variety of apple contributes something the other varieties lack. Sweetness, tartness, flavor, texture."

"And color," Ransom said, eyeing the unusual pink cast.

The blush of the apples was nothing compared to the color rising in Prissie's cheeks as she withdrew a folded paper from the pocket of her skirt and clutched it protectively to her heart. This recipe was special to her for a few reasons, and it was hard to give it away. "There's a secret to the recipe."

"One we'll keep!" her father assured. When Prissie frowned in Ransom's direction, Jayce patted her shoulder reassuringly. "He's already agreed to keep trade secrets."

"Go on, honey. Tell us how it's done!" Auntie Lou urged.

With a tentative smile at her father, Prissie relinquished the recipe. Jayce unfolded the paper and glanced over the instructions with a gleam in his eye. Then, he spread it out on the table so Lou and Ransom could read his daughter's neatly written instructions.

The old lady chortled. "I thought the name referred to the *color*!"

"How long did it take to figure out the proportions for each kind of apple?" asked her father.

"Koji and I must have tried it ten different ways," she admitted. "We didn't get it just right until a couple days before the fair."

Ransom had been reading more slowly than the others because his eyebrows didn't shoot up until right then. "Are you *kidding*?" he asked, pointing to the last line in the recipe. "You actually went a little crazy, didn't you?"

Prissie moved to the coat hooks by the back door. Fishing out a heavy paper sack from her purse, she returned and carefully spilled the contents onto the worktable. The dark red wrappers of cinnamon penny candy from the corner store gleamed against the dull silver of stainless steel. "We were out of cinnamon, so I used these instead," she replied defensively.

"Oh, don't get me wrong," he said, giving her father a sheepish look. "It's good and all. I'm just surprised."

Jayce grinned boyishly. "Some of the best recipes have an unexpected twist."

"Let's get started," Lou said. "Those apples aren't going to peel themselves!"

Moments later, Ransom exclaimed, "Whoa! These are pretty cool!" He'd chosen one of Great-grandmother Mae's favorites apples and discovered the distinctive rose-colored flesh under its pale green skin.

"Aren't they, though?" Prissie's father reached for one and showed off his knife skills, creating a long, unbroken spiral of pink and green. "My grandmother had a real fondness for the color pink, and the apple doesn't fall far from the tree," he said, winking at Prissie. "My grandfather sent for these trees to please her. There's a whole row in the orchard, and these apples were the key to her signature pink applesauce."

Prissie frowned as she worked on one of the other five varieties, an apple as tart as her mood. She didn't think it was any of Ransom's business knowing one of their family's stories, and it bugged her to see how he hung on her father's every word. After all her excitement about spending time with her dad and making her pie together, Jayce was paying more attention to Ransom. It wasn't fair!

Jayce pared a few more apples before leaving the rest of the prep to his able-bodied assistants. Soon, the smell of proofing yeast filled the kitchen, and a batch of poppy seed muffins found its way into the oven. More strong scents filled the air as he chopped rosemary, roasted garlic, and grated nutmeg, and slowly, Prissie began to relax. The bakery was *her* home away from home, and Ransom couldn't take that away.

As they worked, Prissie was pleased to note that she was quicker and neater than her rival. She was mightily peeved that he'd taken all the pink apples for himself, but it looked as though she would be able to finish all the rest before he got through his pile. True, there were smaller quantities of the other varieties, but it was sort of comforting to know she was better than him.

Somewhere along the way, Prissie realized that she missed Koji's company. If the young angel had been there, he would have asked her a hundred questions about everything from their upcoming group social studies project to the reason why cinnamon candy was red when cinnamon was brown. Busywork was nicer if you had someone to chat with, but there was no way she was going to make small talk with *Ransom*. She eyed his progress critically. "You're cutting those pieces wrong."

"You think?" he asked, holding up a chunk of pink apple.

"They're too fat," she pronounced, picking up a long, thin wedge from her own board. "This shape is better."

"You *do* realize it all bakes down to mush?" he inquired, a teasing lilt to his tone.

Prissie's eyes narrowed. "My pie is not mushy!"

Ransom just smirked and turned toward her father. "Hey, Mr. Pomeroy." Holding up the small chunk of fruit, he asked, "Is this okay?"

Jayce glanced over. "Sure, sure. Keep up the good work," he replied distractedly.

The teen quirked a brow at her as he answered, "Yes, sir!"

"Oh, *fine*," she grumbled, returning her attention to her own pile of fruit, which she stubbornly continued to slice the correct way.

In due course, the apples were reduced to six mounds. "I can manage this part if you two take care of those candies," she prompted.

"Sure," Ransom replied. He nabbed one and popped it out of its red wrapper. "So what are we talking about here? Do you use a food processor?"

"Mortar and pestle?" Jayce suggested.

Prissie shook her head and admitted, "Koji and I used a hammer."

The teen's eyes lit up. "Oh, I am *all over* that!" He rummaged in a drawer and came up with a mallet, then rounded on the small pile of candies. "Let's do this!"

With a steely look, Prissie removed the last of the cinnamon candies from its wrapper, and placed them all inside a plastic bag. Holding out her hand for the mallet, she said, "Let me take care of it. I can tell you're going to get carried away."

"No way! I called dibs on the candy-smashing!"

"Don't be ridiculous."

"Aw, c'mon, Miss Priss," he wheedled. "You can supervise!"

"He'll be handling the job from now on," Jayce interjected, giving his daughter a pointed look. "Let him get a feel for it."

With a sour expression, she relented, handing over the bag of candy. Ransom took it over to one of the wooden counters and stood with hammer poised. Glancing expectantly her way, he asked, "Pebbles or dust?"

"Pebbles would be too big, but I don't want dust," Prissie said with authority. "Sand is best."

"Right," he replied, and the hammer fell.

Prissie watched like a hawk, occasionally offering advice that Ransom mostly ignored. Candy-smashing was hardly rocket science, so after a while, she bit her tongue and watched the steady reduction of red disks into pinkish sugar crystals. He certainly seemed to be enjoying the process, which didn't really surprise her. Ransom's hair was too long, his nose was too big, and he did weird things with his eyebrows ... but deep down, he was no different than any of her brothers. Put simply, he was a *boy*.

As if to prove the point, Prissie's dad strolled over to inspect their progress. "May I?"

Ransom turned over his weapon, and Jayce gave the battered bag a gleeful thwack. Shaking her head, Prissie retreated to the other side of the kitchen to lend a hand to Auntie Lou.

While the boys took turns making rubble, the ladies set up a long line of pie plates and rolled the top crusts. They tossed apples with flour and sugar, then dusted them with powdered cinnamon candies before mounding them in the tins. For a while, there was nothing but chaos, but before Prissie knew it, they were crimping the edges on the last of a dozen pies. Auntie Lou smiled in satisfaction before glancing at the clock. "Jayce, you'd better get those two over to the school. I'll bake these off while you're out."

"Yes, ma'am." Nodding to Prissie and Ransom, he said, "Pull yourselves together. The van leaves in five!"

Prissie washed up, hung her apron, and rolled down her sleeves, rushing through a mental checklist — homework, lunch, library book, gym bag. She'd left everything but her purse in the van, so she thanked Auntie Lou and let herself out. In the alley behind the bakery, she found Ransom already waiting, leaning against the side of the van. Drawing herself up, she said, "You'd better not tell anyone about my recipe."

"It's like your dad said. When I signed on, I swore to keep my yap shut about secret recipes and techniques and stuff. Your pretty, pink pies are safe with me."

His entire attitude was far too flippant. "I don't think my dad should be trusting someone like you."

Ransom cocked a brow at her. "Relax, Miss Priss. I know how to keep a promise."

She almost believed him. But *almost* wasn't enough. This was Ransom, after all.

After school a couple days later, Prissie and Koji hurried across the wide lawn in front of town hall. Passing the post office and the *Herald*'s newspaper office, they turned into a small, secondhand bookstore called The Curiosity Shop. They'd skimped on their library time in order to stop in and talk to Harken.

Soft chimes sounded as they slipped through the door, and Harken looked up with a ready smile. "Prissie Pomeroy!" he greeted in a booming voice. "What brings you to my humble establishment?"

"You!" she blurted.

The old gentleman chuckled and stepped out from behind the counter. "Well, now, that's gratifying. It's been too long since you visited."

"Sorry."

"No apologies, Prissie. We've all been busy lately."

She clasped her hands together, suddenly worried that her timing was bad. "That's *true*," she murmured uncertainly.

Koji smiled encouragingly. "There is no one else here. It is safe to ask."

Prissie nodded and glanced back at Harken, who was at once strange and familiar. She'd known him all her life because he'd been a good friend to her father since Jayce was her age, and her mother loved to poke around his shop, looking for bookish treasures. It had been a big shock to learn that the old man wasn't *really* old ... or a man, for that matter. Harken was a Messenger like Milo.

The elderly man gazed at her with a mixture of affection and amusement. "Do you have a question for me, Prissie?"

"Could you deliver a message for me?"

Harken's smile widened. "That happens to be a specialty of mine. Who is it for?"

"You and Milo and Baird and Kester," she rattled off, talking too fast in her nervous excitement.

"A whole company of angels," he replied warmly. "As it happens, Milo is resting in the garden. Shall we join him? Then, you can tell us both at once, and we'll carry your message along to the others."

"Yes, please."

Harken gestured for her to go ahead, and she gladly stepped into the back room. On the far wall, there were two doors — one green, one blue. The green one led to the parking lot behind the store, but the blue door was miraculous. Old and ornate, its carvings of flowers, fruit, and leaves surrounded a pair of trees with intertwining branches. The knob seemed to be made from living crystal, gleaming with shifting colors; when Prissie took hold and turned, it hummed beneath her palm.

Beyond the blue door lay a forest glade that wasn't so much *outside* as it was outside of time. Light rippled and swirled like water in the sky overhead, and soft grass covered the ground. Koji immediately shed shoes and socks and jogged across the meadow toward their friend. Milo was sprawled on his back with his arms behind his head, smiling up at a flock of bright lights that danced above him like fireflies.

Koji all but tackled the unsuspecting mailman, who laughed. "I can tell you've been living with the Pomeroys. You're picking up some of their habits!"

"I have not been here for many days," the young Observer declared happily. "My heart is full!"

Milo ruffled the boy's hair. "Dreams help, but it's not the same," he agreed. "C'mere and rest a while."

Without hesitation, Koji flopped onto his back and spread his arms wide, closing his eyes with a gusty sigh of contentment.

Harken and Prissie reached them, and suddenly worried, she asked Koji, "Do we need to bring you into town more often?"

He peeped at her with one eye, then shook his head. "This light is not required for my subsistence, but I long for it."

With half her attention already caught by the tiny fairy-like angels flitting around them, Prissie asked, "Why?"

The boy's eyes opened fully, and he gazed at her with disconcerting steadiness, which always made her feel as if he could see right to her heart. "Can you not feel a difference?" Stretching his hand toward the sky, he added, "This is unlike starlight."

"I guess I didn't notice," she said, looking at the sky. "It's as bright as the sun."

"The sun *is* a star," Harken gently reminded.

"Oh, right," she muttered, feeling silly.

The shopkeeper patted her shoulder. "The reason young Koji finds so much delight in this place is because we're closer to home here. This is heaven's light."

Prissie's eyes widened, and she managed a dazed, "I had no idea."

Milo smiled up at her. "Now that you know, pay more attention. This is something you'll want to remember."

"I don't see how I could forget," she replied. Then, her

attention was caught once more by Abner's flock. "Are these guys as friendly as Omri?" she whispered to Harken.

The old man's soft chuckle sent the tiny angels into excited spirals. "Have the yahavim charmed you?" he asked, beckoning her closer. "Taweel's little companion is quite possibly the boldest of his kind, but since you can see them, they may respond to your wishes. Like so." Harken extended his hand and crooked his fingers.

Immediately, three of the luminous figures separated from the rest and zipped over. Prissie squinted, for the yahavim were so bright, they were hard to look at. Mimicking the Messenger's stance, she tried to coax one over, and to her delight, one of the tiny creatures dipped closer, then settled on her hand. For several breathless moments, the two simply stared at each other.

When she'd first seen the yahavim, Prissie mistook them for fairies, but Harken had explained that they were the lowest order of angels. They were sort of like pets, not clever enough to talk, but very responsive to the needs of those they served. It was their job to make manna, the food of angels, and in Prissie's opinion, they were the cutest things *ever.*

This particular little manna-maker had chin-length blue hair tucked behind pointed ears. His translucent wings reminded her of a dragonfly's, and his pixie face was dominated by a pair of slanted eyes that had no whites. When he blinked, their faceted depths swirled with jewel-like colors. "Hello," she said with a soft smile. The little fellow considered her for several long moments, than sat down on her palm, tucking his knees up under his chin and wiggling his tiny toes as he smiled back. Prissie was completely smitten.

Eventually, Harken cleared his throat and gently prompted, "Wasn't there something you wanted to ask us?"

"Oh! Yes," Prissie hastily answered, glancing from Harken to Milo and back again. "Maybe. I mean, if you're not too busy with ... everything?"

Milo rolled into a sitting position and crossed his legs, gazing at her expectantly. "What did you have in mind, Miss Priscilla?"

With a glance at Koji for moral support, she replied, "I'd like to make you all dinner."

3

THE MODEL STUDENT

"I asked around, sir. None of the other Flights have noticed an additional yahavim in their flocks."

Abner frowned somewhat, then announced, "You don't need to call me *sir* when we're not working."

"Yes, sir," his apprentice replied pleasantly.

"Where has my lamb gotten himself off to," grumbled the Caretaker.

"If you don't mind my saying so, he is less a lamb and more a lion."

"It took more courage than sense to leave the safety of the garden," Abner conceded. "Was that all?"

"There *is* one more thing, sir. Harken wants you to know that he passed along your message to his former mentor."

Gray eyes sharpened. "And?"

"He says, 'God has chosen the weak things of the world to put to shame the things which are mighty.' "

Abner slowly removed his glasses. "I wonder why that never occurred to me before?"

"What, sir?"

Shaking his head in a solemn manner, he replied, "Perhaps Lavi was *Sent*."

Prissie liked school. Her teachers had always put a great deal of faith in her, and she tried her best to earn their approval. Over the years, she'd climbed through the ranks, from gerbil monitor to crossing guard, from model student to class representative. A few people called her a goodie-two-shoes and the teacher's pet, but Prissie didn't care. She worked hard to maintain her rank and reputation within the classroom, and she walked through the school halls with her head held high.

"I still can't believe your locker *just happened* to be next to mine," Prissie said as she stowed her math things. "Did someone somewhere pull some strings?"

Koji twirled the dial on his combination lock. "It is a providential placement."

Social studies was their last class of the day, and she reached for her textbook. Excited voices and slamming doors filled the busy hallway, but it was easy to tune out the clamor. "It's been a week. How do you like school so far?" she asked curiously.

"It is very interesting."

Prissie lowered her voice a little and asked, "Is it like the school you used to go to? In heaven?"

Koji pursed his lips, then answered, "In some ways. There was more singing."

"You could join the choir, I suppose," Prissie suggested.

"Are you in the choir?"

"Obviously not," she said with a careless shrug. "I've never been very good at singing."

He mimicked her shrug, saying, "Then, I will not."

The young angel's class schedule was identical to hers, right down to the electives, which bothered her a little. Frowning, she pointed out, "You don't have to do *everything* I do."

"I am here so that I can be with you," he replied with a smile.

She couldn't help smiling back. If Koji had been anyone besides himself, Prissie probably would have been annoyed. To other people, he might appear to be one part tag-along, one part stalker, but his constant companionship over the last few days had been a godsend.

Up until this year, Prissie and her best friend, Margery Burke, had always picked up where they left off after the summer break. But things had changed over the summer. Elise Hanson had completely turned Margery's head. Prissie didn't like Elise one bit, and the feeling was mutual. Margery, Jennifer, and April still replied to emails and took her calls, but it wasn't the same. They followed Elise's lead, and whether they meant to or not, they often left Prissie out of the loop.

"You coming, Prissie?" called Jennifer from across the hall.

Brightening, she hurried over to walk next to her friend. Jennifer Ruiz was a bit of an airhead, but her bubbly personality made her popular with just about everyone. She was sweet and silly, and Prissie sort of envied her big brown eyes. At the moment, they were wide with excitement. "Eeee!" Jennifer squealed. "I'm *so* glad that Marcus is in our class again!"

Prissie's lips thinned, but she kept her opinions to herself as she followed Jennifer's gaze to the boy sitting next to Ransom in the back of the classroom. She supposed Marcus was good looking enough. Her friend certainly liked to go on and on about his warm brown skin, full lips, cleft chin, and gold-flecked brown eyes. Still, Prissie didn't really approve of Jennifer's current crush. A wide section of his hair had been bleached platinum blond, and there were rumors about him being shuffled from one foster home to another. You could tell at a glance that he was trouble with a capital T.

Unless you were Jennifer. "I would kill to have lashes like his!" she gushed.

"Everybody has eyelashes," Prissie retorted.

"Not like his!"

The boy in question seemed completely ignorant of his admirer. Slouched in his seat, he tapped his pencil against the desk while listening to Ransom describe something using broad gestures. With a huff, Prissie turned her back on the both of them. Eventually, her friend had to run out of things to drool over. There couldn't be much left. Maybe his shoelaces?

At the last possible second, Prissie marched to her desk and slid into the seat, which was right in front of Ransom's. Only then did she realize that Koji had been quietly following her the whole time. With a little half-smile, he took the desk in front of hers, another *providential* placement. The young Observer was always very attentive — unlike certain class clowns she could mention — and she wholly approved of his serious attitude toward their studies.

The bell sounded in the hallway, and Miss Knowles snapped her fingers for attention. "Today, we'll divide into groups of three for a special project," she announced, looking quite pleased with her plan. Miss Knowles loved group projects; last year, there had been one every couple of months. Prissie didn't particularly like them because she always ended up doing all the work. "Choose your own teams, and be quick about it!" their teacher said with another series of snaps.

Prissie straightened and glanced Margery's way, but the blonde girl was already arm-in-arm with Elise. Koji turned to her with a hopeful expression, and she smiled gratefully. That just left Jennifer and April, who exchanged a long look before parting company. April slipped over and leaned against Prissie's desk. "I'm with you guys," she said, her gray eyes bright behind the rectangular frames of her glasses.

"We are a team," Koji acknowledged seriously.

April Mayfair kept her mousy brown hair in a sleek bob, with baby bangs forming a sharp line across her forehead. She was a smart girl with quick wits and plenty of opinions, and she planned on becoming a journalist. "Are you two sticking around for the pep rally after school?" she asked eagerly.

"Yes!" Prissie confirmed. Tonight was the first home game of the season, and there was no question that all of them would be attending. Margery and Jennifer were both on the cheerleading squad, and April covered the games for the school's paper. Usually, she and Prissie stuck together for at least part of the evening.

However, April nodded. "Perfect! I promised to make sure Elise has fun tonight. Sounds like she wants to stalk some of the players, so we'll probably be on the sidelines, but whatever! You'll be doing the same for Koji, am I right?"

"R-right," Prissie replied brightly, hoping April couldn't

tell how disappointed she was. Why couldn't things go her way for once?

Game nights had been a Pomeroy tradition ever since Neil was in the peewee leagues. Grandpa was a huge football fan, so he'd been delighted that one of his grandsons had taken an early interest in the sport. Neither Tad nor Beau had wanted to play, but Pete was already encouraging Zeke to follow in Neil's footsteps.

Though the whole family didn't always attend every game, the Pomeroys were out in full force tonight. Grandma Nell and Momma carried blankets to sit on, and Beau had a book tucked under his arm. Tad wandered off to talk to some friends, and Jayce tried to corral the two youngest in the stands. Zeke and Jude scampered like monkeys up to the topmost tiers of the bleachers, with the rest following more slowly. "Careful!" Prissie called after them, but then she turned her attention to the bottom row, gave the plank a flick to make sure it was clean, and sat down.

Koji didn't question her choice, taking his customary place by her side. He gazed thoughtfully after her younger brothers. "Too high?"

"*Way* too high," she agreed. Prissie peeked at the young Observer out of the corner of her eye. The more time they spent together, the more he seemed to understand her. It was a nice feeling, being known. "You can sit with them if you want," she said. "I'm sure it's a better view."

"No, thank you."

A few minutes later, Jude turned up and plopped down on Prissie's other side. "Dad said I can sit with you, okay?"

"Sure, Judicious," Prissie agreed with a smile, giving her brother a quick squeeze.

The West Edinton Warriors were warming up on the field, and it didn't take long to pick out their brother from among the other players wearing red and white jerseys; *POMEROY* was printed in neat block letters across Neil's back. "I see him!" Jude exclaimed. Lifting a megaphone he'd made from red construction paper, he yelled, "Hi, Neil!" Prissie didn't think he actually heard the call, but as the stands continued to fill, Neil looked at their family's usual seats, giving them a quick wave.

Just before game time, the athletes jogged off the field, and the cheerleaders made an appearance, their short, red and white pleated skirts flaring out as they bounced up and down on the sidelines, waving pompoms. Many of the locals filling the stands wore the school colors. Prissie's thick red sweater was her traditional game day attire, and as an added touch, she'd redone her hair so that red and white ribbons wove through the braids.

Jude's red hoodie had the team logo, a warrior with a shield brandishing his sword. While her little brother shouted encouragement through his megaphone, Prissie turned to Koji and asked, "Why don't Jedrick and Taweel and Tamaes carry shields?"

The Observer's brows lifted, but then his eyes took on a mischievous shine. "I will ask if you can watch *our* team practice one day. Then you will see."

"They fight one another?"

"They do," Koji replied seriously.

"Why?"

"Shimron says that it is impossible to *be* what you must *become*."

She gave that a little thought before asking, "Does that mean you have tournaments and things?"

"Battle is not for sport," Koji answered. Meeting her gaze steadily, he explained, "They cross swords to improve. Iron sharpening iron."

"That makes sense," she said. "I'll bet it's more exciting to watch than football."

"It can be." Leaning closer, Koji confessed. "However, I like singing together more."

Under the lights, referees in black and white uniforms took their places, and in the big tower at the center of the field, their school's announcer introduced the starting lineup. As a sophomore, Neil wasn't a starter; he was the backup quarterback, slated to step up next year, after their current quarterback graduated. As the reserve players ran the pom-pom gauntlet and charged out onto the field, Prissie cheered as loudly as anyone.

A whistle blew, and the game began. Koji watched with rapt attention, but Prissie was soon distracted by other things. Out of habit, she searched for Milo, who rarely missed a home game. Eventually, she spotted him on the sidelines, talking with a small knot of people that included Derrick Matthews, whose wife, Pearl, worked at Loafing Around, the two EMTs whose ambulance was parked in the end zone, and the reporter from the *Herald*.

During a time out, the school band launched into West Edinton's fight song, and as many of the people in the stands started singing, Prissie leaned close to Koji and said, "I'm just going to walk up and down a couple of times."

"Shall I join you?"

Shaking her head, she answered, "You stay with Jude. I'll be right back."

Many teens loitered around the concession stand, which mostly sold hot dogs, nachos, candy bars, and soft drinks. There was also a coffee cart, which always did a brisk business in cocoa and other hot drinks when the temperature took a plunge. This evening was still mild enough that kids were buying ice-cream sandwiches and lemon ice. Prissie was just considering bringing back a treat for Koji and Jude when some people under the nearest set of bleachers caught her eye.

A couple of teenagers had cornered a little boy with tear-stained cheeks. She immediately recognized Marcus's distinctive two-tone hair, and a moment later, she realized that the boy on the ground was Gavin Burke, Margery's little brother. His shoulders were hunched, and his lip trembled as he stared at Ransom, who'd hunkered down in front of him. Quick as a flash, Prissie rushed over and demanded, "What did you do?"

"Nothing," Ransom replied, rising from his crouch. "The kid won't tell me his name, though."

"He's hurt!"

"Nah, he just took a digger," her classmate said. "You know him?"

Gavin sniffled and dragged the back of his hand across his nose, leaving a long smudge of dirt across one cheek. He looked so miserable, and it was clearly Ransom's fault. Furious, Prissie wheeled and shook her finger in his face. "How *dare* you?"

"How dare I *what*?" Ransom asked incredulously.

"You are *such* a bully!" Prissie exclaimed hotly. This was something she could do to prove that she was still a good friend. While Margery was busy on the sidelines, Prissie would protect Gavin. "Picking on a little boy? He's only four!"

Ransom glanced at his friend. "We just got here, Miss Priss. Ask Marcus!"

She treated the other teen to a skeptical look before accusing, "You made him cry!"

"I didn't," Ransom said in exasperation. "He was already crying when we stopped to check on him!"

Gavin's lip began to tremble again, and Prissie said, "I think you've done enough damage. You should go."

Ransom looked from her to Gavin and back again, and for the first time, he looked angry. "Are you accusing me of something?"

"Yes," she said haughtily.

"Based on *what*?" he asked darkly. "Did you *see* me hurt that kid?"

"It's the sort of thing you would do," Prissie retorted, blue eyes snapping in righteous indignation.

"Since when?"

"Since always!"

Ransom took a deep breath, and when he released it, he said, "You have *no idea* what happened, but you're blaming me anyhow."

"I can't stand bullies," she said scathingly.

He cocked a brow at her. "Me either."

That threw her off for a moment, but she rallied. "Your innocent act isn't fooling anyone. Get out of here before I report you."

"You don't know how to listen, do you?" Ransom inquired.

"I'll scream."

Marcus cleared his throat, "Maybe we should leave her to it."

Ransom stubbornly jammed his hands into his pockets.

"Miss Priss, you're jumping to crazy conclusions. We didn't hurt the kid. We were trying to help!"

"Well, you're not very good at it," she said, pointing imperiously toward the parking lot. "Go away!"

"Come on," Marcus said, touching Ransom's arm. "As long as the kid's all right, it's good. Let's get out of here."

"Guess so," he muttered, allowing his friend to lead him away.

Prissie glared after them, so she saw when Ransom looked over his shoulder at her, a troubled expression on his face. Giving her braids a toss, she turned to Gavin, helping him to his feet. "Did those awful boys give you a hard time?"

Green eyes that were so much like Margery's stared up at her, and the little boy sulkily answered, "Nooo."

"No?" Prissie echoed, startled.

"Uh-uh," he clarified, giving a shake of his head. "Were they bad?"

Prissie wasn't sure anymore, but she took his hand. "It doesn't matter. Come on, Gavin. Let's find your mom."

4

THE STEADY HAND

Koji concentrated on the dream. His cheek rested against cold stone, and darkness pressed against his eyes. "Is that you?" he asked softly.

"It is me," came a ragged whisper.

"Why is it so dark?" Koji asked, sitting up and blinking in an unconscious effort to clear his vision.

"Because I am in the dark," the low voice replied tiredly.

"But we are children of light," he earnestly pointed out. "Our raiment at least . . . ?"

"You see what I see, young Observer."

Koji turned this revelation over and over in his mind, and when understanding came, so did his tears. "I am sorry, Ephron."

"I can still taste its sweetness, and tiny wings whisper of its presence," he murmured. "My eyes are not needed to confirm heaven's light."

"Shimron calls you a poet," Koji offered shyly. "I can see why."

"Am I?" he asked bemusedly. "I only say what I am thinking."

"Your thoughts fall in pleasant ways."

"Will you stay for a while?"

"For as long as I am permitted."

"Thank you."

Jayce poked Ransom's shoulder. "Come on. It's high time you tagged along on one of my rustles. You've got the rest of this covered, right Lou?"

She poured two cups of coffee and moved toward the table in the corner. "I'll mind the ovens. You two go on and bring back something nice!"

"Who's Russell?" asked Ransom.

"My mom used to say she was going out to the garden to *rustle up* some supper," Mr. Pomeroy explained. "Come to think of it, she *still* says that. Anyhow, ditch the apron, young man. We're going foraging."

"For what?"

"Inspiration and ingredients, not necessarily in that order," he replied with a grin, sauntering out the front door. "Some days, I get restless, and that's when I like to play with my food."

"Right," the teen replied, quirking a brow at his boss.

"You'll see," Jayce said. "It's the best way to figure things out if you're a hands-on learner like me." They walked into the corner store, and he headed straight for the produce section, eyes alert. "I'm pretty spoiled because I'm a country boy, and we grow a lot of our own produce. That's why I usually pick something we don't put in."

"Like oranges and bananas and stuff?"

"Sure, sure," Jayce agreed. "And I try to stick with the seasons. Summer is the most fun because everything is fresh. Plenty to choose from. Fall is next best, I think." He patted a pumpkin in passing and wandered over to inspect some pineapples. "I switch to nuts and spices in winter when produce is scarce, and there's always preserves. Jams, jellies, compotes, chutneys," he listed, half talking to himself.

"What about spring?" Ransom asked curiously.

Jayce grinned. "Chocolate."

"Right."

"Here's a good one," he said, nabbing a couple bags of cranberries and tossing them to the teen. "Very autumn. Very interesting."

"I don't think I've ever had cranberries that didn't come from a can," Ransom admitted, prodding the hard, red berries through the plastic.

"One of the best ways to get new ideas is to learn everything you can about the ingredients you work with," Mr. Pomeroy said. "Chop it, mash it, boil it, grate it. See how it bakes down, how it fries up, how it tastes with other ingredients. Think about moisture, texture, sweetness, acidity."

Ransom followed along, listening intently and nodding at intervals while Jayce pulled random items out of bins and off shelves. "Something sweet, something salty, something heavy, something light. Contrasts are good. Two things that are nothing alike can bring out the best in each other."

"Maybe with food," Ransom said skeptically. "People don't seem to mix very well."

"Oh?" Jayce turned and gave the boy his full attention. "What makes you say that?"

"Eh. Some girl at school," he replied. "She doesn't approve of 'people like me' for some reason."

"People like you?" Jayce inquired lightly. "Someone who knows what he wants and works hard for it?"

"Guess so."

"You know, I really respect that about you. I have a boy who's a year older than you, and I don't think he's given much thought to his future. You're a step ahead of most people your age."

"Thanks, sir. I wish more people thought like you."

Jayce chuckled and grabbed a box of candied ginger off a shelf. "Like that girl?" he inquired. "I take it her opinion matters to you?"

The teen's brows drew together as he thought it over. "It's not so much that her opinion matters. It's more that I don't understand her opinion. I don't like being written off."

"Girls are confusing, and women are a mystery," Mr. Pomeroy said. "Since I have a mother, a mother-in-law, a wife, a sister, and a daughter, I speak with the voice of experience."

Ransom snickered, then juggled his armful of groceries to make room for a tub of mascarpone cheese. "Guess I should be glad it's just me and Dad."

"Oh, don't get me wrong," Jayce said. "I treasure each and every one of them, but I can do that even when I can't figure out what they're thinking."

"I really doubt she's gonna get past whatever I did to get on her bad side."

"Well, for what it's worth, you're on my good side," Jayce assured.

"What about the whole religion thing?" Ransom asked nonchalantly.

Jayce's blue eyes shone. "I told you I won't push, but the invitation's still open. I'd be pleased and proud to have you join me and my lot on any Sunday."

The teen grimaced. "That's really not my thing."

"Okay. What about an evening service?" Jayce ventured. "There's a place down in Harper, and they hold services on Wednesdays and Saturdays. It's pretty casual, and the music's good. Might be more your speed?"

"I'll think about it, sir."

"Fair enough," Jayce replied. "Until then, I think it might be good to set you up with firsthand information. I keep a few spares lying around. Remind me to give you one when we get back to the bakery."

"A spare what?" Ransom asked.

Mr. Pomeroy balanced a tin of pistachios on top of the boy's increasingly precarious pile and answered, "A Bible."

The farm was always busy during harvesttime, but Saturdays were the craziest. Locals showed up early to beat the crowds, and city folks brought their families and made a day of it. The cool, dark apple barn was filled with the tangy-sweet smell of cider, and long tables held lines of overflowing bushel baskets. Plates of sliced apples were set out at intervals so people could taste each variety, and a glass case by the register was filled with applesauce doughnuts and apple turnovers, courtesy of Loafing Around.

Momma and Grandma Nell took care of customers inside, and Grandpa Pete alternated between the cider press and the kettle corn machine, with Beau and Koji lending a hand. Tad and Jude helped the people who came especially to pick their own apples, and Prissie kept busy pouring cider and handing out fliers to everyone who came through the door.

As lunchtime drew near, Momma came over to give Prissie a break, and she gladly escaped out into the sunshine. She took a deep breath of crisp air that meant summer was truly at an end. Strolling past green picnic tables, she chased down a blowing napkin, dropping it into the garbage barrel before following the fence line to the footpath that led to the prettiest spot on their farm — Pomeroy's Folly. The beautiful garden was more than a decade in the making, a father-daughter collaboration between Pete Pomeroy and Jayce's younger sister. Grandpa still added something to it every year, even though Aunt Ida had married and moved away.

Prissie paused as a southbound flock of Canadian geese flew overhead in vee-formation. Once their honking faded, the clear blue sky looked empty, but she wondered if it just *seemed* that way. Milo had once said their farm was a busy place, with Protectors, Guardians, and Messengers always coming and going. If you added all their customers' escorts to the mix, wouldn't there be an angelic traffic jam? Maybe there were angels whose main job was directing traffic, like Neil, who was down in the turn-around at the end of the driveway, overseeing parking. It was a silly idea, but Prissie sort of wished Koji was around to ask.

For now, she was on her own, or as alone as one person could be in the midst of visible and invisible crowds. Prissie looked at the roof of the barn where Tamaes apparently spent most of his time, then frowned at another passing thought. Why would Tamaes spend most of his day *sleeping* on the barn roof if angels didn't need to sleep? Funny how the questions always occurred to her when there was no one around to answer them. Prissie patted the pocket of her work apron, wishing she had a piece of paper to write them down. Koji liked it when she asked questions, but his answers weren't always easy to understand.

Just then, someone on the pond's bridge caught her eye. The young man rested his forearms against the bright red railing, and there was something familiar about the glossy, auburn hair that fell across his face. He peered at the ducks paddling below, and while Prissie watched, he straightened and nodded pleasantly to a couple of older women with cameras who climbed the graceful moon bridge. Lots of people came to take pictures of the fall display Grandpa and Aunt Ida had planted — golden birches, red Japanese maples, orange firethorn, and mounds of purple asters.

Prissie slipped through the green gate and hurried along the footpath, not taking her eyes off the slender man, because the last time she had, he'd disappeared. Turning toward her, he tucked his hands into his pockets and welcomed her with a genial smile.

"Hello, Adin. What are you doing here?"

"I came to see you, of course."

Once again, this angel had chosen clothes that complemented her own. His neat, woolen pants were a perfect match for her pleated skirt, and he wore a vest in the same shade of dark green as her apron. She thought they looked as if they belonged together, which made her happy. "Really? Why?"

"I thought we should compare notes," Adin replied, leaning casually against the railing. "I see you decided to have an adventure after all."

"I don't know if I'd call it an *adventure,*" she protested.

"You're consorting with angels, Prissie," he said. "That's not exactly commonplace."

"Well, when you put it *that* way ..." She turned her attention to the ducks that swam in tight circles below, hoping for a handout. Although he had a point, she didn't like being corrected. "What did you want to talk about?"

"Oh, this and that."

"So do you like apples?" she asked, immediately feeling foolish. Angels ate manna, not apples.

Adin chuckled softly. "They have their uses. You appear to have a bumper crop this year."

"Yes! Grandpa's very pleased."

"It's said that a good harvest is a sign of divine favor."

"Oh! Are you a Caretaker ... maybe?" she asked curiously.

"Would that I were!" Adin replied with an ironic smile. "It might interest you to know that Caretakers are few and far between. They are earth-movers and storm-bringers, angels of cataclysmic power."

"R-really?" she asked, startled.

"Truly," he affirmed. Then, he gave her a speculative look. "I was just thinking. It's taking a long time, isn't it?"

"What is?"

"Finding the one who was lost," Adin replied with a sad shake of his head.

"Oooh." Prissie glanced nervously into the orchard. "I'm sure everyone's doing their best. They're all very worried about their friend."

"Are you worried as well?"

"A little, I guess," she said. "It's creepy to think that there might be dangerous things on our farm."

"So you're worried for yourself, not for him."

"Well, I don't *know* him," she said defensively. It was hard to feel much for someone she'd never met, but Koji's sadness over Ephron's suffering had made a deep impression on her. With a stubborn tilt to her chin, she declared, "I *do* hope they can rescue him."

"Hope, hmm?" Adin sighed heavily before asking, "A little omniscience would be more effective, don't you think?"

"But Jedrick says that only God is all-knowing."

"True." Then, he casually inquired, "Have you ever wondered why God lets people flounder around in the dark? After all, He must *know* where Ephron is being held. Poor fellow."

Prissie's brows drew together in confusion. "It does seem a little strange."

Adin's gaze wandered over the surrounding area, lingering from time to time at different points. His jaw tightened, but when he turned his attention back to her, his expression smoothed. "Maybe that's where you'll come in."

"Me?" she echoed, taken aback. "I don't see how."

"Still, you know what they say. The unlikely ones are chosen." His gaze sharpened, and he softly said, "I'm curious, Prissie. Do you have a favorite brother?"

The sudden change in topic threw her off. "A favorite?"

"Yes. Is one more important to you than the others?"

She slowly shook her head. "They're *all* my brothers. I don't think it would be right to play favorites with family."

"No? How admirable. You're right, of course," he agreed. "And, you're about to gain another brother by the looks of things."

Prissie's eyes widened in shock. "Momma's not having another baby, is she?"

"I'm referring to the young man your father's been spending so much time with," Adin explained. "The one who's planning to follow in his footsteps."

"Ransom," she said dully.

"That's the fellow," he said amiably. "You and he don't get along very well, do you?"

"Not hardly."

"Such a shame, but understandable. I mean, wasn't that *your* plan? To work alongside your father?"

She fidgeted uncomfortably. "Maybe when I was little. I'm not so sure anymore."

"Oh, well. Since you don't mind, it probably doesn't matter." Adin's eyes drifted skyward again as he mused aloud, "Playing favorites only ever leads to trouble. Abel over Cain. Jacob over Esau. Mankind over angels."

Prissie followed his gaze, wondering what had distracted him, but the sky was as clear and blue as ever. And when she glanced back, she was alone.

5

THE FRANTIC HOSTESS

With their keen eyes, the archers had spotted them first, a blackening upon the earth, a blot against the sky. Soon, the other Flights sensed their encroachment and rose to meet them. Foul smells, vile words, and the constant gnashing of teeth filled the air as the enemy swarmed over the nearby ridge like a plague of locusts. Twisted blades, cruel smiles, and malicious intent sent Protectors and Guardians alike into a terrible clash that had lasted until sundown.

In the aftermath, Jedrick strode through the orchard, sword drawn as he scanned the gathering shadows for any sign of further malice. His apprentice followed close on his heels, similarly armed but far less silent. "It's weird they pulled back just when it was getting dark. Not that I'm complaining."

The Flight captain calmly said, "By the same token, we could say it was strange for them to attack when the sun was high in the sky."

"Say, do you think maybe ... was this a *bad* sign?"

A stern look warned him to say no more, and Jedrick firmly replied, "There is no reason not to take this at face value."

The younger angel scowled, and his mentor favored him with a long look. "You don't agree?"

"Here? Now?" he asked incredulously. "I don't buy it."

With a faint smile, Jedrick said, "Nor do I."

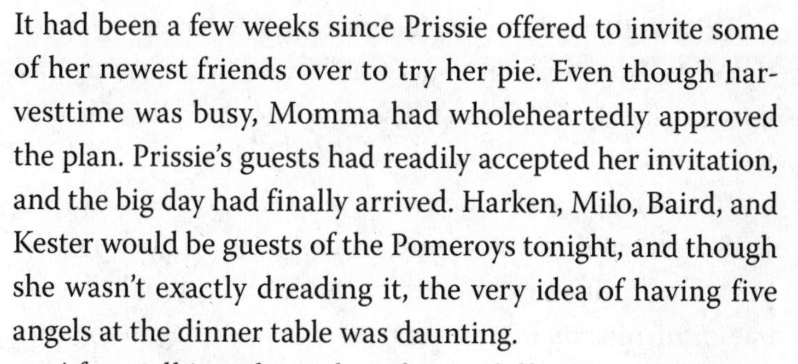

It had been a few weeks since Prissie offered to invite some of her newest friends over to try her pie. Even though harvesttime was busy, Momma had wholeheartedly approved the plan. Prissie's guests had readily accepted her invitation, and the big day had finally arrived. Harken, Milo, Baird, and Kester would be guests of the Pomeroys tonight, and though she wasn't exactly dreading it, the very idea of having five angels at the dinner table was daunting.

After talking through a dozen different possibilities, Grandma Nell finally persuaded Prissie to fall back on their usual company fare. As soon as they returned from church on Sunday morning, the two of them retreated to the smaller of the two houses that shared the Pomeroy's lawn. In Grandma Nell's kitchen, they fried enough chicken to feed a crowd, then returned to the main house to check on progress there.

Prissie inhaled deeply and smiled. The smell of yeast always meant that Dad was home, messing around in the kitchen. Zeke stood guard over two towel-draped pans cooling on the sideboard, and when he spied his sister, he proudly announced, "Me and Dad made fancy potato rolls! I grated the cheese myself!"

Jayce's bakery was famous for their potato rolls, but when he made them at home, he often added a twist. The cheese-topped variety was a family favorite, and Prissie nodded briskly. "Perfect!"

"Is it almost time?" Zeke asked, a whine of impatience creeping into his voice.

"Not until four," his mother replied patiently. She was perched on a tall kitchen stool, humming quietly as she peeled potatoes.

"That's *forever,*" grumbled the eight-year-old.

Prissie glanced at the clock, which was creeping up on three. As far as she was concerned, *forever* was rushing past far too quickly. "There's still so much to do," she muttered worriedly.

"Can I help?" Koji inquired.

She started, for the boy had padded up behind her unawares. Still, she was grateful for the offer. Koji had a talent for turning up in times of need. With the beginnings of a smile, she asked, "How do you feel about flowers?"

Armed with pairs of scissors and a basket, Prissie led the young Observer into the garden — or what was left of it. The bean trellises stood empty, and most of the vegetables had already been harvested. Much of the ground had been turned and composted in readiness for winter, leaving nothing but perennial herbs, a few root vegetables, and some hardy flowers that would bloom right up until the first killing frost.

"Grandma said I can take the rest of the zinnias," she explained. "We'll be filling jam jars, so the stems need to be this long," she said, demonstrating the height she needed.

"I can do that," Koji replied and crouched down beside the long row of brightly hued flowers.

For a while, all that could be heard were the soft rustle of leaves and sharp snips, but eventually, the young angel began to hum softly as he worked. "That's pretty," said Prissie.

He looked thoughtfully at the bright red flower in his hand. "It is," he agreed.

"I meant your humming."

Koji seemed surprised. "I did not realize my joy had spilled over."

"You're happy?" Prissie asked, feeling a little envious. With so many last minute details to take care of, she was trying her best not to fly to pieces.

"Very."

Studying his face, she realized that Koji *did* look happy. "What's put you in such a good mood?"

"The others are coming, and I am glad," he replied simply.

"Aren't there lots of angels around?"

"Indeed." He returned to snipping flowers. "I am acquainted with almost all of the angels whose responsibilities keep them close to your home."

"Almost?" she asked teasingly.

"Almost," he replied in all seriousness. "The others are certainly my comrades, but after living here, I have come to understand something new about my teammates." Koji sat back on his heels and waved in the direction of Prissie's home. "You have a family, and I have a family. Today, they will be together."

"Well, let's hope everything's ready before your family gets here. Otherwise, they'll have to pitch in!"

"I do not think they would mind."

"Well, I *would*!" He gazed at her with eyes that seemed to search her very soul, and to distract him, she exclaimed, "Oh! I thought of something to ask you!"

"I will answer if I can."

"Who directs traffic in crowded places?" He stared uncomprehendingly at her, so she clarified. "I mean like yesterday, when we had so many customers visiting the orchard. Doesn't it get busy having all those angels in one place?"

The Observer's expression flickered, his happiness now tempered by concern ... or sorrow. "It varies," he replied carefully. "Yesterday *was* uncommonly busy."

"That must be a colorful sight," she said, holding up their basket. "Like bouquets of zinnias in the sky!"

The shine returned to Koji's eyes. "Indeed."

Prissie almost dropped her handful of silverware when Zeke's whoop sounded from the front porch. "They're here! They're here!" he hollered before hot-footing it down the driveway. Jude, who'd been waiting patiently on the steps, trotted after him.

Grandma Nell pulled back the edge of a curtain to peer out the window, but Prissie's mother simply shook her head and smiled as she stirred the gravy. Jayce emerged from the little computer nook off the kitchen where he did his bookkeeping. With a wink at his daughter, he exclaimed, "Smells good enough to eat!"

"Hope so," she replied breathlessly. Prissie followed him to the front door and peered past his shoulder, suddenly very nervous. Would her brothers be embarrassing? How would Grandpa react to Baird? Would the food taste good? "Oh, no!"

Koji's head tilted. "What is wrong?"

"Kester didn't like fried food at the fair, and we made fried chicken for dinner!" she whispered tragically.

The boy's forehead creased in thought. "I do not think he would refuse the good food your family has prepared. Do not fret."

Almost before Harken's car rolled to a stop beside the family van, one of the back doors popped open and Baird sprang into view. The Worshiper was dressed as always in faded jeans and a somewhat rumpled shirt thrown over a tank top. His shoulder-length red hair was pushed behind his ears, one of which was adorned by a cuff.

Prissie hovered uncertainly, but Jayce tucked her arm through his and escorted her down the front walk. "They're *your* guests, my girl. Let's go make them welcome."

After turning a circle, Baird threw his arms wide and exclaimed, "Wooo! This place is the real deal!"

"Hey, Mister!" Zeke greeted. "Are you sure you're one of *Prissie's* friends? 'Cause you're *old*!"

"Out of the mouths of babes," dryly remarked Kester, who exited the car from the other side. He had a large nose, olive skin, and glossy black curls, and he paused to slip a suit jacket over his starched white shirt.

"Welcome to Pomeroy Orchard!" Jude greeted, offering his hand to the tall man. "Since you're already a friend, you can call me Judicious!"

He stooped to accept the six-year-old's welcome, speaking with a faintly foreign accent. "It is a pleasure to meet you. My name is Kester Peverell."

"Where are you from?" the boy asked curiously.

Dark brown eyes crinkled at the corners, and Kester

answered, "I have been to so many places, it is difficult to say where my travels began. With your permission, I will make myself at home *here* for the time being."

"That's really smart!" Jude exclaimed in delight.

Meanwhile, Zeke was answering Baird's rain of questions, most of which consisted of pointing to random items and asking, "What's that?"

The eight-year-old barely contained his laughter as he answered, "Apple barn ... chicken coop ... machine shed ... tractor ... my house ... Grandpa's house." He finally snickered at the last and bluntly asked, "You don't know what a *cat* is, Mister?"

"Baird!" the redhead corrected. "Everyone calls me Baird, and I was just checking with the cat. Does he have a name?"

"*She,*" said Zeke. "That's Tansy, and she's a mama kitty."

As Baird ran back and forth, his shirt flapped, giving peeks of the vivid red tattoos that twined around his shoulders. "It's all ... *farm*!"

Kester shook his head and blandly replied, "Perhaps that is because this *is* a farm?"

The redhead wasn't paying him any mind. "Oh, man! *Ducks*!"

"You've never seen a duck?" asked Zeke skeptically.

"I've never seen *these* ducks," Baird said with enthusiasm. "Hey, have you ever tried to *walk* like a duck?"

In the next moment, he and Zeke were duck-waddling across the lawn, following a line of quackers toward the pond. By this time Harken and Milo had emerged from the car, and the mailman leaned against its roof. "There he goes," Milo said with a smile.

Harken stepped up to Prissie's father and offered his hand. "Afternoon, Jayce. I appreciate your generosity in opening your home to us."

"You're always welcome," Mr. Pomeroy replied with a grin. "But this time around, we have Prissie to thank for the fellowship."

All eyes turned to their young hostess, who smiled uncomfortably. "I'm glad you could all make it."

Jude's attention was still fixed on Kester. "Have you been to a farm before?"

"I have, but never one dedicated to the production of apples," he replied solemnly.

"Do you wanna look around before dinner?" the boy invited. He was always eager to show off the place he loved best.

Kester inclined his head. "I would appreciate a tour, Judicious."

With a bright smile, the boy led the way. The orchard was closed on Sundays, and after the previous day's hustle and bustle, the farm seemed especially peaceful. Leaving Harken and Jayce chatting on the front porch, Prissie, Milo, and Koji trailed after man and boy, listening in as Jude made Kester welcome.

"I like apples and chickens. What do you like?"

"Music is close to my heart."

The boy gazed up at the tall man and asked, "Do you know lots of songs?"

"I do."

"How many?"

Kester admitted, "I have never tried to number them."

"That's okay," Jude assured in a confiding tone. "I've never

counted all the apples before. Or all the chickens. They don't hold still long enough."

Milo chuckled at this, and Kester cast a bemused glance at the mailman before saying, "It would be like trying to number the stars."

"Or snowflakes," the mailman interjected.

"Or sparrows," said Koji.

"Or my hairs," Jude said happily. "I learned that in Sunday school this morning."

"Very true," Kester agreed.

Jude drew to a halt and frowned in consideration. "I do have a favorite chicken, though. Would you like to meet Maddie?"

"That would be acceptable."

Milo stepped up and offered, "Would you like some help catching her, Jude? Since Maddie and I are old friends, I'd love to say hello."

The boy's smile grew sunny, for Milo had rescued the hen once before. His gratitude to the mailman knew no bounds. "That'd be real good!"

"I will help as well," said Koji.

"Really? Okay! I know just where she'll be right about now!" Without further ado, he trotted off, the Observer at his side. With a wave and a wink, Milo followed, leaving Kester in Prissie's hands.

"Come on, I'll show you Pomeroy's Folly," Prissie said, leading the serious-faced Worshiper to the gate. "It's very popular. People come from all over to see it."

"Most people are eager to hide their folly," he remarked.

Prissie was about to explain about architecture when she caught the faint smile lurking on the Worshiper's lips, and she realized that, in his way, Kester was joking.

They strolled past the barn, and the familiar bow of the bridge came into view, along with the red-haired angel and his young escort. Zeke hung precariously over the railing, and from the looks of things, Baird's firm hold on the boy's belt loops was the only thing keeping him from taking a plunge into the chilly water below. Prissie groaned. "Sorry, he's always like this."

"Yes, he is," agreed Kester, whose gaze was fixed on his partner. Sometimes it was hard to believe that Baird was the mentor and Kester was the apprentice.

They leaned against the fence and watched Zeke's latest adventure unfold, and in the calm silence that settled between them, Prissie remembered. "May I ask a question?"

"You may."

Kester was easy to talk to, so Prissie didn't mind bringing her odd questions to him. "I was just thinking ... Koji says that angels don't need to sleep."

The Worshiper laced his fingers together. "That is true."

"Then why does Tamaes sleep on top of the barn?"

Kester hummed, lifting his gaze toward the rooftops. "He is not sleeping. He is dreaming."

"What's the difference?"

He pondered for a moment before confessing, "I have never had to put our dreams into words before, but I will do my best to explain. We do not dream as you do, yet you are able to dream with us." Noting Prissie's deepening confusion, Kester tried again. "It may be simplest to think of it as an avenue of communication. Messengers are best equipped to open the way, but each of us is able to find respite by inhabiting dreams. They carry us to different places. Some bring us closer to home, and others bring us closer to those that are far away."

"You dream about heaven?" Prissie asked, trying to make sense of Kester's words.

The angel's smile took on a wistful quality. "I do."

"And Koji dreams about Ephron."

Kester nodded. "Since Ephron was taken, Tamaes has been searching for him in dreams. He is coordinating the search with Harken's assistance."

"Why is Tamaes the one doing all the dreaming?" Prissie asked. "Isn't Jedrick in charge of your team?"

"Our captain has his own concerns, and Tamaes volunteered. Jedrick entrusted the task to him."

"But isn't he supposed to be following *me* around all the time?"

Gazing off into the orchard, Kester replied, "Tamaes and Ephron were very close, and their affection for each other fosters a sense of remorse, as well as a sense of urgency." Offering a small smile, he added, "However, you can rest assured that your Guardian knows his place."

"Oh." Quickly changing the subject, Prissie asked, "So dreams let you talk to each other when you're apart, almost like cell phones?"

"I do not think technology can replicate the experience, but yes, we can reach out to each other across distances."

"Does that mean you can hear Harken's voice in your head?"

"I can, provided he has a message for me," Kester replied. "In fact, he says the meal is ready."

Right on cue, the dinner bell that hung just outside the kitchen door rang out, summoning everyone to the house.

Dinner was served family style, so after the respectful hush that settled while Jayce gave thanks for the meal, the kitchen burst into happy confusion. Exclamations and laughter rang out on every side as platters and bowls filled with home cooking made the rounds.

Koji was fairly bursting with happiness to be sharing the table with four of his teammates, and every so often, his fingertips tapped the back of Prissie's hand. It was a habit he'd adopted in recent weeks whenever he wanted to catch her eye, and now she wondered if he was making do since he couldn't send her the kinds of silent messages Kester had described. When she turned to see what he wanted, he rolled his eyes toward Baird, who was so engrossed in his conversation with Naomi that he passed everything on to Kester without taking any food. The redhead might have gone hungry if it wasn't for his apprentice, who calmly filled both their plates.

By the time all the individual conversations ebbed and expanded to include everyone at the table, Prissie was feeling much more comfortable in her role as hostess. The four angels were teammates behind the scenes, but there was no need to hide the fact that they were good friends. Harken and Milo lived in neighboring apartments over The Curiosity Shop, and Baird and Kester led music at the DeeVee, where Milo attended midweek services. Their intertwined relationships seemed perfectly normal.

"Rehearsals start in a few weeks," Grandpa Pete remarked. "You boys are helping out this year, right?"

Baird had just taken a huge bite of a potato roll, so he elbowed Kester, who promptly answered, "Yes, sir. The first rehearsal is the second week of October, and this year Baird is in charge of the band and orchestra."

"So it'll be *both*?" Pete asked, frowning slightly. Prissie knew her grandfather wasn't very pleased that the committee had decided to mix things up this year by performing an updated arrangement of Handel's *Messiah*. Despite assurances to the contrary, he was pretty sure their newfangled ideas were going to ruin his favorite part of the holiday season.

"Yes, sir," Kester repeated politely. "The orchestra has been retained, but other non-period instruments have been added."

Baird jumped in, excitedly explaining, "Choir members shouldn't have any problem picking up the new arrangements. It's the same old *Messiah*, but we played with the pacing."

Tad surprised everyone by quietly interjecting, "I was thinking of maybe joining the choir this year."

Grandpa Pete looked like Christmas had come early. "Good! That's good, m'boy!"

Grandma Nell leaned forward to catch Neil's eye and asked, "What about you? Your voice has settled."

The sixteen-year-old's face scrunched thoughtfully as he chewed, and Prissie suspected him of drawing out the suspense before he finally answered. "Guess so. If Tad does."

"There's a bunch of young people from the DeeVee that'll be joining the choir this year, and every one of them is a first-timer," Baird said with a sidelong glance in Grandpa's direction. "They'll be relying on those with more experience to learn their parts." Pete harrumphed, and the redhead went on to reveal, "Milo's a newbie, too."

"How *wonderful*," Grandma Nell enthused, passing the biscuit platter along to the mailman. "What about you, Harken?"

"I wouldn't miss it," the old shopkeeper assured with a ready smile. "This year's performance is sure to be memorable."

Prissie couldn't help but notice that for angels who only needed manna to survive, their heavenly guests could put away a lot of food. It made her feel good to watch people enjoying something she'd helped prepare, and they lingered at the table for quite some time after the empty plates were pushed aside. Finally, Naomi stood and announced, "I'll put the coffee on. Shall we move to the family room?"

Immediately, Baird raised his hand and waved it like a schoolboy hoping for attention. "If you don't mind, ma'am, I did promise Prissie that if she could wrangle us a place at your table, we'd sing for our supper! Kester and I came prepared!"

Jayce shook his head and kindly said, "There's no need to repay us for your company."

Baird nodded, but countered, "Just the same, we'd love to sing with you. I guess you could call it our kind of hospitality."

"Meals and music are often best when shared with friends," said Kester.

"Fair enough," Jayce agreed. "What did you have in mind?"

The red-haired Worshiper bounced from his chair and swept the table with an assessing gaze. "When we packed Harken's trunk, Kester here got a little carried away. There must be half a dozen pieces of precious cargo out there, which means I need at least six hands. But God only saw fit to give me two! I'm taking volunteers!"

All five of the Pomeroy boys and Koji scrambled to follow

Baird out the door, and Kester quietly gathered his dishes and carried them over to the sink. Grandma Nell was quick to scold. "Let us take care of that, young man."

The serious-faced musician inclined his head and graciously replied, "Pardon my intrusion."

Grandma Nell tutted. "You're not intruding. You're just being over-helpful! We'll exercise our gifts, freeing you up to exercise yours."

Kester's dark eyes warmed with the smile that graced his lips. "I shall bow to your wisdom. Thank you, Mrs. Pomeroy."

Grandma Nell shook her dishtowel at Pete, Jayce, Kester, Harken, and Milo, chasing them out of the kitchen. "Off you get, the lot of you! And call me Nell!"

Naomi laughed at her mother-in-law's good-natured bossing and accepted a quick one-armed hug from Jayce, who kissed the top of her head. "Thank you, ladies," he said, including all three generations. "We'll get out from underfoot."

Prissie moved to help with the clearing up, and a moment later, there was a *clatter-bang* as the boys returned with Baird. She peeked into the front hall long enough to see that they were weighed down by four instrument cases and two amplifiers. Jude popped into the kitchen to report, "Mister Baird's guitar is *blue*!" before disappearing back into the living room.

A few moments later, the strains of a wistful melody filled the house, and Prissie realized that one of those cases had held Kester's violin. Grandma Nell sighed happily as she loaded the dishwasher, and Naomi's expression grew dreamy as she transferred leftovers into storage containers for the fridge. While she dried the pots and platters that needed to be done by hand, Prissie stole peeks into the living room where Beau and Neil were giving Baird a hand setting up the equipment.

The three women didn't take long getting the kitchen squared away, and they joined the menfolk. Naomi walked around the room, lighting candles, and Grandma Nell cozied up to her husband on one of the love seats. Tad, Zeke, and Jude watched with undisguised interest as Kester opened another case and withdrew an acoustic guitar. The black instrument gleamed in the lamplight, and Zeke boldly reached out to touch the pattern of paua shell insets that ringed its sound hole. "What's this for?" he asked.

"That is called the rosette," Kester answered. "It is purely aesthetic."

The eight-year-old stared at the tall man with a blank expression until Baird leaned over and translated, "He means it's pretty."

"Oooh!" the boy breathed, staring critically at the decoration. "I guess that's okay."

At that moment, Baird turned expectantly to the room at large and held up the end of a cord. "Juice, please?"

Jayce chuckled and guided the redhead over to the corner so he could help himself to an outlet. Neil smirked and said, "Baird likes it loud!"

"I do at that," the worship leader readily agreed.

"And Kester is the lyrical band member?" guessed Naomi.

"Hey, I can *do* lyrical!" Baird protested. So saying, he plugged his blue guitar into the power supply, made himself comfortable, and gave an experimental strum. Then, he deftly picked out a sweet melody that sounded like it belonged in a music box or maybe a merry-go-round.

Koji glanced around the room, located Prissie, and sidled up to her. Tapping the back of her hand, he whispered, "Kester's music made everyone sigh, but Baird's music makes everyone smile."

"Which is better?" she wondered aloud.

The young Observer said, "Both are good."

Baird finished with a small flourish and waved off the smattering of applause. "Everyone get comfy," he invited, for most of the family was still standing around. "We'll do one song for you, but then let's sing together. All of us ... any old thing ... I totally take requests ... and have yet to be stumped!"

As he rambled, Prissie's brothers vied for seats in the wide couches and deep chairs arranged around the room. There was plenty of space for everyone, but that didn't stop the siblings from jostling. Neil and Tad tossed a few throw pillows around until their mother sent them The Look. Prissie ended up on one of the sofas, tucked between Beau and Koji.

A hush fell while Kester tuned his guitar, plucking stray notes as he fiddled with the knobs. It wasn't a melody, but the notes didn't clash. Prissie thought they were like the tunings of an orchestra, not the main event, but a signal that something was about to happen. Slowly, a tune emerged from the random cascades, and Baird picked up a harmony line. The two Worshipers exchanged a brief glance, then switched roles, with the mentor taking the melody as his apprentice modulated through the opening bars of an old hymn that just *happened* to be Grandpa Pete's favorite.

The old man harrumphed, but he looked rather pleased

as the young men sang their way through every verse. Once the song ended, he gruffly said, “Not many people know that hymn, nowadays.”

“Many things are forgotten as time passes,” Kester replied gravely. “However, I believe there will always be those who remember.”

Prissie settled back into the couch cushions and stared in amazement at the two Worshipers. What Kester said was true. He and Baird would live forever, so all the songs they knew would *never* be forgotten.

“Now taking requests!” the redhead warbled.

For a few seconds, the Pomeroys just exchanged glances, but then Jayce reached into the bookshelf next to his chair and started passing out books with deep red bindings. “These should help,” he declared.

Baird’s eyes widened. “Oh, man! You keep hymnals in the family room?”

“Doesn’t everyone?” quipped Neil as he ferried copies over to Harken and his grandparents.

The redhead actually got a little misty-eyed as he laid his hand over his heart. “You guys make me so happy!”

Harken accepted one of the books and casually checked the printing information. “These are quite old. I’ve seen a few of them come through my store.”

Pete Pomeroy nodded. “When the church replaced their hymnals the last time, they gave folks the chance to purchase the old ones. I bought a stack.”

“More like two stacks,” countered his wife with a teasing smile.

The old man explained, “I remember when these were new. My mother headed up the fund-raiser that brought ’em into the church, so I wanted to hang on to some and pass them along."

"I can understand that," Harken said as he flipped through the pages reverently. "Wasn't she the church pianist?"

"That's right." Grandpa Pete nodded to the upright piano tucked into one corner. "That was hers. Ida learned to play it," he said proudly.

"My younger sister," Jayce explained to the two who were newcomers.

Prissie had good memories of what Grandma Nell always called "hymn sings." Aunt Ida would play, and everyone would gather around with the hymnals. It had been a winter tradition, and snowy days were right around the corner. Quickly, she called out the number of the hymn that Aunt Ida had always requested, and Kester struck a chord.

"Prissie?" Koji's black eyes sparkled as he studied her face. "Which part do you sing?"

As the others began, breaking into four-part harmony, Prissie murmured, "I always sing the melody with Momma."

"I will sing with you."

She glanced around at the others. Neil attempting to growl out bass notes that were just under his range, and Milo coaxed Tad into joining him on the tenor line. Feeling enormously self-conscious with so many angels in the room, Prissie tentatively joined in, adding her voice to the mix.

They took a break for pie and coffee, then migrated back into the family room, anxious to return to the music. Kester traded his guitar for a harp, and Milo requested a gentle hymn that Prissie couldn't remember ever hearing before. It was sweet and beautiful, and she noticed Grandma Nell dabbing at tears before it was over. The hour had grown late, and

Zeke was yawning when Kester changed to the lullaby that Prissie now thought of as *his*.

It was as if everyone was reluctant to let the evening end, but finally, Harken said, "These two could probably go on all night, but this old man has a shop to open in the morning."

He began the goodbyes while Kester played softly, and Baird stowed the instruments and coiled the cords. The older boys helped him carry the gear back to Harken's car, then returned so the redhead could enthusiastically thank Naomi and Nell. He caught Prissie's eye and gave her a wink that let her know he'd be getting around to her soon enough.

In the midst of the noisy leave-taking, Kester returned to the family room and opened the piano, running his fingers over the keys. Prissie and Koji listened curiously as he once more chose random notes before slipping into a few practice scales. Grandpa Pete ambled over and said, "It's fallen out of tune and isn't much used these days. Our Ida married a fine man, and she travels with him. They're missionaries."

Kester hummed thoughtfully, then offered, "I would be pleased to tune this for you sometime. It is within my abilities to do so."

"Really? We're hoping Ida can visit for the holidays, and it'd be good to have it ready for her. How much would you be asking?"

The Worshiper shook his head. "I would ask for nothing."

"That wouldn't be right," argued Pete. "Either set a price or work out a trade."

Kester bowed his head. "I will give the matter some consideration."

"You do that," Grandpa said with satisfaction.

The rounds of goodbyes seemed to go on forever, but

finally, Momma worked it so that Prissie could have the last word with her guests. Shooing her out onto the porch with them, she herded the boys toward their bedtime routines.

"Thank you for coming," Prissie said, looking from one angel to the next. They all smiled at her, but it was Baird who stepped forward. She supposed that made sense, because Milo had said he was older than the other three, which probably gave him some kind of seniority. She sort of expected him to say something grand. He didn't.

Baird wasn't very tall. In fact, he and Prissie were the same height. He searched her eyes for a moment before blurting, "Will you freak out if I hug you?"

Prissie blushed and awkwardly said, "It's okay, I guess."

Taking her at her word, the Worshiper stepped closer and wrapped his arms around her shoulders, giving her a friendly squeeze. "Thank you for today, Prissie," he said seriously. "I thank you, and I thank God for this day of rest. Your family has been *such* an encouragement."

"R-really?"

"Totally," he said with feeling.

Searching her mind for some kind of response, she lamely offered, "I didn't know angels needed encouragement."

Baird released her, stepping back. "Even an angel's wings grow heavy once in a while," he confessed with a little half-smile. Glancing at Kester, he brightly announced, "Tonight, I'm gonna write a song!"

"That is good."

"Nope. It's *awesome*!" his mentor countered, then turned to Milo. "Race you to the car, fly-boy!"

The two took off, Harken following much more sedately, leaving Prissie and Kester on the steps. With a gentle smile, the tall Worshiper took her hand in both of his. "It has been many months since Baird composed something," he revealed. "Indeed, it has been a considerable source of concern on my part. *Thank you* for extending your generosity to one whose need was great."

"But I didn't *know* Baird needed anything."

"God knows what we do not," Kester said with confidence. "His plans encompass yours, and His purposes are always good. Have faith in that, Prissie."

6

THE LOST LAMB

Green light exploded into rainbows as Jedrick burst through the ring of stones set into the floor of Shimron's tower. The old Observer glanced up and serenely smiled at his captain before turning his attention back to his task. The big warrior strolled across the chamber to peer over his shoulder. "I know your subject matter very well," Jedrick remarked.

"The Protector should know that which he protects," the Observer said, adding a daub of color before sitting back to consider the effect. The painting alongside rows of neat text was a close-up of a smooth stone pillar topped by an ornate capital involving carved netting, pomegranates, and leaves.

"A valid point," his captain replied. "Still, I am near those columns daily without paying much attention. Seeing one of them upon your page makes me appreciate them anew. They are well made."

"Their craftsman has had time enough to hone his skills. The gate is a testament to his patience."

"Yes," Jedrick agreed with a solemn expression. "If there is one thing Aril has in abundance, it is time."

"Have you ever been here?" Prissie asked Koji as they stepped off the school bus.

"Indeed," he replied. "However, I have never been underground. I am very curious."

Today's field trip had been planned by their science teacher, who'd just wrapped up a unit on caves. "I've been through them a few times. We take field trips here *every* year."

Sunderland State Park occupied a large section of the northeast corner of Milton County, and the sprawling acreage included a river, hiking trails, wildflower meadows, a deer garden, orienteering courses, picnic pavilions, camping sites, and a learning center, but its main attraction was the vast network of caves. Miles of underground passages had been mapped, and spelunkers came from all over the area to explore the network of interconnecting chambers.

"Every year since you were little?" Koji asked.

"Yes. Nature walks, a class on bat colonies, bird watching, things like that."

"Then you have met the rangers?" he pressed, as they filed through the entrance with the rest of their classmates.

"I suppose," she replied. "I'm not sure about the volunteers, but I remember an old man in khaki shorts. He's always here. He's usually the one who teaches the classes."

There was a sparkle in Koji's eyes. "Do you remember that old man's name?"

"I always just called him Mister Ranger. Why?"

Koji's fingers brushed the back of her hand, and he whispered, "His name is Abner."

Prissie wandered along the fringes of the chattering group, eager to steer clear of Margery's group. She wasn't in the mood for any of Elise's sly remarks today. Sunderland's learning center was filled with interesting things — mounted insects, old bird nests, animal pelts, deer antlers, porcupine quills, and even a few glass cases containing live animals. Since she'd been here so many times either for classes or with her younger brothers, Prissie had seen it all before.

Koji had wandered off at some point, and she spotted him in front of the relief map of the park. The Observer was talking animatedly to one of the rangers, a young man with high cheekbones and long black hair neatly parted and gathered into a glossy plait down the center of his back. Glancing at her watch, she sighed. In fifteen more minutes, they needed to meet at the entrance to the main cave. "Might as well get a head start," she muttered.

Without a backward glance, she aimed for the side door, which opened onto the short trail leading down to the caves. The way was overhung by pines and ash, and a few stray leaves and needles littered the path. She hunched her shoulders as a short burst of chill air sent a shiver through the trees and down her back. Rain was in the forecast, and the gray skies looked like lead. "I hope it doesn't storm," she said to a sugar maple. "Then all your pretty leaves will be gone."

"Torn away by wind and rain," agreed a pleasant voice.

She whirled to find a familiar figure standing nearby, his hands in his pockets as he leaned against a trail marker. "Oh, it's you! You startled me, Adin!" she exclaimed. "Why are you here?"

"To see *you*, of course."

"Oh," Prissie managed, pleased to be attended by the handsome angel once more.

"Actually, I don't have much time, but I needed to speak with you."

"About what?" she inquired, picking up on his sense of urgency.

"I'm curious how far you're willing to go in order to help your friends."

Prissie shook her head. "I'm not sure what you mean."

"It's simple. Here, let me show you." He slipped around behind her and pointed over her shoulder. In a sing-song voice, he inquired, "Do you see what I see?"

At first, Prissie didn't notice anything out of the ordinary, but then a flash of brightness caught her eye. The small spark spiraled upward in lazy circles, then darted purposefully through the cave mouth. "It went inside?" she whispered.

"Into the darkness," Adin confirmed. "Odd behavior for a yahavim, don't you think?"

Prissie thought back to what she'd learned about the tiny manna-makers. "They need light to survive." Peeping into her companion's face, she asked, "Isn't it dangerous for one to go underground?"

"Perhaps," answered Adin as he took a step back. "Maybe you should follow."

Biting her lip, she stared at the huge, black opening. "Do

you really think so?" she asked uncertainly, but when she turned around again, he was already gone.

For several long moments, Prissie wallowed in indecision, but the thought of one of the little fairylike angels in trouble gave her the courage to start forward. "I'm coming," she said, whispering her promise. Nothing bad could happen. After all, wherever she might go, Tamaes would be there as well.

The soft sparkle of the yahavim flitted further along the main tunnel, then disappeared into a side passage that was barred by a simple chain. Prissie hurried to follow, until a voice called, "You're going the wrong way, Miss Priss." Ransom loafed just inside the entrance, looking bored.

"What do you care?" she snapped.

He pushed away from the wall and ambled over. "That's one of the spelunking paths, so it's not lit."

Prissie poked her head around the corner. She could still see the light of the little manna-maker. "I have a light," she said stubbornly. "And I'm in a hurry."

"For what?"

"None of your business," she said, climbing over the chain.

"You can get really lost in here if you're not careful."

With a toss of her braids, she retorted, "I'm *always* careful."

As she turned away, Ransom caught her arm. "What's *wrong* with you?" he asked sharply. She tugged, but he didn't let go, meeting her glare evenly. "Stop being childish, Priss. It's not safe."

"I know what I'm doing," she stubbornly argued.

"Show me your light." When she couldn't, Ransom muttered a curse under his breath, then fished in a pocket with his free hand. "If you're going to be a complete idiot, at least take this," he said, pressing a small flashlight into her hand.

"I don't need it!" Prissie insisted, pushing it back at him, but Ransom stepped out of range, hands raised. She glanced anxiously down the passage again, but before she took off, she asked, "Are you going to tell on me?"

"Sure am." Walking backwards toward the entrance, he said, "I'll go get your conscience. You mostly behave yourself when he's around."

If he was talking about Koji, that would be a big help. Nodding briskly, she replied, "You do that." Then Prissie plunged into darkness.

She flicked on Ransom's flashlight and hurried as fast as she dared after the tiny sprite. Luckily, yahavim didn't seem to be built for speed, and she was able to catch up. "Hey, little one," she called gently. "What are you doing in here?"

He turned back to face her, and Prissie crooked her fingers just as Harken had taught her. When he hesitated, she asked, "Are you one of Abner's flock, or do you belong to another Flight? Either way, you're awfully far from home. Well, *probably*."

Small feet settled on her palm, and the tiny creature peered up at her in surprise. "I'm Prissie. I'm already friends with Omri, so maybe we could be friends, too. I wish you could tell me your name."

Faceted eyes blinked several times, and Prissie smiled. He was easily distinguishable from Omri, for unlike Taweel's constant companion, this yahavim had short hair. Fine strands stood up around his head like a dandelion tuft, and its dusky shade of green reminded her of old copper. "Where are you going, little angel?"

He pointed along the passage, indicating his desire to keep going. "Aren't you afraid?"

The yahavim's expression grew solemn, and with a jolt, Prissie realized that she could see his face clearly because he wasn't very bright. Omri's happiness nearly blinded her when he was near, which meant that this little guy was sad, or possibly sick. "Maybe I should take you to Abner?" she asked worriedly. "He's a Caretaker, and you look like you need someone to take care of you."

He shook his head and pointed even more insistently into the depths. "Right. Can I help, then?" she offered. "I have a flashlight. I know it's not the same, but maybe it's close enough?"

When she showed it to him, he immediately launched off of her hand, twirled through the narrow beam of light, then hovered right in front of her. He smiled with such sweetness, she had to swallow the lump in her throat. "I guess you like it. Which way, then?"

The yahavim sat upon her upraised palm and pointed in the direction he'd been flying, humming softly. They walked on together, and for a while, they remained on the well-trod path. Prissie had been on it twice before and mostly remembered the way. It was a beginner's loop. In less than a mile, the trail would rejoin the main tunnel, where she hoped to catch up to her classmates before her absence was noticed. But then the green-haired angel pointed at a narrow opening in the wall Prissie had never noticed before. "Are you sure?" she asked, and he nodded grimly.

Before long, she lost track of the twists and turns. The

caves really were like a labyrinth, and Prissie was hopelessly lost. Down here, the air was still, and the silence was suffocating. Darkness seemed to take on a life of its own, pushing against her, playing tricks on her.

When they reached another turning, her tiny companion leapt into the air, then spun and flung himself over the end of the flashlight, giving her a pleading look. Somehow understanding, Prissie switched it off, leaving only the little angel's glow to see by. However, he dove closer and burrowed down inside her jacket's collar, effectively snuffing out the last glimmer.

He was trembling, which frightened Prissie even more than the pitch black. Crouching down, she made herself as small as possible against the tunnel wall. From somewhere in the darkness ahead came a sour note, off-key and unpleasant. She held her breath, listening with all her might. A dull *clink* was followed by a crunching sound that reminded Prissie uneasily of a barn cat eating a mouse. She cupped her hand around her little passenger and curled more tightly, hiding her face on her knees as her heart sent up a silent plea for help.

Seconds ticked by, though Prissie forgot to count them, and eventually, the yahavim's trembling eased. He popped back up, and when she straightened, he fluttered to a perch on her upraised knees. For several moments, he seemed to be listening to something in the silence, but then he faced her squarely. Putting a finger to his lips, he then pointed to the ground. "I'm supposed to stay?" she asked breathlessly. His nod was accompanied by a slight increase in brightness, but Prissie couldn't be glad. "Does that mean you're going?" Another nod.

Impulsively, she asked, "Then do you want to take this?"

Faceted eyes widened, and for a moment, he was too bright to see. With a joyous somersault, he gave thanks for the blue plastic flashlight, then held out both his arms to accept her gift. He tested its weight with a couple of short hops on her outstretched hand, his wings humming with the effort, and then he nodded. It would work. Before leaving, he placed something on her palm. "Manna?" she gasped. He took flight, hovering close until Prissie held the precious wafer between her fingertips, and then he fluttered away, dipping and bobbing under the burden of Ransom's flashlight. "Be careful, little angel," she whispered after him.

Prissie watched until there was no light left, then slipped the manna into her mouth and blinked back tears as its sweetness spread over her tongue. "I did the right thing. Right?" she asked tremulously. It was a very good question, but no one answered. Prissie couldn't remember the last time she'd felt so alone.

Sounds were too loud because there weren't enough of them. To blend into the silence, Prissie found herself talking shallow breaths. Could the enemies hear the beating of her heart or the dripping of each tear that seeped between her lashes? She'd never been so scared in her whole life, even when she was falling, because *then,* there had been someone to catch her. No, it was *much* worse to be alone.

Suddenly, she heard a scrape. Prissie curled more tightly, and tried to be quiet, but a sniffle escaped.

"Prissie," someone called. "I'm coming, so sit tight."

She didn't recognize the voice, but in a few moments, the clatter of loose stones came closer, and light blazed around her, hurting her eyes. Hiding her face, she squinted until she was able to make out a pair of heavy boots and blue jeans in the pool of flashlight. Her rescuer crouched down in front of her, and Prissie's eyes widened in alarm. "Y-you?"

After all the twists and turns she'd taken, she'd expected it to take days for anyone to find her — man or angel. The last thing she'd expected was Marcus Truman. "What are *you* doing here?" she asked numbly.

"You've gone astray, and I'm here to lead you back into the fold," he replied, sounding rather put out.

"That doesn't make any sense," she groused. "Why would the rangers send you?"

"Oh, I'm Sent," he said grumpily. "I'm here to lead you back onto the right path, so come on."

"Did Ransom send you?" Prissie asked suspiciously. "Why should I trust you?"

"You really are turned around ... in more ways than one," he said. "Actually, Harken sent me down here."

"Y-you know Harken?"

Marcus shook his head as if she'd said something particularly dense. "This may be the only chance I *ever* have to say this, so let's make it good. You should *trust* me because I'm an angel Sent by God." Marcus offered her a hand, saying, "Fear not, and all that."

"You're an angel?" she asked skeptically.

"Yup. A cherubim."

Prissie frowned in consternation. "Which one is that?"

"Protector."

"Like Jedrick?" she asked, startled.

Marcus grinned broadly. "Just like him, yeah."

"Prove it!"

He gave her a baffled look and cautiously asked, "How'm I supposed to do that?"

"Well Jedrick has wings ... and armor ... and a sword. You have scruffy clothes ... a bad haircut ... and a worse attitude. You *can't* be one of them."

"What's wrong with my hair?" Marcus growled, running a hand over the top of his bristling two-tone hairstyle.

"It's weird," she muttered, eyeing the platinum section.

He gazed at her for several heartbeats, then sighed in resignation. "Evidence, huh? Fine, we'll give that fragile faith of yours a boost. Hold this," he commanded, thrusting his flashlight into her hands.

Prissie might have snapped at him for the insult, but Marcus shrugged out of his ever-present brown leather jacket, draping it around her shoulders. Its warmth stopped her shivering, but it didn't calm her nerves as her classmate next unzipped his hoodie and let it drop to the floor. Jagged patterns that ranged from cream to soft yellow decorated his warm brown skin, and while she watched, they began to glow. With a harmony of whispered notes, they unwound from his bared arms, lifting and spreading until a set of luminous wings fanned out above him, filling the cave with a warm glow. Prissie stared in amazement at the brilliant display, then met Marcus's waiting gaze and gasped. "Your eyes are different!"

"Very observant," he replied with a smirk. Deep brown had been traded for an impossible shade of gold. "Abner said they would stand out too much, so he changed them for me. Kinda like Koji's ears."

"You really *are* an angel."

"*Now* you're making sense. You can't trust everything in wings, though," he cautioned. "Plenty of the Fallen have 'em, too."

"Oh. Okay."

This time when Marcus offered his hand, she took it, and he pulled her to her feet. Shaking his head at her, he remarked, "It's beyond me how you even found this place."

"Where are we?"

"The Deep."

That sounded ominous, and she gazed around nervously. Marcus's radiance stretched far enough for her to see more of the narrow path that cut through rough stone. "It looks like this tunnel ends?" she said, worried about what had become of her little friend.

"Kinda," he replied. "You came this far. Might as well see the rest." Gesturing for her to follow, he strolled a short distance down the passage. As he moved, his wings relaxed, draping in neat folds that barely swept the floor. Prissie stared in fascination. She was tempted to touch them, to see if the translucent cascade was made of intangible light.

When he reached the opening, Marcus scooped up a stray pebble and casually tossed it into the darkness. Long seconds passed before a distant patter sounded somewhere far below. Then he propped his forearm on the edge of the opening and peered into the echoing space beyond. "If you stand in front of me, I'll show you what's out there," he offered.

"Do I *want* to know what's out there?"

"I dunno, but you have an opportunity to see something none of the cave explorers will ever discover," he said. "Your chance is now if you want to take it."

Part of her wanted to run away, but she remembered

Harken's warning when she'd been nervous about trying manna for the first time. Some offers only came once in a lifetime. Prissie hung back and asked, "Why do I have to be in front?"

He favored her with a long look. "I'm gonna turn up the wattage, and I really doubt Tamaes would thank me for blinding you."

"Oh." She hadn't expected to face her fear of heights while under the earth, but her knees were already knocking. With a shaky nod, she edged past him, nearly screaming when he placed a hand on her shoulder.

"Aw, c'mon! Calm down or Jedrick is gonna chew me out!" And then, golden light swelled behind her, spilling across the few paces that remained between them and a precipitous drop. "I might only be an apprentice, but I'm still a Protector, Prissie. I'm just trying to keep you safe."

Even though she knew Marcus was telling the truth, it was hard to trust him. She was too used to thinking of him as a troublemaker. "I really, *really* don't like high places," she confessed through clenched teeth.

"Don't I know it," he replied. "Tamaes gave the whole Flight a schooling after that Ferris wheel thing. You can take the inside. It's not far."

"Is it safe?" she begged, needing reassurance.

"Yeah, Prissie," he assured. "I'll let you take a quick look, and then we'll get out of here."

The path that curved along the cavern's wall was broad, and Prissie was able to hug the sheer rock face as they slowly approached an enormous slab of stone that was set into the wall with chains. She brushed the polished surface with cold fingertips and asked, "What's this doing way down here?"

Marcus tested one of the chains and grunted softly. “It’s kind of a lock-up.”

“Like a prison?” she asked tentatively.

“Yeah, just like a prison.”

Her eyes widened in dismay. “You mean there are *people* inside?”

“Enemies,” he clarified. “Many who have Fallen await God’s judgment.”

Horrified, Prissie snatched back her hand and stepped away from the square barrier. “Shouldn’t there be guards or something?”

“Oh, there’re guards,” Marcus replied nonchalantly, nodding to a few points in the vicinity. “Beats me why you’ve got such selective vision.”

“I’m sorry,” she murmured, glancing around uncertainly. “I can’t help it.”

“Nothing to apologize for,” he said gruffly. “Come on, let’s head back.”

They turned and retraced their steps, and the going was easier with the Protector’s wings to lend them light. After the first few twists and turns, Prissie dared to ask, “Marcus, why are you here?”

“I already told you. I’m here to lead you out.”

“I know *that,*” she huffed. “What I meant was … why are *you* here instead of Tamaes.”

Marcus tapped her shoulder, and she turned to look at her rescuer. “Tamaes is up to his whatsis in trouble,” he said seriously. “Knowing him, he’s having kittens and slaying lions.”

“Having kittens?” she echoed incredulously.

“He’s *worried* about you,” Marcus clarified. His golden eyes narrowed for a second, and without warning, he leaned forward and gave her forehead a flick with his middle finger. "Don't even think for *one* second that he let you down!"

Rubbing the spot, she grumbled, "Are angels *allowed* to be this mouthy?"

"Am I wrong?" he challenged.

Prissie turned her back on her classmate, resuming her upward march. "Are you *sure* you're an angel?" she flung over her shoulder.

"True facts, kiddo!"

"Don't call me kiddo," she snipped. Then a thought occurred to her and she paused. "Hang on. How old *are* you?"

"Older than you by a long shot, but what you see is what you get. Until Koji showed up, I was the youngest member of the Flight."

"So, you're still learning?"

"Yep, I've got a lot to learn."

Prissie wasn't sure if she should be worried that her life was in the hands of a novice, but it was sort of nice to know that Marcus wasn't perfect. "How much further do we have to go?"

"A lot further, actually. We're a *long* ways down. Gives me the creeps," he said, hunching his shoulders. "Why'd you come all this way in the first place?"

"I followed one of the little angels down here. He seemed to be in trouble."

Marcus stopped in his tracks, and she turned to peer into his baffled face. "There's nothing but darkness down here, and they need light to survive."

"I *know* that!" she retorted sulkily. "That's why I was so worried about him."

"Are you sure you didn't imagine it?"

She glared at him. "Obviously!"

The young Protector's face grew serious, and he gazed back down the way they had just come. "The need must be desperate," he mused, and then his eyes widened. "Oh, man. I wonder if there's any chance ...! Hey, Prissie, did you get close enough to see the little guy?"

"Of course," she said in exasperation. "We were together the whole way!"

"What did he look like?" Marcus pressed.

"Just like all the others, except for his hair. It was short ... and stood up like a little mane ... and it was a very pretty shade of green."

With a stunned expression, the Protector whispered, "Lavi."

7 THE PARK RANGERS

A bent figure skulked through the shadows, stubbing gnarled toes on a tumble of stones and cursing as he pitched onto his knees. "This wasn't there before," Dinge muttered sourly.

"You're just clumsy," taunted Murque. The lumpish demon patted the untidy heap of stones in a proprietary gesture. "I picked 'em up. Thought it might be fun to pitch them down the hole."

"Might be at that," his companion replied with a hoarse laugh. He squinted down into the pit and said, "A few rough knocks to teach him not to let his guard down."

"Sleeps too much, that one," Murque grunted.

"Yes. I don't trust it," Dinge muttered. "I was a Messenger, wasn't I? There's dreams to consider."

"I remember dreams," the other demon murmured, then his lip curled. "Taken, weren't they."

"That they were," his companion said in a dull voice. Reaching down, he picked up a stone and hefted it experimentally. Crossing to the edge of the pit, he sneered and let the missile drop. A soft grunt echoed from below, and a cruel smile cut across Dinge's misshapen face. "Yes, this might be fun."

"Who's Lavi?" Prissie asked.

"One of Abner's yahavim," Marcus said. "They all have names since Abner dotes on them so much. They know his voice. He knows their names. Stuff like that."

"Like a shepherd?"

"Just like that, yeah," he replied, gesturing for her to keep walking. The passage had widened somewhat, and they could travel side by side again. "Of course, Caretakers are responsible for a lot more than those pipsqueaks, but Jedrick says Abner is good at getting lost in details. Lavi went missing not long ago, and Padgett has been beside himself looking for any trace of the little guy."

"Padgett?" Prissie repeated, feeling like a parrot.

"Abner's apprentice," he said with a sidelong glance. "Him and Padgett both work as rangers at this park. Koji didn't tell you?"

"*He* and Padgett," she corrected automatically. "And *no*. Koji didn't get around to telling me *anything* before I followed the little manna-maker. Lavi." Prissie liked the way the name rolled off her tongue and quietly confessed, "I was wishing he could tell me his name."

"They don't talk."

"I *know*!" Her brief flare of temper fizzled fast. "Do you think he's okay? He wasn't shining very brightly."

"If he flew all the way to The Deep, then he's pushing himself awful hard."

"I carried him most of the way."

Golden eyes flashed her direction once more. "You like those little guys?"

"Yes," she replied, bristling because he seemed to be laughing at her. "Is that so strange?"

"Nah, they're cute and all," Marcus admitted. "I was just wondering why you think my hair is weird, but you think Lavi's wild, green frizz-job is pretty."

"That's hardly the point," she grumbled.

"You got that right," he agreed with a smirk. "There *is* something important about that little guy, though. He was Ephron's special favorite. They weren't as close as Taweel and Omri, but headed that way."

"Does that mean you think your friend is down there somewhere?"

"Could be," Marcus replied grimly. "Abner's gonna knock something loose if he finds out Ephron's been right under his nose all this time."

Prissie once again lost track of all the turns as they wound their way upward. "Do you come down here a lot?" she asked, hoping her guide wasn't as confused as she was.

"Nope."

"How do you know your way, then?"

They reached a fork in the trail, and he led her to the left. "I'm just retracing my steps, but I had help coming in."

"Harken's?"

“Nope,” Marcus replied, and once again Prissie felt as if he was teasing her. She clammed up, but in a little while, he said, “Took you long enough to call for help.”

“I guess,” she mumbled sulkily.

“Y’know, there’s only so much we can do on our own,” the Protector said seriously. “When you need help, don’t wait to ask. Sometimes that’s all God is waiting for. It’s *so* frustrating to stand by and wait to be Sent, but Jedrick says I’m too impatient.”

It occurred to Prissie that Marcus was actually pretty talkative. At school he mostly just shrugged and grunted. Of course, at school, he didn’t have strange eyes and shining wings, either. “Why are you pretending to be a student?”

“Harken will be retiring soon, and Jedrick wanted to have another Graft in place.”

“Why would Harken retire?”

“He’s getting old,” Marcus replied nonchalantly. “By human standards anyhow. People would notice if he hit his hundredth birthday and kept ticking, so he has to move on.”

“No!” Prissie gasped. “Harken’s always been there! I don’t want him to go!”

Her classmate turned, and his expression softened. “Don’t panic. I’m not talking about next week or nothing. In the next decade, maybe. By then, I’ll fit in somewhere, and I can help Milo keep an eye on things. In fact, we’re kinda thinking if Harken pulls out, I can just move in with Milo. Nobody would be surprised if he befriended me, since he’s friends with everyone.”

“Would you run The Curiosity Shop, then?”

“Dunno for sure. Maybe.” Marcus paused at the next turning and frowned. “I should probably switch back just in case we run into someone. I'm only allowed to freak *you* out today."

Prissie watched in awe as he shook out his wings. The shifting shades of butter and cream pulled together, winding into tight strands that settled onto his skin in jagged patterns. She stared until the last little bit of light left with them, then sighed with regret.

"Turn my flashlight on?" prodded Marcus.

She'd forgotten she still had it, and when she snapped it on, her companion was untying his hoodie from around his waist. Marcus pulled it on and zipped up, then squinted at her in the beam of light. His eyes were back to being brown, and he looked like a normal teenaged boy again. Well, as normal as someone with two-toned hair *could* look.

They stepped onto a path that was much wider and smoother than the way they'd been going, and Prissie realized that they must have reached one of the mapped tunnels. Though the passage was once more wide enough for them to be side by side, Prissie's steps lagged. They'd been walking for what seemed like forever, but there was no end to the darkness. She couldn't remember the last time she was this tired. "Are we almost there?" she asked, whining a little.

"Hang in there, kiddo," the Protector replied. "Not much further."

For a while, the only sound was the scuff of their feet, but suddenly, Marcus stuck his arm in front of her, and she jerked to a stop. "What's wrong?" Prissie whispered.

"Someone's coming," he announced. The heavy tread of boots came from the direction they were traveling.

"Do you have a sword or something weapony?"

"*Weapony*?" he snorted.

Prissie gave him an impatient look. "Yes! Don't Protectors carry sharp pointy objects?"

"Not on the school bus."

"So should I be worried?"

"Nah," Marcus replied nonchalantly. "There's no reason to get bent out of shape." Low voices carried along the passage, echoing slightly in the darkness, but he didn't seem at all concerned ... until two figures came into view. "Or not," he muttered.

"What?" she hissed, wondering if that was her cue to run for it.

However, Marcus ran to them, calling, "Tamaes, oh *man*! What happened?"

Prissie's eyes widened in alarm as soon as she realized what she was seeing. Her guardian angel leaned heavily on Jedrick, whose drawn sword caught flashes of the colored light radiating from their wings. Marcus reached them and pushed himself up under Tamaes's other shoulder, though it didn't do much good because of their height difference. Still, the Guardian smiled faintly at his young teammate and said, "Thank you, Marcus."

"You're going the wrong way, you know," the teen grumbled. "Abner's waiting in the garden."

Jedrick shook his head. "Tamaes was quite insistent."

The sagging warrior murmured, "I just needed to be sure."

Looking her way, Jedrick studied her dirty clothes and tear-stained face with concern before asking, "Prissie Pomeroy, are you well?"

"I'm ... fine?" She was stunned to realize that her guardian was clutching a wound in his side. "Why is he hurt?"

"Tamaes was beset," the tall Protector explained. "We

have been battling the enemy since the buses arrived on the park grounds, and it appears that their purpose was to separate the two of you. Did something happen?"

Prissie nodded mutely, and Marcus quickly said, "Can we talk and walk at the same time?"

Jedrick tried to maneuver Tamaes around, but the Guardian dug in his heels. With a small shake of his head, the green-winged warrior beckoned. "Please, Prissie. Let Tamaes reassure himself?"

Shuffling forward, she peered up into her guardian angel's scarred face. "I'm fine," she repeated, more confidently this time. For once, Tamaes didn't avoid eye contact, and there was a warrior's fierceness in his attitude.

The Guardian carefully withdrew his arm from around Marcus's shoulder and lifted his wings, increasing the intensity of the light that surrounded them. His fingertips rested atop her head, and he pronounced, "I thank God for guarding your steps while I could not."

"You're hurt," she whispered, taking in the gouges in his armor and the tears in his raiment.

Marcus casually remarked, "It takes an awful lot to keep a Guardian from his charge."

"Doesn't he need a doctor or something?" Prissie asked anxiously.

"We will take him to Abner," Jedrick said, adjusting his grip on Tamaes. "Marcus, if you take Prissie to the garden, Tamaes will have no choice but to follow. Use the stone door."

"Yeah." Waving urgently for her to follow, the teen said, "The sooner we get there, the better. Tamaes isn't the *only* one who wants to reassure himself."

"Who ...?"

With a faint smirk, Marcus said, "What did Ransom call him? Your conscience?"

"Oh, no!" she gasped. "Koji!"

Before long, the passage opened onto one of the well-lit thoroughfares, and Prissie glanced around, trying to get her bearings. "That isn't where I went in," she said in consternation.

"Nope. This way," Marcus directed.

She glanced behind to be sure that Jedrick and Tamaes were still following, then hurried after her classmate. When they rounded a bend, she reached out to tug at Marcus's sleeve. "One of the rangers is up there," she whispered, pointing.

"Yeah. He's holding the door for us," Marcus replied. "I'll introduce you."

"Is that Abner?"

"Nope. That's his apprentice," he corrected. "Padgett's nice and normal. You'll like him."

The stone door wasn't a proper door, meaning there weren't any signs of hinges or a handle. A part of the wall had simply been pushed outward, creating an opening from which soft light spilled into the cave. Prissie recognized the ranger who stood in the gap. He was the one Koji had been talking to just before she left the learning center. As they drew near, he stepped aside to let them pass. "Welcome back, Prissie Pomeroy," he said politely.

"Th-thanks."

"*In* first; introductions second," Marcus urged, hustling her through so Jedrick could maneuver Tamaes over the threshold.

She barely had a chance to take in the new setting when

Koji barreled into her. Without a word, the young Observer hugged her tight and hid his face in her shoulder. "Mercy," she groused. "You really have been spending too much time with Zeke."

To her embarrassment, that was the moment when all her pent up emotions decided to break loose. Sniffling, she turned her face, trying to hide her tears from Marcus. With a snort, the apprentice Protector patted the back of Koji's head and said, "Looks like you're in good hands here. I'll just go help Jedrick."

Prissie was grateful to see him go, and immediately felt awful because it was the wrong reason to be glad. "M-marcus?" she called, her voice barely carrying across the distance between them. He paused, though, and she whispered, "Thank you."

He smirked over his shoulder, then disappeared through the trees.

"Trees?" she mumbled, looking around in confusion.

"Promise me?" Koji begged, backing up enough to grab her arms and give her a small shake. "I have asked, and it is permitted for me to request a promise from you. Because we are friends."

"What are you talking about?" Prissie asked, wishing desperately for a tissue.

"It's unusual for an angel to secure a promise," interjected the ranger. Padgett wasn't exactly smiling at her, but his dark eyes were attentive as he offered her a handkerchief. "But Koji's desires coincide with the will of God."

The boy let her go so she could blow her nose and dab at her wet cheeks. Once she pulled herself together, she asked, "You want me to make a promise?"

"Yes." Koji reached out, and his fingertips grazed her hand. "Promise me that you will not go off without me again. Let me stay by your side for all the time that remains to us."

Prissie's brows drew together. "I didn't *mean* to go alone. It just sort of happened," she said defensively.

"From now on," Koji pressed. "Promise to keep me close. *Please*?"

This was obviously very important to him, and after the experience she'd just had, Prissie really didn't want to be alone again. "Okay," she agreed. "I promise, Koji."

The Observer's sigh might have been relief or contentment. Either way, he brightened considerably. Turning to their quiet companion, he said, "This is Padgett. He is the Caretaker apprenticed to Abner."

For the first time, Prissie *really* looked at this new angel. He wasn't particularly tall, yet he stood tall. With his black hair and eyes, Padgett appeared to be Native American, and he fit into the same hard-to-figure age group as many of the members of Jedrick's Flight — grown up, but not old. His park service uniform was neatly pressed, with short sleeves that left his arms bare, and she glanced at them, curious to see what color his tattoos might be. "My sort doesn't have wings," he said.

The gold name tag over his shirt pocket read, *Padgett Prentice,* so she courteously offered, "How do you do, Mr. Prentice?"

He gave a small shake of his head. "Padgett will do, miss."

She nodded and glanced back the way they came, frowning in confusion when she found nothing but blank stone. "Where's the door?"

"Caretakers can *make* doors," Koji said in awed tones.

Prissie thought back to what Adin had told her about this kind of angel. "You can move earth and bring storms?"

Padgett smiled. "As you might imagine, Caretakers take care of things. Creation is our concern, and we have been given the means to tend it by God."

"So you care about the environment and stuff?" Prissie guessed.

"That is a part, but not the whole," he replied, gesturing for Koji to lead the way through the trees. "We are not limited to this earth. A Caretaker renders his service to heaven as well."

"They sing with the stars," Koji whispered, as if sharing a great secret.

"The universe is vast," Padgett said calmly. "But my place is here."

Suddenly, Prissie realized that there was something very familiar about the forest Koji was leading her through, and she looked up between green leaves that belonged to an eternal summer. Sure enough, shifting lights filled the sky. "Is this the garden behind the blue door?"

"It is," Padgett replied.

"But we didn't use the blue door."

"There is more than one way in," the Caretaker explained. "The blue door was given to Harken and Milo so that they could enter this place. Baird and Kester also have a door, and there is a way in for Shimron, which Koji also used once upon a time."

"Do you have a door, too?" Prissie inquired.

"Of course," Padgett acknowledged. "Abner needs easy access so he can care for his flock, and we tend the garden."

"I like gardening, too," Koji shared, giving his teammate a shy smile.

"Yes, it is a pleasant pastime," agreed the Caretaker. "Here's Abner."

The forest opened up ahead, and when Prissie slipped between some saplings and into a small clearing, she was met by a fantastic sight. Upon a mossy knoll stood the most beautiful angel she'd ever seen. He was dressed in raiment similar to the kind Koji had been wearing when Prissie first met him. However, the beige tunic was longer, and the stitching that edged the collar and cuffs was black. The creamy hues of the cloth shimmered in subtle contrast to Abner's gleaming silver hair, which fell nearly to his ankles.

It took several moments for Prissie to realize that half the light that dazzled her eyes was coming from yahavim. The flock swarmed their shepherd, twirling around his upraised hands as he hummed softly. She didn't recognize Abner's melody, yet it seemed familiar somehow. As the notes flowed together, peace settled over Prissie, and fears she hadn't realized she'd carried back with her from The Deep lost their grip and faded away.

His song tapered off, gently giving way to silence, and then the Caretaker turned to face them. Prissie blinked as reality seemed to flicker. The brilliant angel was gone, replaced by a balding man in his fifties wearing a park ranger's uniform. With a gentle *tsk-tsk*-ing sound, he shooed away a playful little sprite who attempted to perch on the wire-rimmed glasses that he straightened as he strolled over. He studied her with icy gray eyes, then exclaimed, "The girl!" Without waiting for an answer, he looked to Padgett. "You found her?"

"Marcus brought her, sir."

"You don't have to call me *sir* when we're in here," Abner chided.

"Have you tended to Tamaes, sir?" Padgett asked quietly.

"Hmm?"

His partner patiently said, "Tamaes was injured in the recent fracas."

"He certainly was," Abner agreed. "I did what I could. Jedrick and Marcus are wrapping him up somewhere over there," he said, doing a little finger twirl in their general direction. Immediately, several yahavim started turning cartwheels in the air, causing the Caretaker to chuckle. "I was counting the ninety-nine," he explained distractedly. Then suddenly, Abner peered at Prissie with new intensity. "Lavi is still missing, but Marcus tells me you've found my lost lamb."

"I met a little manna-maker with green hair ... sir." The name tag pinned to his shirt said *Abner Ochs*, but she thought it best to follow Padgett's lead.

"Nonsense," he scolded. "My name is Abner, and that is what I wish to be called."

"Abner," she repeated obediently, still boggled that the old man in front of her was the beautiful angel she'd seen just a minute ago. His features were similar, yet unremarkable in his new guise. "I'm Prissie."

"Of course you are," he said, clasping his hands behind his back as he peered at her. "I've heard much about you from your friend."

At first, Prissie wasn't sure who he meant, for she'd gained many new friends within Jedrick's Flight over the past several weeks. Then, Koji shuffled his feet, giving himself away. It seemed to her that the young Observer was more than a little in awe of the Caretakers, and she planned to ask *why* the next time she had the chance. Remembering her manners, Prissie said, "Thank you for the apples."

His brows arched. "God created apples, not me."

"Oh, of course! I meant thank you for finding *ripe* apples," she clarified.

"Did I?" he asked, glancing at his apprentice.

"You did," Padgett confirmed.

"Ah," Abner murmured. "That explains that, but not that which needs explaining."

Prissie took a deep breath and said, "I'm sorry if I did something wrong, but I was only trying to help."

The senior Caretaker focused on her, and the keenness was back in his gaze. "You don't need to explain yourself to *me*, Prissie."

She was relieved to hear it, but Padgett quietly reminded, "Time holds no sway in this place, but it's running on schedule out there."

Abner nodded seriously. "Yet we are here, and here I hold a little sway. I'm permitted to bend the rules, but Prissie's choice will still have its consequences."

"Consequences?" she asked nervously. Hours must have passed while she was missing in the caves, and she felt a little sick at the thought of all the people who must be worried. "I'm in a lot of trouble, aren't I?"

"No," the Caretaker replied, peering over his glasses at her. "You're safe here."

Prissie didn't know how to respond, so she glanced at Koji, hoping for a clue. The young Observer helpfully explained, "This garden is outside of time." She shook her head, and he tried again. "Abner will open an earlier door."

Padgett stepped up and quietly murmured, "Excuse me,

miss. You're a little worse for wear after your ordeal." He gently cupped her cheek, and while she blinked up at him, he almost-smiled at her. "What Koji means is that we'll return you before you're entirely missed."

"No one will know I was gone?" she asked.

"Only those Ransom Pavlos spoke to," Padgett replied.

Glancing from him to Abner, she asked, "Who did he tell?"

Marcus sauntered through the trees at that moment and answered, "Me for one. Koji for the other."

"And he came to me as well. Angels one and all," the head ranger announced as his apprentice dropped his hand and stepped back. "Not bad, not bad," Abner remarked, looking critically at Prissie.

Startled, she glanced down at herself and found that the grime had disappeared from her clothes. Prissie felt better, too, less tired and more clearheaded. "What did you do?"

"I ministered to you," Padgett answered.

"Oh," she replied, not entirely sure what that entailed. With a tentative smile, she mumbled, "Thank you?"

"You'll need it," he replied seriously.

"Why?"

"Because we have to go back into those caves, kiddo," Marcus answered for him. "The field trip. Remember?"

Prissie paled. "Do we have to?"

"C'mon," Marcus said, jerking his thumb in the direction of the trees. "Let's get this over with."

Abner nodded and led them to the stone wall. "I'll meet you back at the cave entrance," he instructed. "Be quick, and be quiet." That said, he placed his hand upon the featureless gray rock, and it opened before them, leading into inky darkness.

"Flashlight?" prompted Marcus.

"Oh ... umm," Prissie murmured in confusion, trying to remember what she'd done with it.

Padgett smoothly placed it in the young Protector's hands and said, "Jacket?"

"Yeah, you'd better give it back," Marcus agreed. "That'll only add fuel to the inevitable fire."

Prissie slipped out of the heavy leather jacket, feeling more vulnerable with its weight gone. "Where does this lead?" she asked in a small voice.

"*This* is where you came in," Marcus explained. "A quick jog will put us back where we belong, and only a little late. Koji, you go ahead and let him know we're coming."

With a nod, the young Observer darted through the opening. Abner nodded approvingly, then said, "Take courage, Prissie. Not every shadow is something to be feared."

Clicking on the flashlight, Marcus hooked his hand through her elbow and steered her through the opening. Darkness swallowed them up, and she fought back a whimper of protest. Using the flashlight to point the way, he hustled her along the passage. "Tamaes is okay, by the way," he announced. "He'll need to rest for a while, but that's to be expected after he was mobbed like that."

Prissie was pretty sure he was trying to reassure her, but the mental picture of swarming demons wasn't helping her battered courage. Seconds later, she could see a light ahead, and she hastened her steps. Marcus willingly picked up his pace as well, and by the time they clambered over the chain barring the side passage, she was breathing hard. Several heads turned, and someone called out, "They're over here, Mrs. Solomon!"

"*There* you are," their science teacher snapped in exasperation. She gave them both a stern look, then made a point of checking their names off her list. Lifting her voice, she called, "All present and accounted for, Ranger Ochs! You can begin the tour. *Finally.*"

Prissie wilted under her teacher's disapproval, but was quickly distracted when she realized that Ransom and Koji were talking to Abner, who certainly didn't look as if he'd just raced in from someplace else. Padgett walked in and spoke softly to his mentor, who nodded before clapping his hands for attention and launching into a quick run-down of some of the cave formations they'd be seeing today.

Ransom hurried over and punched his best friend's shoulder. "I was starting to worry."

"Wasn't nothing," Marcus replied with a laconic shrug.

"You okay, Miss Priss?" Ransom asked with a frown.

"Fine," she muttered. "Stop making a big deal out of it."

"Yeah, okay," he said, glancing at the rest of the class. "At least Marcus was able to haul you out before Mrs. Solomon finished roll call. I would *not* want to cross that woman. *Yeesh.*"

With that, he and Marcus took off, falling in line with the rest of the class to be fitted for helmets with flashlights set into them. As soon as they were out of earshot, Padgett strolled over and said, "I'll be bringing up the rear. You may walk with me if it would help."

"I have never been underground, and Prissie is still frightened," Koji frankly admitted. "I would be glad for your company."

The Caretaker nodded, the Observer smiled, and as Abner led the way into Sunderland State Park's famous caves, Prissie hoped that no one would notice just how tightly she clung to Koji's hand.

8

THE BENCH WARMER

Sit still."

"I must get back!"

"You must rest and heal," Shimron countered. "You can watch from here."

"Do not ask it of me," growled the warrior. "I cannot sit back and watch like you, Observer. She could be in danger!"

"Injuries need time to mend," the white-haired angel said, patient and firm. "You will do your young lady no good if you are endangering yourself."

Tamaes frowned miserably at the small flock of yahavim hovering anxiously around his head. "My place is with her."

"This is why active Guardians are paired with a mentor," Shimron remarked, giving the bandages a firm tug. "Taweel is watching over Prissie."

Wincing at the sudden pressure against his wound, Tamaes stubbornly argued, "Leaving Milo at risk!"

"Jedrick is with him."

Eyes widened. "What about . . . ?"

"Padgett is there." With a serene smile, the ancient angel said, "We are a team, Tamaes. Let the other members of the Flight cover for you while you heal."

Broad shoulders sagged as the Guardian finally relented, allowing Shimron and the yahavim to meet his needs.

Over the next few days, the school buzzed with rumors about the good girl and the bad boy who'd snuck out of the tour group in order to meet in the caves. It was Prissie's first brush with scandal, and she didn't care one bit for the attention. She walked through the halls with her nose in the air and her ears burning, horrified that so many people would believe such complete and utter nonsense.

The worst part of the whole mess was her friend's reaction to the gossip. Prissie had spent what seemed like twenty unchaperoned minutes alone with the boy Jennifer was crushing on, and Jennifer believed the rumors.

"I don't like Marcus!" Prissie said, rolling her eyes in exasperation. "Far from it!"

"I know you do!" Jennifer argued. "You'd be crazy not to!"

"Then I'm crazy."

Jennifer's brown eyes flashed with anger. "We talk about him all the time!"

"*You* talk about him. I just listen!"

"I trusted you with my private feelings." Drawing herself up, she accused, "All this time, you just wanted him for yourself!"

"You're being stupid," Prissie protested. "If that's what you think, you don't know me at all!"

"I guess not!" Jennifer stormed away. A few steps later she called back over her shoulder, "I *thought* you were my friend!"

Prissie could only watch her go with a bewildered expression on her face. "I thought you were, too." Turning to find Koji right at her elbow, she muttered, "Why won't she listen?"

Koji gazed after the girl. "She is angry."

"That's not a good reason to accuse me of something I never did!"

He peered thoughtfully at her, but simply answered, "No, it is not."

Prissie stalked off toward their lockers. "Me and Marcus," she muttered. "Impossible! And even if I *did* like a boy, I wouldn't sneak around to meet him!"

"There is no truth to what is being said," Koji agreed quietly.

"No one cares about the truth," she replied waspishly.

"I do," he replied, his dark eyes shining.

She hated it when he did that. It was so hard to stay angry when Koji smiled.

During classes all week, Prissie took extra care never to look in Marcus's direction. In her experience, if you ignored something long enough, it went away. Not that Marcus actually went away. He stayed put, acting just the same as he always had. According to April, he shrugged off all the rumors, so people were already losing interest. Prissie supposed she should thank him, but it was still too strange to think of him being an angel. Even stranger, he was an angel who willingly hung out with Ransom, of all people. Risking a glance in their direction, she puzzled over his reasons for sticking so close to someone who didn't even believe in God or church or anything.

Light fingertips brushed the back of her hand, and she guiltily looked to see what Koji wanted. The boy asked, "Why do you ignore Marcus?"

"I *always* ignore Marcus."

Koji nodded solemnly. "Why do you *continue* to ignore Marcus?"

"Why wouldn't I?" she asked, sitting a little straighter.

"Your perspective has not changed?"

"Technically, yes," Prissie said in a low voice. "But I can't suddenly act friendly with someone like him. He's *not* the kind of person I would *ever* be friends with. Plus, it would make it seem like the rumors were true."

"But they are not."

"I know that, and you know that," she replied patiently. "But people would think differently of me if I acted differently toward him."

Koji tipped his head to one side, considering her closely. "The opinion of others is important to you."

"Oh, I wouldn't say *that*," Prissie quickly protested.

"Why not?"

"That makes me sound shallow!"

His gaze sharpened, then softened, and he gently asked, "Does my opinion mean more to you than those of your other classmates?"

Prissie had to think about that one, because it had never occurred to her that Koji might have an opinion. For some reason, she'd assumed he was just taking everything in with those clear eyes of his. Now that she was thinking along those lines, she knew deep down what her answer must be. "Yes."

At noon on Friday, Prissie and Koji carried their lunches to their usual table and slid into the two remaining spots on the end. The conversation was well underway, so there were just a few quick hellos before everyone picked up where they left off. Prissie wasn't really surprised when Jennifer didn't bother to make eye contact.

"I usually dress as a cat," Elise announced as she poked at her salad. Her dyed black hair was pulled back with an electric blue headband that perfectly matched the makeup rimming her hazel eyes.

"I can't see you as a cute little kitten," giggled Margery.

"Not *cute*," the girl replied scornfully. "I have two words for you. Black. Leather. 'Nuff said."

"Meow," April said, making a little cat's paw motion before fishing around in her lunch bag and coming up with a container of yogurt.

"So what are you doing for Halloween this year?" Jennifer asked Margery.

Prissie smiled, for she already knew the answer. Every year, she and Margery always took part in West Edinton's Fall Festival by helping out at Loafing Around. During the last weekend in October, the whole town turned out for an annual celebration of its founding, and this year, the big deal was even bigger because it was West Edinton's bicentennial. Main Street would be roped off at both ends, and with a corn roast, food vendors, live music, and dancing, it would be like a huge block party. Prissie hadn't had the chance to talk to

Margery yet about the plans they'd made for the bakery, but there was still plenty of time for that.

However, Margery clapped her hands and announced, "Party at my house!"

"R-really?" Prissie asked, startled. "But what about the Festival?"

The blonde girl smiled sweetly. "Well, you don't really *need* me this year. You have Koji, right?"

Prissie carefully said, "I'm sure he'd be happy to help out."

"Indeed," Koji acknowledged.

"And you're invited, of course," Margery breezed on. "If your parents let you out early, you can come over! It'll be so much fun! We're doing all kinds of spooky stuff, and everyone will wear costumes!"

"Your Mom is being so cool about the whole thing," Elise said smugly.

Prissie could feel the color draining from her face. Not only had Margery made plans that excluded her, she'd made them with Elise. She clenched her fists in her lap and stared determinedly at her untouched sandwich, feeling sick to her stomach. Koji shifted in his seat so that their arms touched, and she leaned slightly into his silent offering of comfort.

The conversation spun on without her when Jennifer said, "I have a gypsy costume this year, with tons of scarves and beads, and I found an ankle bracelet with little bells on it!"

"Hey, did you make up your mind yet on your costume?" Elise asked Margery. "I still think you should be a witch, so I can be your familiar."

"I'm still not sure," she said. "I haven't looked around yet."

"We should shop!" Jennifer exclaimed.

"Yes. Yes, we should," agreed April. "I still need some props for my costume. I'll be a pirate this year."

"With a corset?" asked Elise eagerly.

"With a *plume*!" April countered with a grin. "Best. Hat. Ever!"

Ten minutes later, the warning bell rang, and everyone at the table hurried to finish their meal. Most of Prissie's friends trailed after Elise without a backward glance, still talking about Margery's party. Only April stopped to check on her and Koji. With a sympathetic smile, she called, "Will you be at the game tonight?"

While Prissie only managed a mute nod, the young angel brightly replied, "Yes, we will be there."

That night's game was against the Predators, the Warriors' toughest rivals, so everyone in the stands was keyed up. When the Predators took the field in a flood of green jerseys, the visiting team's bleachers sent up a roar of support. Their school had some boys on their cheer squad, and they were doing some impressive formations on the sidelines. They even had a team mascot — someone dressed as a toothy dinosaur.

At halftime, the Warriors were holding their own, and not long after play resumed, Coach Hobbes sent Neil to the sideline to warm up his arm. Prissie wondered if that meant her brother would be playing tonight. She really hoped so.

Whistles blew as a timeout was called, and Koji nudged her and asked, "Do you want something hot to drink?"

Prissie frowned in surprise. "Do you have money?"

"I do," he answered with a pleased smile. "Harken gave

me some, and I have not found many reasons to use it. May I treat you?"

"I'd like that," she replied politely. "Cocoa, please?"

Koji was barely out of sight when Milo slipped into the vacant spot the Observer left behind. "Good evening, Miss Priscilla!"

She smiled. "What, are you Koji's backup?"

"I just thought you looked a little lonely."

"In the middle of a crowd?"

"You'd be surprised," the Messenger replied. "Are you enjoying the game? It's been a real nail-biter!"

"Oh, I guess so," she hedged. "I don't know very much about football."

Milo's eyebrows lifted. "You're here for every home game, but you don't know what's going on?"

Prissie nodded. "I follow along. If everyone else is cheering, I cheer, too."

"Are you saying that you have no idea why you do what you do?"

"Yes."

"So, you're just going through the motions?"

There seemed to be a shade of disapproval in his tone, and Prissie's conscience twinged. "Isn't it best if I cheer for our guys no matter what? I want to support Neil and the team."

"I think it's wise to understand the whys and wherefores, but this *is* only a game," Milo conceded. "Other things have far greater importance."

"Like what?"

"The kinds of things that last forever."

"Oh," Prissie replied awkwardly. "So it's okay if I don't understand what's going on out there?"

"Yes, understanding the ins and outs of football is optional," Milo assured. "However, it might be good if you tried to understand the people who are playing that game."

She looked out onto the field where the players were taking up their positions once more. "Why?"

The mailman clapped his hands as the game resumed, his eyes on the field. "Because *they're* eternal."

"Oh," she said again, feeling like a dunce. "I didn't think of it that way."

"I can't help but think such things."

"Because of your *job*?" she asked, peeking uncertainly over her shoulder in case anyone was listening in.

"Yeah," he said with a crooked smile. "I also happen to enjoy football. Would you like me to explain what's going on?"

"I guess," she agreed. "I should warn you, though. Grandpa's tried, and Dad's tried, and Neil's tried. They get all excited and use words I don't understand, so once it starts sounding like blah, blah, blah, I stop listening."

He laughed. "I can say with some authority that it's no use trying to give a message to someone who isn't listening."

Blushing in embarrassment, Prissie promised, "I'll listen. Just don't expect too much."

With another chuckle, Milo pointed to the players of the field. "The boys in red uniforms are trying to carry the football across the line at that end of the field, and the boys in green are trying to carry the ball across the line on the other end. If either of them succeeds, they earn points."

Prissie stared up at him, feeling insulted. "I know *that* much, Milo."

"I'm not patronizing you, Miss Priscilla." The Messenger

held up his hands in a gesture of innocence, saying, "I've simply eliminated all the jargon from my explanation."

"Go ahead, then," she said with a sigh.

As the Warriors battled their way down the field, Milo simplified the game to such a degree that Prissie actually started to see the big picture. His commentary made a lot more sense than that given by the announcers up in the press box, and the more she understood, the more she cared about what was happening. "It's like a battle," Milo explained. "Both sides have a goal, but only one can achieve it. To do that, they must prevent their opponent from making progress."

She tapped his arm to get his attention. "Do you fight?"

Passion flashed fiercely in his blue eyes. "I don't carry a sword, but I carry messages for those who do. I would see the will of God carried out," he declared earnestly.

Prissie's heart thudded at the sudden change in her friend's demeanor. It was as if she was catching a glimpse of the *real* Milo, an angel who served God with all his heart, and to be honest, it was unsettling. She still sort of preferred the old Milo, the mailman who was always ready with a kind word and an easy smile. "Well, be careful," she said briskly.

He took the time to consider her demand, then answered, "I'll do whatever God asks of me."

"Then I hope He doesn't send you into danger."

The Messenger's expression softened, and there was affection in his tone when he replied, "Thanks for your concern, Miss Priscilla."

She fidgeted under his gaze and turned back to the field. "What's happening now?"

Milo resumed his lesson by pointing to the various players, giving the names of their positions, and explaining their roles. Before she knew it, Koji came into view, carefully carrying two steaming cups. When he reached them, Milo quickly relinquished his seat, saying, "If you'll excuse me? I'm needed elsewhere."

"You are?" she asked in surprise.

"Yep." Placing his hand on his young teammate's shoulder, he said, "Koji's learned many of the finer points of football, so he can continue your lesson."

"You *are* taking turns!" she accused huffily. "I don't need a babysitter, and I already have a Guardian!"

"Don't scold us for doing what we must, Miss Priscilla." With an uncommonly serious expression, Milo added, "And don't worry. It'll be all right."

As he strolled off down the sideline, Koji placed a cup of cocoa into her hands. She curled cold fingers around its welcome warmth and asked, "*What* will be all right? Do you know what he's talking about?"

Koji gazed after the Messenger. "No."

She'd always thought angels should be a little mysterious, but Prissie was beginning to think she preferred straight answers that made sense. With a gusty sigh, she took a cautious sip of her cocoa. "Mmm, this is good! Thank you, Koji."

Her friend beamed. "I agree, and you are most welcome."

Prissie felt a burst of affection for the angel who'd taken on the appearance of a boy in order to be by her side.

Late in the final quarter, Prissie was actually paying attention to the game. She knew the names and faces of all the football players, but it was harder to tell them apart with their helmets on. The announcer up in the press box called out the play-by-play, which helped a little. Still, it was odd to hear the boys referred to by their last names or by their uniform numbers. Over the cheers of the crowd and the blare of their school's fight song, the announcer's voice rang out.

"...And Blake is on the move, looking for an opening ... and there's the throw! It's a quick slant pass to Number 14, Mueller!"

The stands roared with excitement as Mueller tucked the ball snugly against his chest and started toward the end zone. It took a moment for Prissie to realize that the wide receiver the commentator kept referring to as "Mueller" was actually Joey, one of Ransom's friends.

The lanky teen was quick on his feet, but not fast enough to outrun one of the Predator's linebackers. A cry of disappointment rang across the field when the green-clad opponent gained enough ground to wrap his arms around Joey's chest and slam him into the turf.

"Down on the forty-six yard line. It'll be third and four."

An uneasy murmur rippled through the crowd while the linebacker picked himself up, but Number 14 didn't move. One of his teammates hurried over, then waved furiously at the sideline, calling, "Coach! Better c'mere!"

Whistles blew, the clock stopped, and Coach Hobbes jogged out onto the field to check on Joey. Prissie glanced up to where the rest of her family was seated in the stands and saw that her grandfather was on his feet, frowning as he rubbed his chin. Her father said something to him, and Grandpa Pete grimaced, pointing to his shoulder as he answered Jayce's question.

Around her, Prissie heard concerned voices. "That poor boy!"

"He's not moving! Do you think he's been knocked out?"

Turning to Koji, Prissie asked, "What just happened?"

"A player has been injured."

That much was obvious. Fleetingly, she wondered why Joey Mueller's Guardian hadn't stepped in. "Is it bad?"

"He is in a great deal of pain," Koji replied frankly.

Prissie didn't know *what* to do, but while she looked on with the rest of the crowd, someone hurried past, another person slouching after him. With a start, she recognized Ransom and Marcus. They headed straight for their team's bench, and Ransom punched one of the big linemen on the arm. The back of his red jersey read *EVANS*. Brock Evans was Ransom's other close friend, and all three of them stared onto the field with tense expressions.

Derrick Matthews eased Joey onto his back and was talking to him. It'd been a long time since they'd had a serious injury during a game, but that's one of the reasons Coach Hobbes kept Mr. Matthews around. Although a carpenter by trade, Derrick was also a first responder with West Edinton's volunteer fire department. And an avid football fan. He acted as the Warriors' trainer and provided first aid when necessary.

Cheerleaders huddled together, looking nervous as they whispered, and members of both teams removed their helmets and knelt along the sidelines. She spotted Milo kneeling next to Brock. At the mailman's beckoning wave, Ransom and Marcus climbed over the bench to join them, showing support for their downed friend. "Is that why Milo was needed?" Prissie murmured curiously.

"I believe so," Koji acknowledged.

A grim murmur from the crowd, and Prissie heard someone say, "Here comes a stretcher."

The referees urged everyone to back up and make room for the two EMTs. When they carried Joey off the field a minute later, everyone clapped and called encouragement, and the wide receiver managed a clumsy wave before disappearing into the back of the ambulance.

The injury put a damper on the rest of the game, but the Warriors rallied, pushing their way into field goal territory. They brought out their kicker, and the game ended with West Edinton winning by three points. As the stands began to empty, Prissie again caught snatches of conversation, and she had to agree with those who said the victory had been a costly one.

During the ride home, Prissie sat between Neil and Tad on one of their van's wide bench seats. The Pomeroy's overall mood was subdued, but her two older brothers fell into conversation.

"Did you learn anything more about Joey while you were in the locker room?" Tad asked.

"Only that they took him to the hospital down in Harper to do some X-rays and stuff," Neil replied.

Tad hummed. "Was he that bad off?"

"I think it was just a precaution," Neil said. "Joey was alert and everything before they carted him off. He was more embarrassed than anything that he had to be pulled out of the game."

"I thought he was really hurt," said Prissie.

"Yeah, he was definitely banged up," he confirmed. "Derrick said he thought the collarbone was broken, which means he's out for the rest of the season."

"Too bad."

"No kidding."

Prissie sternly asked, "Since when do you call Mr. Matthews by his first name?"

Neil grinned and tugged her braid. "He invited all of us on the team to call him Derrick, so don't fuss at me about my manners. You call his wife by her first name."

"Pearl and I are *friends,*" she retorted.

"Yeah, well, Derrick's part of my team, and an important part, too," he replied seriously. "He was really great tonight."

Tad eyed his brother. "You were right out there with him and Coach."

Neil rubbed his hands together, and he looked as if he was back in that tense moment. "I wanted to *do* something, but I didn't have a clue how to help. Derrick did, though. He took charge and calmed Joey down. Even made him laugh a couple times. And rode with him in the back of the ambulance since his folks weren't at the game."

"That's good," Tad said neutrally.

Neil gazed out the van window at the starry sky and quietly repeated, "He was really great."

9

THE FIRST REHEARSAL

Rough voices filtered through Ephron's darkness, stirring him from a dull stupor of pain.

"Did you see that?" growled Murque.

"Be more specific, idiot," Dinge sneered.

Scuffling and scraping sounds grated against the Observer's sensitive ears, and finally the first captor said, "There it was again! Just a bit of light out of the corner of my eye!"

"Down here?" scoffed his companion. "Your eyes are playing tricks on you."

"I'm going to check," insisted Murque, and the ominous *snick* of a drawn blade sent a shiver down their prisoner's back.

With a hiss of impatience, Dinge snapped, "Fine! It's a waste of time, though."

"Not if I'm right!"

"You're *never* right!"

While the demons' bickering faded from earshot, Ephron lifted his face toward the whisper of tiny wings. He opened the front of his shirt with fumbling fingers, offering refuge to the little one who risked so much to meet him in his dank prison. Small hands patted his cheek, then pressed a thin wafer to his lips, and as the manna dissolved upon his tongue, Ephron's hope was renewed.

"Mind your wings," he murmured as he pulled his raiment over the yahavim. Its inherent glow would help to mask the little angel's presence. Tucking his chin against his chest, the Observer curled protectively around his precious visitor, smiling softly as Lavi snuggled against him.

Koji didn't ask for much, so when he asked Prissie if they could attend the first *Messiah* rehearsal at Holy Trinity Presbyterian, she talked to Momma. "Could we go?"

Her mother seemed surprised. "Are you planning to sing?"

She shook her head, saying, "Koji wants to see. Do you think it's okay?"

"I don't see why not, as long as your homework is done," Naomi replied. "Tad's driving separately from your grandpa, so let him know he'll have two more passengers."

"Thanks!" Prissie hurried off to locate her big-big brother, and found him in the machine shed, tinkering with his hunk-of-junk car. Grandpa had given it to him when he was sixteen, and they'd taken it all to pieces. In their spare time, when work on the farm slowed down, they'd been putting it back together. According to Grandpa Pete, the vehicle was a practical puzzle, and it was pretty obvious that in his own quiet way, Tad enjoyed figuring it out. "Say, Priss, do you see a small metal thingamabob on the floor anywhere?"

"Is that the technical term?" she asked.

Gray eyes slanted her way. "Of *course* it has a proper name, but you don't need to know it to find it."

"Did you drop it?"

"Yeah, just now. It's a tiny little thing," he said, giving her an idea of the size with his thumb and forefinger. "But if it's missing the whole lot is useless."

"So it's an *important* thingamabob."

"No more important than any of the other thingamabobs. I need them *all* in the right place if this thing is ever going to make it out of the shed."

She crouched down and peered underneath the car, scooting around until she spotted something in the shadow of one of the tires. Holding up the doodad, she asked, "Is this what you lost?"

"Lost and *found*!" Tad took the part from his sister and went back to tinkering. "Did you need something?"

"Can Koji and I go with you and Neil tonight?"

"No problem. Guess I shouldn't be surprised."

"Why?"

"The kid likes to sing."

Prissie tugged at the end of one braid. "How do you know?"

He paused, wiping his hands on a greasy rag as he gazed thoughtfully at the ceiling. "Mostly because he sings while he's slopping the pigs. It's interesting to listen to him because his songs are never the same."

"R-really?"

"Yep. It's like he's always making it up as he goes along." Tad shook his head as he went back to work. "Koji's not what I'd call normal, but he's a nice kind of odd."

The Presbyterian church on Main Street was a beautiful building constructed from locally quarried stone. As Prissie trailed after her brothers up the front steps to the big, double doors, her attention was caught by the bronze plate beside the entrance or, more specifically, by the smooth surface to which it was affixed. Many of the buildings in town were faced by the same gray stone, including Town Hall and the post office. Lightly running her fingers over the polished surface, she murmured, "I remember this."

"Which part?" asked Koji, who was reading the plate that commemorated the completion of Holy Trinity's construction.

"No, this," she replied, tapping the wall. "It's like the stone I saw in the caves. The one with chains."

Koji's eyes widened, and he placed his hand on the building. "I did not know, but Tamaes says you are correct. This is the same stone that was used to seal the Deep."

Shivering at the stark reminder of her time underground, Prissie slipped through the doors and hung her coat in the foyer. Everything about the Presbyterian church felt fancy, from the rich red carpet underfoot to the wood that gleamed darkly against more gray stone. She and Koji tiptoed into the back of the sanctuary, whose high ceilings always made her wonder if this was what a cathedral might be like. The spacious room smelled of candles and furniture polish, but Prissie's favorite things were the windows.

Tall, stained glass windows depicting various scenes from the Old and New Testaments reached upward to the vaulted ceilings. The sun had already set, but floodlights illuminated the colored panes from outside. Prissie thought they were even more beautiful when daylight streamed through, but they were still impressive at night.

"Pastor Bert is here," she whispered, pointing to Albert Ruggles, the preacher from her home church. He was in his usual navy suit, and this evening he wore an October-appropriate orange tie. A quick check confirmed that his wife Laura wore a matching orange sweater. They did things like that.

"And I see Kester," Prissie said softly. He was listening to the choir director, who gestured broadly even when he talked.

"I *hear* Baird," Koji replied, as an electric guitar filled the sanctuary with a swiftly ascending set of scales. He crooked his fingers. "I have been here before, and there is a good place this way."

She followed him back out into the foyer, feeling rather sneaky. "Is it somewhere only an angel can get to?" she asked softly.

"No. Follow me," he urged. Just around a corner was a stairway leading up, and over it was a sign that read, *BALCONY.*

Prissie hesitated. "Is it high?"

"I believe you will feel secure," Koji said, offering his hand.

"I'll manage." She put her hand on the banister instead. As they climbed the stairs together, she asked, "Why were you here before?"

"Harken has joined this congregation," he explained. "He invited me."

"Was that before anyone else could see you?"

"Yes."

Prissie didn't protest when Koji led her to the very back of the balcony because it kept her well away from the edge. Bright silver pipes in all shapes and sizes took up the entire rear wall of the sanctuary, flanking a central console and its tiny bench. They looked curiously at the confusing series of knobs, and Prissie asked, "Do you think Kester knows how to play a pipe organ?"

"I am not sure," he admitted. "We could ask him afterward."

They faced forward and Prissie swallowed hard. The view was great, but that was only because they were up so high. Below, sections of pews fanned out in front of a series of wide steps that the choir would use as risers. The pulpit stood on the topmost tier, and the orchestra would use the open space between the choir and the first row of pews.

Grandpa Pete and Grandma Nell were already there, laughing and talking with friends and neighbors, and she could see Tad and Neil sitting with a bunch of other teens from the DeeVee's youth group. Unplugging himself from the equipment, Baird bounded down to greet a batch of newcomers, his guitar still slung from his shoulders.

Focusing on her friends and family helped a little, but Prissie was still nervous when she edged forward enough to quickly drop into a seat. She braced her arms against the pew in front of her, feeling a little dizzy. Koji sat beside her and laid his hand on her arm. "Would you like Tamaes to join us?"

"Is he on the roof?"

"No, he is here," Koji replied. He gestured to the side and relayed, "He wants you to be at ease."

With a nervous half-smile, Prissie admitted, "I'd like it if he joined us."

At first, there was only a faint blooming of orange light, which deepened in color and intensity before spreading. Then, it unfolded to reveal Tamaes, who was leaning against the arm of the pew across the aisle, his large hands folded together. Shifting colors of bittersweet and amber stretched wide for a moment, displaying the Guardian's impressive wingspan, then settled, spilling across the wooden seat behind him as if his wings were made of fabric instead of light. The last time Taweel had dropped into sight, it had been instantaneous … and startling. This gradual revelation was more to Prissie's liking, and she wondered if Tamaes had been hiding behind his wings so she wouldn't be frightened.

Reddish-brown eyes lifted to meet her gaze, and Tamaes said, "There is nothing to fear, little one."

Prissie was grateful for the reassurance. "How are you feeling now? Are you still hurt?" She hadn't seen her Guardian since he was injured during the field trip two weeks ago. For someone who was almost always with her, he was actually pretty scarce.

"I am well," he said with a gentle smile.

"Sit with us!" Koji eagerly invited. He stood and scooted past Prissie, sitting on her other side and encouraging her to slide down to make more room for the angelic warrior. "You would like that, right, Prissie?"

She nodded. After a moment's hesitation, Tamaes slowly unfastened the sword that was strapped to his back, propping it within easy reach before carefully taking a seat. Prissie barely noticed how high up she was anymore. It was much too distracting to have the big Guardian sitting so close.

Tamaes's wings had flicked up to settle behind the pew, and though the shifting lights didn't come close enough to touch her, she thought she could hear a whisper coming from them. The faint ripple of sound wasn't the same as the soft notes that Kester's wings had made. This was less like a wind chime and more like lapping water. It was hard to tell if the warmth she felt was coming from the wings, the angel, or her own face, which was turning red. She glanced at Koji for help, but the young Observer merely smiled as if the awkward silence was the most natural thing in the world.

Finally, she leaned forward to try to see past the curtain of sleek auburn hair that hid Tamaes's scarred face. "Do you like music?"

He smiled faintly. "Yes, I do."

"I do, too," she admitted.

The Guardian's smile deepened enough to reveal a dimple, and he replied, "I know."

Of course he did. He probably knew her better than anyone. A soft giggle bubbled up, breaking the tension. Rolling her eyes, she said, "Obviously."

Just then, Baird plugged in his guitar and struck a chord for attention, and the choir director stepped to the front, getting the first rehearsal underway. Prissie was a little disappointed because it didn't sound like there would be much singing tonight. The director spent most of his time dividing the newcomers into their appropriate parts and introducing the various section leaders.

Tad was sorted into the tenor section with Milo, and Neil ended up a baritone, joining Derrick Matthews in their section of the pews. Grandpa and Harken were basses, of course, and Grandma Nell was in the alto section.

After a time, Koji leaned into Prissie and said, "Shimron would like to meet you."

"Now?" she gasped.

"No," he said, looking amused. "When the time is right."

"He's your mentor, right?"

"Indeed."

"What's he like?" she asked, glancing at Tamaes to include him in the conversation.

"Shimron is very patient with me," the young angel said seriously.

Prissie snorted softly. "Dealing with *Zeke* requires patience. Why would Shimron need patience with *you*?"

"Koji asks many, *many* questions," said Tamaes.

The apprentice Observer swung his feet. "Shimron says he does not mind. I can only learn if I seek answers."

"Seek, and you will find," Tamaes acknowledged, his jaw tightening once the words were out of his mouth.

To Prissie's surprise, Koji's eyes widened, and he reached across her to pat the big angel's arm. "We *will.* I am sure of it."

She realized the angels must be talking about Ephron. It was awkward to see so much sadness in their eyes, so she tried to distract them. "Does Shimron mind that you're going to my school instead of learning how to be an Observer?"

Koji said, "I am still learning from my mentor as well."

"Really? Does he give you homework or something?"

"Shimron listens to my accounts and checks my records." With a small squirm, he confessed, "He says that my writing could be neater."

"Accounts?" Prissie asked suspiciously.

Tamaes said, "Observers do not simply watch. They are archivists."

This was news to Prissie. "So you're *reporting* on me and my family to Shimron?"

He slowly shook his head. "No. That is not my purpose."

"But you're watching," she accused.

"Indeed."

Her Guardian briefly touched Prissie's shoulder, and she turned her gaze on Tamaes. He met it evenly. "An Observer watches that which can be seen, but he is looking for evidence of that which is unseen." When she still seemed baffled, he explained, "Even if Koji is watching you, you are not his focus."

Even more confused, Prissie asked, "Then what *are* you looking at?"

Koji said, "We watch for the hand of God, for He is always at work in the lives of those who are His."

"So when you look at me, you don't really see me?"

The boy quickly reacted to the note of dismay in her voice by seizing her hand. "We are *friends*," he said with earnest emphasis. "I see you clearly."

"Jedrick has threatened to reassign Koji to Taweel," Tamaes remarked, a glint in his eye.

"Why would he do that?" Prissie asked, giving the younger angel a questioning look.

"Our captain is only teasing," Koji said. "Since becoming your friend, my perspective has changed. Shimron says I sometimes act more like a Guardian than an Observer."

"You seem the same to me," Prissie replied defensively. She didn't like the idea of Koji being teased just because they were friends.

"I am me, but I *have* changed," Koji said, releasing her hand. "I have become isolated."

Prissie frowned. "I suppose we *do* live in the middle of nowhere."

Koji shook his head. "No, you live in the middle of ..." he began, but he was swiftly interrupted when Tamaes reached from behind and tweaked his ear.

"... an orchard," the Guardian firmly finished. "But that is not what Koji means."

"I don't understand," she said.

"Let me try to explain," Tamaes requested, looking to Koji for permission to proceed. The boy pulled one knee to his chest and swung the other leg, an expectant expression on his face, so his teammate pointed to the nearest stained glass window, which depicted Daniel in the lion's den. An angel dressed all in white was holding back a pair of lions while the old prophet prayed with hands lifted to heaven. "Do you see that single piece of clear, orange glass just above the closest lion's right eye? It is shaped like a leaf."

It didn't take long for Prissie to locate the fragment Tamaes was talking about. As he described it, the small piece of lion's mane jumped out at her. "I see it."

"Look carefully at that single piece of glass," Tamaes instructed. "Give it your full attention."

It was a strange request, but Prissie did as she was told. "That's almost the same color as your wings," she noted.

"So it is," he said, a smile lurking in his tone. "It is a small thing, but it is in my nature to appreciate small things. I would be pleased to spend many hours simply studying the shape of that piece of glass, how it looks by day with the sun shining through it, by night when the moon glows in the sky."

Prissie was amazed by her Guardian's quiet eloquence. Since he rarely spoke, she'd assumed he had nothing to say, yet here he was, rambling on about something as random as window glass. She stole a peek into his face, earning a small smile. Maybe he was getting over some of his shyness as well?

Directing her attention back to the stained glass window, Tamaes continued, "While I look, I might wonder what it feels like to be orange, if it wishes it were blue, or if it knows how carefully the window's maker fitted it into its setting."

Koji nodded. "Yes, I would want to know all those things, too."

With a sidelong look at the boy, Prissie said, "That sounds kind of crazy."

Tamaes pointed insistently at that bright patch of orange glass. "If that one part was under my watch-care, that is how I would feel."

Prissie straightened, finally realizing that they weren't *really* talking about stained glass windows. They were talking about *her*, and that made it more interesting.

"However, Shimron's role as a master archivist is much different," Tamaes patiently explained. "He does not often enter the created world."

"Does he stay in the garden behind the blue door?" Prissie asked.

"No, Shimron looks down on West Edinton from on high," Koji answered. With a straight face, he added, "Harken calls it his Ivory Tower, but the stones are actually white."

Tamaes seized control of the conversation once more. "Observers see patterns. While I keep my eyes on one special piece, Shimron sees *all* the pieces as they fit together and finds beauty in the picture they form."

"It sounds like *he's* the one who's isolated," Prissie said. "He's locked up in a tower!"

"Not at all. Shimron is well acquainted with the world," assured Tamaes. "He is one of the First, so he remembers the day when time began. And for the last two centuries, he has been watching pieces fall into place *here*."

"In West Edinton?" Prissie asked.

"In and around," the Guardian replied vaguely.

Prissie looked at Koji and asked, "So you're isolated because you're out of touch with the ... the grand scheme of things?"

"Indeed."

"And that's bad?"

To her relief, Tamaes declared, "The plans of God are only good."

"I already told you my mentor is *glad* that I made a human friend," Koji reminded. He waved confidently toward Daniel and the lions. "Shimron says that it is good to remember that just as the many are gathered together in the whole, the whole depends upon the many. So, for a season, I will watch over you with Tamaes."

"Apprenticed to an apprentice?" she asked skeptically.

"*Sent*," the young angel corrected. "I have been Sent."

"Why would God do that?"

"I do not know," Koji admitted. "I cannot see the whole picture."

"Can Shimron see it?"

"You could ask him when I introduce you," the young Observer suggested. "He often says that the ways of God are mysterious, so even angels must have faith."

10

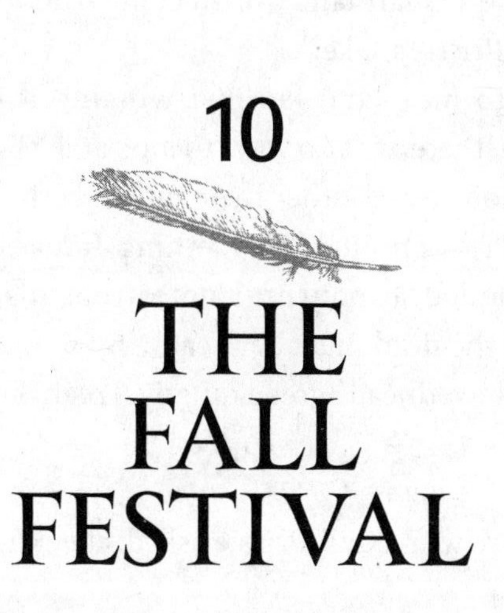

THE FALL FESTIVAL

I have a question," Kester announced.

"For *me*?" Baird asked, glancing up from where he was fitting a new string onto his guitar.

"You *are* my mentor."

"Good point," the redhead conceded. "Shoot."

"Why did God allow a Guardian and his charge to meet?"

"No clue," Baird fired back. "And don't give me that disappointed puppy-dog look. I'm totally out of the loop on this one."

Kester nodded solemnly and picked up his bow, but did not draw it over the cello strings. "I am merely concerned."

His mentor fiddled with his instrument some more, then said, "I get where you're coming from. In fact, I did a little asking around. No one around here has even heard of such a thing. It's like a Guardian's dream come true."

"Is it for Prissie's sake?"

"Seems to me — and I'm just winging it here — but it seems to me, there are two ways to look at it," Baird said with unusual seriousness. "Either their time together will provide something Prissie needs, or something Tamaes needs."

Kester pulled a mournful note from his instrument. "Either way, the need must be great."

"Yeah," the redhead agreed quietly. "Yeah, I think so, too."

"Is that it? Are we ready?" Prissie asked, checking for the fifth time.

"Talk to Auntie Lou," her father replied with a laugh. "She stole my list."

Prissie swept through the door to Loafing Around's kitchen with a satisfying rustle of full-length skirts. It was the last day of October, and all of West Edinton was readying for a local celebration that was one part Founder's Day and one part Fall Festival. Like most of the other businesses on Main Street, the Pomeroys were adding the final touches to their front doors because the center of town would soon be filled with trick-or-treaters. Everyone chose a theme because there was an annual contest headed up by the *Herald,* with prizes awarded for the most creative displays. People were *still* talking about the corner store's clever arcade setup from a few years back, which had sent local kids up and down aisles haunted by Inky, Blinky, Pinky, and Clyde.

Jayce enjoyed being in the thick of things, so his bakery always took part in the festivities. He and Momma chose the theme each year, and all the staff pitched in to help pull it off. Naomi inevitably chose kid-friendly settings, and this year, they were doing a more generic castle theme — lords and ladies, knights and pages. Prissie was enormously pleased with the fancy dress Pearl Matthews had sewn for her. It made her feel like a princess in a fairy tale.

In the kitchen, Grandma Nell was ladling thick chowder into an old brown and beige crock she usually used for baked beans. Koji, whose bicolored squire's tunic was a match for those that would be worn by Beau and Tad, sat on a stool beside the wide work table, munching on a heel of bread. Spying Prissie, Auntie Lou said, "Come on over here and give the cocoa a stir, then fill the thermos, dear." She bustled over to the oven and pulled out fresh loaves. "Heaven knows there will be enough candy floating around town tonight, but it'll mostly go to the kids. That's for Harken's sweet tooth."

Prissie sniffed the steaming pot, which had a vanilla bean floating in it. It was really strange, thinking back. For years, ever since she was a very little girl, she'd helped pack Harken's dinner on the night of the festival. Since the shopkeeper had his own preparations to make, he bowed out of supper with the Pomeroys and the bakery staff. Still, Jayce always made sure the old man received a portion of the special dinner. One or more of the kids delivered a picnic basket, and Prissie was pretty sure she'd been along for the small errand every single year. In the past, she'd always just dropped off the basket, but back then, she'd thought of Mr. Mercer as nothing but a nice old man. This year was different. Now, she thought of him as *her* friend, not just her dad's.

"Koji and I will take the basket over," Prissie volunteered.

"Thank you, sweetie," Grandma Nell replied. She wrapped

the crock in a towel and packed it in an oversized basket. Adding smaller containers of side dishes, she asked, "Is the thermos ready? It'll go here."

Prissie carried it over and tucked it in, and Auntie Lou added two loaves of hot, crusty bread. "There!"

As soon as the basket's lid was secured, Prissie grabbed the handles and lifted. "Oof! This is *heavy*! Are you sure Mr. Mercer needs this much food?"

"Milo lives over there, too. They can share," Grandma Nell said in her kindly, bossy way.

Outside, Prissie lugged the heavy basket with as much grace as she could muster. A large section of Main Street had been cordoned off, and a band was setting up in the gazebo. As she and Koji hurried past Town Hall and the newspaper office, she hoped Milo would be there this year, for even though she knew it was silly to still care, Prissie wanted to show off her dress to him.

There was nothing scary about The Curiosity Shop's decorations, and Harken didn't dress up in any kind of costume. On Halloween, he invited children into his store just as he always did. In fact, when Prissie and Koji carried their burden over his threshold, he greeted them with his usual smile. "Jayce told me there was a royal theme this year!" he exclaimed. "My compliments to your seamstress!"

Prissie curtsied. "I'll make sure to tell Pearl."

Just then, Milo ducked out of the back room. "Hey, Miss Priscilla, Koji! Do I smell fresh bread?"

"Yes, hot from the oven," she said, as the mailman hurried forward to take her burden. "Isn't this the first time you're here on Halloween?"

"It is, actually," he replied. "Taweel asked me to stay close to home, so to speak."

Harken's expression grew serious. "By the looks of things, it'll be a rough night. I haven't seen this much turmoil in some time."

Prissie's eyes widened. "Is that bad? I mean, is it safe for all the kids?"

The old shopkeeper came forward and placed a reassuring hand on her shoulder. "To everyone in town, including you, this will be a night of fun and games. Don't fret over things best left in the hands of God."

"I suppose."

Milo carried the picnic supper into the back room, and a moment later, he leaned through the doorway. "Say, Miss Priscilla, while you're here, why don't you come through and say hello to the others? Baird and Kester are here."

Gladly accepting his invitation, she and Koji slipped into the back. The blue door opened onto the bright glade with its carpet of soft grass, and Prissie admired the green-gold forest. "Is it always summer here?"

"The seasons don't turn in a place untouched by time," Milo said. As he gestured for her to precede him over the threshold, his gaze lit on the pair of Worshipers relaxing in the glade, and he exclaimed, "*Oh!* Miss Priscilla, I probably should have warned you ..."

"Is that a costume?" she asked in an undertone.

"Nooo," the mailman replied. "It would be the other way around. That's their true appearance."

Koji smiled up into her face, dark eyes sparkling. "Did you forget that we are not what we seem?"

"Maybe I did," she admitted, allowing Koji to lead her toward the others.

Kester, who stood gazing into the sky, turned to them as they approached. Instead of the usual suit, he was dressed in shining raiment, a long tunic over a pair of loose pants. Varicolored stitching in rainbow hues edged the collar and cuffs, and for the first time, Prissie realized that the decoration might actually indicate his angelic order.

Just as striking as his new wardrobe was Kester's hair. Glossy black curls went on and on, gathered back with a series of thick leather bands. With his olive skin and large nose, Prissie thought the apprentice Worshiper looked like a foreign dignitary or perhaps the prince of a faraway land. She gaped at him with all the manners of a goldfish, and his dark eyes crinkled at the corners. "Good evening, Prissie. I trust that you are not alarmed by appearances?" With all seriousness, he reminded, "They are not the most important consideration."

"N-no. I was just so ... You look very ... angelic," she ended lamely. It was true, though.

Kester merely smiled and glanced at his mentor. Baird was sprawled on his back in the grass, arms behind his head and one foot propped on his knee; his eyes were closed, and he was humming softly to himself. "He is lost in song," Kester remarked calmly.

Prissie could only nod, for Baird's transformation was equally distracting. His raiment was the same as Kester's, and he looked right at home in the loose clothing. What grabbed her attention, though, was his hair. It was no longer the orange-red of human hair. Baird's hair was *red*-red, just like the vibrant hue of the furled wings that decorated his skin like an audacious set of tattoos. "Is it *possible* for hair to be that color?" she mumbled dazedly.

"Most assuredly," said Kester.

Hazel eyes drifted open, distant and dreamy, as if Baird

was seeing something far away. "Say, Kester, I think I have that bridge figured out." In that instant, Prissie thought he finally looked the part of an angel, and she found herself holding her breath as awe built up in her heart. Then, Baird grinned.

"Prissie!" he exclaimed, bounding to his feet. "You're here! Harken said you might be dropping by!" Giving Koji a quick cuff on the shoulder, he continued, "Aw, man, this is *awesome*! Your town sure knows what it's doing when it comes to throwing a party! I can't *believe* I've never come up for it before now!"

Though she knew it was rude, Prissie couldn't stop staring. While Baird had been lying down, she hadn't noticed, but now that he was on his feet, it was impossible to ignore the Worshiper's shaggy mane. From one ear to the other, sections of hair had been twisted into small knots; they looked almost like a headband, with the loose ends standing up like a fuzzy, red halo. The rest was longer, but hardly tame; the ends flew away in every direction at once.

He screeched to a verbal halt. "Prissie? Uh-oh. Am I freaking you out?"

"You do look different," she mumbled uncomfortably.

Baird sobered quickly and took a step back before gently pointing out, "So do you. Dresses like that went out of style *ages* ago."

She glanced down at her full skirts. "This is a *costume*."

"Okay," he said, then thumped his chest. "*This* is the real deal. Think of it as me having a pajama day!"

Kester gave his mentor a pained look. "Raiment are *not* pajamas."

"Nope, but they're just as comfy!" Baird cheerfully countered. Turning back to Prissie, he added, "You know, this is the first time I've seen *you* without braids."

Prissie self-consciously touched her hair, which she'd left loose for once. The comparison hardly went far enough, for changing your hairstyle wasn't the same as changing your hair. Still, Baird was certainly the same guy she knew. Only his appearance was altered. "You fixed your hair like this during the fair," she recalled aloud. "Only with little clips."

Baird propped his hands on his hips and beamed at her. "You noticed! Yeah, I do that a lot, actually. It helps me feel like myself even if no one else realizes why it suits me so well!" With a sly glance at Milo, he added, "By now, I think you've realized that none of the Grafts look quite the same when they're off duty."

The mailman promptly changed the subject. "Miss Priscilla and Koji brought loaves and fishes for dinner."

"Old school!" Baird exclaimed.

"It's actually chowder, but Dad did bake bread this afternoon. I think Grandma packed enough to go around," Prissie said.

"Thank your family for extending their hospitality to us again," Kester requested.

"I will," she replied with a blush. In a valiant effort at small talk, she addressed Baird. "You sounded excited about the festival. Does that mean you're planning to go?"

"Jedrick would rather I lay low for tonight," he replied. "I haven't decided what to do."

Prissie's brows furrowed, and she said, "He's your captain. Don't you *have* to do what he says?"

The redhead fiddled with the cuff that decorated his ear. "Strictly speaking, no. He's responsible for me, but I don't answer to him."

"So you can just go off and do whatever you want?"

Baird laughed. "Not quite. If I do take a quick turn around downtown, I'll let Jedrick know, and he'll make sure I have backup."

"So it would be dangerous for you?" she asked worriedly.

"No more than usual," he replied. "Grafts take a lot of flak."

"Then why would you . . . ?"

"Rush in where angels fear to tread?" he finished teasingly.

"Yes."

"It's hard to explain, so let's call it a hunch," Baird replied. "I can't put up much of a fight, but there are times when all that's needed is a light in the darkness." He tucked her arm through his and escorted her back to the blue door. "Don't dawdle on your way back, and don't talk to strangers. Once you're with your family, stay put."

Koji fell in step on her other side. "Prissie promised to stay with me. We will remain inside."

"Glad to hear it!" Baird replied with a broad grin.

There were two ways to enjoy trick-or-treating in West Edinton's business section. The first was to come knocking at the front doors, which faced all the lights, music, and festivities underway up and down Main Street. From one end of downtown to the other, kids were sure to find smiling faces and crazy fun. However, for those who dared, several buildings could also be approached from behind. In the alley that ran behind four blocks of businesses on the western side of the street, tricks and traps were laid for those who wanted to be spooked.

Those who came knocking on back doors were met by creepy cobwebs, strange mists, and eerie faces, but only if they made it past all the obstacles. Rattling trash cans, cloaked figures, low growls, and maniacal laughter kept kids on their toes, and costumed adults did their best to send them screaming. Most of the back alley lurkers were local school teachers, who took great pleasure in spooking their students. Prissie was strictly a front door kind of girl, but Tad, Neil, and Beau ran the gauntlet every year. Zeke coaxed hard for the chance to see the horrors for himself, but when offered the opportunity, Koji had politely declined.

Prissie and Koji made the quick trip from Harken's to the bakery without incident, and as soon as they were through the door, Auntie Lou put them to work pulling tables together for their traditional pre-festival dinner. The Pomeroys were joined this year by Auntie and Uncle Lou, Derrick and Pearl Matthews, Ransom, and Koji, so it would be crowded.

Once the tables were ready, Prissie noticed that Koji had moved to a spot before the front window. Instead of looking at all the busyness on the street out front, he was staring fixedly into the sky.

His seriousness made Prissie nervous. "What do you see?" she whispered.

"Colors," he replied, glancing at her with a smile. She followed his gaze, and indeed, the clouds above were painted pink by the setting sun. "There are so many colors, it is like a stained glass window, and I was looking for a certain piece."

"Do you see Tamaes?" she gasped, searching the sky. "Is he very far away?"

"No, he is on the roof," Koji replied. "But I can see Taweel."

"Really?" Prissie asked in awe. "Is Omri with him? Isn't it too dangerous for the little guy to be up there when there might be a battle?"

"I do not think there is anywhere else Omri would want to be."

"Why are he and Taweel always together?"

"That is not my story to tell."

"Oh. Isn't it strange, though?" she ventured. "Do any of the other angels have their own little manna-maker hanging out with them?"

"Not that I have seen," Koji admitted. "However, I have not seen all there is to see."

Auntie Lou called them to ferry all the food from the kitchen. There was a lot of hustling back and forth, followed by jostling to fit everyone around the tables. Grandma Nell was stationed at one end, ladling bowls of steaming chowder, and Jayce stood at the other, wielding a long knife as he sliced thick chunks of warm bread. Midway through the serving, Auntie Lou exclaimed, "Oh, the pitchers! Prissie, be a dear and fill the water pitchers for us?" "Yes, ma'am," she replied, scooting back her chair.

Compared to the din in the front, the bakery's empty kitchen was hushed. Prissie crossed to the shelves where several pitchers were lined up and carried four of them to the sink to fill. Before she had the first one half-full, there was a knock on the back door.

Now, it was too early for the trick-or-treaters to be coming around. She knew for a fact that the back alley was blocked off from both ends to keep kids from stealing a sneak peek while the crew got into place. Front doors opened at six, and back doors waited until seven, when it was good and dark.

Jayce generally left the back door to Derrick Matthews, who enjoyed finding something spooky about Momma's fairy tale themes. More than once, Prissie had been surprised to learn that an innocent-seeming story had something dark and dangerous lurking within. When they'd done a pretty gingerbread house like the one in Hansel and Gretel, the back door had led to the witch and her oven. When Momma chose Little Red Riding Hood, Derrick had created a wolf's den. This year, the back door led to the castle's dungeon, complete with ominous chains and cages. Neil and Ransom made a fine pair of creepy guards who would try to lure the unwary aside for Derrick to lock away in the cage he'd built.

The knock came again, and Prissie turned off the tap and walked to the door. Neil had told her that his football coach would be inhabiting the dumpster just behind the bakery, so she thought it might be him. "Is that you, Coach Hobbes?"

A voice called back, "Prissie? That's good. You're the one I wanted to talk to."

"Who's there?" she asked curiously, trying to place the voice.

"Adin."

"Oh!" With a quick twist of the lock and turn of the knob, she opened the back door.

Twilight was deepening, but even in the shadows, she could make out Adin's handsome face. "What are you doing here?"

"Taking in the sights. Having a little fun. Calling upon a lady fair," he replied with a courtly bow.

Prissie smiled, for his gentle flattery pleased her. The angel was dressed in princely attire, right down to the tights her brothers had flatly refused to wear. She curtsied and said, "Good evening, sir."

"Can her ladyship join me for a turn around the square?" he inquired.

"I can't," she said regretfully. "We're just sitting down to dinner."

"It wouldn't be for long," he coaxed.

Again, she shook her head. "I'd have to ask my dad, and I *really* don't think he'd let me go off alone with someone he doesn't know."

"Understandable," Adin promptly agreed. "He has every right to be overprotective when his daughter is so lovely."

"Prissie blushed and murmured, "I don't know about *that*."

"Are you *sure* you couldn't just step out for a minute?"

It was tempting. So tempting, but her conscience pricked her fiercely. "I *really* shouldn't. I promised to stay inside tonight. You know?"

"Ah, I see," Adin replied with obvious disappointment. Then with a flourish, he produced a single, red rose and held it out to her. "Another time, perhaps?"

"I'd like that," she admitted.

He proffered the flower, and it was almost like a scene from a real fairy tale. Prissie knew they must look just like a prince and a princess, and her heart gave a flutter. Almost without thinking, she reached out, but the rose was too far away. Leaning forward, her fingertips just brushed one dewy petal when Ransom pushed through the kitchen door behind her, calling, "What's *taking* so long, Miss Priss? Your dad wants to pray or something so we can eat already!"

Prissie glanced over her shoulder to glare at her classmate. Ransom was already in costume, a dingy gray smock, disheveled hair, and dirty smudges on his face. He was frowning deeply at her, but the brown eyes searched her face with a mixture of surprise and concern. When she turned back to the alley, Adin was gone. Her beautiful moment had been stolen, and she was furious.

"Did someone come around already?" Ransom asked, stepping past her to gaze up and down the alley.

Koji hurried into the kitchen, his eyes wide. "Prissie, are you safe?"

"Obviously," she grumbled. "Why wouldn't I be?"

"I am not certain," he admitted, glancing between the two. "May I help with the water?"

"Sure," she muttered, turning her back on Ransom and stalking back to the sink.

Dinner was a hasty affair, for everyone was in a hurry to finish. Zeke was understandably eager for the sun to set, and Jude hardly touched his food. Their mother would take them around as soon as the clock struck six. At thirteen, Beau was now considered too old to join the kids who trick-or-treated up and down Main Street, so he was helping out inside the bakery for a while. Once the back alley opened up in an hour, he was meeting up with some classmates to run through it together. After he got back, Tad would take Zeke through. Neil planned to wander out later, but he'd helped Derrick so much with the setup that he already knew too much behind-the-scenes information for anything to be scary.

While the clearing away, sweeping up, and washing were underway, Prissie pointedly avoided Ransom, but eventually he cornered her by the glass-fronted bakery case, which had special, limited edition cookies shaped like knights' shields, castles, dragons, and crowns.

"Hey, Miss Priss," Ransom said in a low voice. "What gives?"

"I don't know what you mean," she retorted breezily.

"What's got you all worked up?" he tried again. "Normally, I'd say your hair was wound too tight, but that can't be it."

She scowled. "If you must know, you interrupted me."

"There *was* someone at the back door?"

"Yes. A friend came by to say hello."

"Who?"

"No one *you'd* know."

"*Not* someone from school, then?" he pressed.

Prissie stuck her nose in the air. "It's none of your business!"

"Look, you're acting all weird, like you're *hiding* something," Ransom said reasonably. "You did the same thing when we were at the park, right before disappearing into a cave. I just want to make sure you're not about to do something stupid."

Her blue eyes sparked. "I'm *not* doing anything wrong!"

"Neither am I," he replied stubbornly. "You're the boss's daughter. It's really obvious that he thinks the world of you. I'd hate to see you mess that up!"

"Stop butting in!" she snapped. "Don't talk about me and my dad like you know anything!"

Ransom lifted his hands and backed down. "All right, already," he said. "Never mind. Sorry to intrude."

From the front window, Prissie could see people gathering in the square. The band started up, and people wandered around with hot dogs sold by the Lions Club or plates of barbeque that the fire department had been smoking since before sunup.

Jayce had changed into his kingly attire right after dinner, so he looked rather regal when he pulled Prissie aside. "Is there a problem between you and Ransom?"

"Of *course*," she replied huffily. "He's impossible."

Her father shook his head and said, "Enough, Princess. You're dressed like a lady, and I want you to *behave* like one. A little grace would go a long way."

She didn't appreciate the warning. It proved that Ransom was coming between her and her dad. The only bright side to the whole evening was that her nemesis was working the back door, so she wouldn't have to deal with him for the rest of the night.

As soon as six o'clock rolled around, the bakery doors were flung wide, and their busy evening began. Somehow, Auntie Lou had convinced Uncle Lou to be fitted for a suit of armor, and he stood on the front step, eyes twinkling and moustache bristling. He made the perfect greeter. "Good evening, my dear damsel, are you by any chance in distress?"

Trick-or-treating tapered off by eight thirty, but plenty of adults still drifted in and out of the Main Street stores, checking out the décor. Prissie carried the goodie bowl into the kitchen in order to refill it and caught the sound of high-pitched screams coming from out back. Just then, Ransom strolled to the table as well, twirling a ring of keys on his finger and whistling. "How's it going up front?" he asked.

"Fine."

"Well, the back door is awesome. That Derrick guy is some kind of genius, rigging things up like he did," he said with a grin that showed several blacked out teeth.

"What are the keys for?" she asked, curious in spite of herself.

"Oh, I have a couple girls from our class in the cage," he replied smugly. "The one dressed as a black cat kept trying to rub up against Neil, and it was freaking him out. Funniest thing ever."

"Elise?"

"Yeah. Her and Margery, who asked if I would bring her a cookie. I told her sure. Which kind should I get?"

"She'd want a crown," Prissie replied faintly. "One with blue jewels."

While Ransom looked over the trays of frosted cookies, he set down his keys, and for the first time, Prissie noticed that they were real keys, not props. "What are those for?" she asked sharply.

"Huh? Oh. It looked silly for the jailers to only have two keys on their key ring, so your dad let me have the main set."

"He gave you *all* the keys?" she asked, astonished.

"What's the big deal?"

"The lock box and everything?" Prissie demanded fiercely.

"Of course," he replied nonchalantly. "You know, I *do* help open the store every morning. Your dad trusts me."

She couldn't believe it. "But that's *terrible*!"

Ransom located Margery's cookie. "I'm not a thief, Miss Priss. I have no idea where you got the idea that I'm a gang member or some kind of delinquent. I've never stolen anything in my life."

"You are *too* a thief. You're trying to steal Dad!" she cried. "It's a mistake to trust someone like you!"

Ransom's head reared back, and his face registered hurt ... or anger. Prissie wasn't sure which, but either way, she knew she'd crossed a line. He turned his back and walked out without a word. When she turned *her* back, she realized Koji had joined her, and she looked to him for support. The young angel's sorrowful expression hit her like a blow. "Prissie, that was not true," he quietly asserted.

"I didn't mean it."

"Then why did you speak it?"

"I was angry!"

"That is no justification," he replied seriously.

"I didn't mean to," she muttered miserably.

"You did." Koji's soft assertion startled her into looking at the Observer, and he quietly repeated, "You wished to hurt him, and you succeeded. Did you consider the consequences?"

Prissie felt nauseous. She'd been spiteful, hateful, mean, and now that she'd lashed out at her classmate, she really wished she hadn't. Her petty triumph left a bitter taste in her mouth, and she didn't know how to make it go away. "What do I do?" she whispered, afraid she already knew the answer.

"Ask for forgiveness," Koji calmly directed. "From Ransom ..."

"And me," interrupted a low voice.

Prissie whirled. "Dad!"

"Koji, you may wait in the front," Jayce calmly directed. "My daughter and I need to have a little talk."

"Yes, sir," he replied, leaving without a backward glance.

Jayce rubbed his chin as he gathered his thoughts, then folded his hands together and sought his daughter's gaze. "Prissie, what has Ransom done to deserve your treatment of him?"

Her jaw clenched. "He's annoying."

"He must have done *something*?" he prodded. "You can tell me."

"I told you. He's annoying," she repeated.

"That's all?" Jayce pressed. "He's never bullied you. Or given you trouble here or at school?"

She hunched her shoulders in a defensive shrug. Though she didn't like Ransom, her conscience wouldn't let her accuse him of something he'd never done. "No," she admitted.

"So you think he's *annoying,* and that justifies the way you've been treating him?" She stared sullenly at her father, who considered for a moment. "You know, I've always tried to make Ransom feel welcome. I've invited him to church, but he's under the impression that all Christians act like … well, like I've seen you behaving tonight."

"So it's *my* fault Ransom won't go to church? That's not fair!"

"No. But you certainly haven't helped matters."

Cold settled in the pit of her stomach. Koji was disappointed in her. Her father was mad at her. And it was all Ransom's fault. Why did her dad care more about him than her? She doubted tonight could get any worse. Except … it did.

"Prissie, I want you to apologize to him."

"*What*?"

"You heard me," her father said seriously. "I'll be praying that you find an opportunity. When it comes, I expect you to take it."

11

THE ALMOST TWIN

The clash of blades rang above the forest, and with a quick twist, one sword spun free of its wielder's grasp and plummeted from the sky. Marcus glided down to the grassy meadow and bent double, hands on his knees as he tried to catch his breath. "Think before you act!" chided Jedrick as he joined him on the ground.

"Yeah, I blew it," his apprentice admitted. He straightened and kneaded his sword hand with a grimace. "I didn't realize you were setting me up until it was too late."

"The enemy delights in deception, so you must be wiser than the serpent," instructed the Protector as he crossed to retrieve Marcus's blade.

"But gentle as the dove?" he asked with a smirk. He accepted his weapon and tested his grip.

"On the contrary," Jedrick replied with a glint in his eyes. He extended green wings and launched back into the shifting lights overhead. "I intend to make an eagle of you, so rise up!"

November rolled around, and with it came Beau's birthday, which had always been a big deal for the Pomeroy family. Since he and Prissie were only ten months apart, for the next two months, they would both be fourteen. The novelty of being *almost* twins was part of the reason why Prissie was closer to Beau than any of her other brothers. Though they weren't quite what she considered *friends,* they operated under a sort of siblings' truce. She didn't nag him, and he didn't criticize her, all because they shared their age for seventy days of the year.

"What do you want for supper?" Momma asked with a knowing smile.

Beau glanced up from his cereal bowl. "Macaroni and cheese, I guess."

Neil snorted. "Big surprise, little brother."

The birthday boy rolled his eyes, and Prissie fondly shook her head. Beau's favorite food hadn't changed since he was two.

Today's celebration would be so different from the way the Burkes did birthdays. Margery's mother threw parties that took weeks of preparation, and the resulting events could have been photographed for a magazine. Whenever the Pomeroys celebrated a birthday, the kids were given their choice of dinner and dessert. A few presents found their way onto the table after the meal, and the rest of the evening was usually taken up by board games and embarrassing stories.

Just before dinner that evening, Jayce rounded up the kids and led the procession to the measuring wall. Grandma Nell had started this part of their family traditions back when he and Ida were little, marking their height on the laundry room's door frame. When Jayce's lot came one after the next, it became necessary to spread out. The entire laundry room wall was filled with neat lines and notations in Momma's tidy handwriting. Somewhere along the way, color coding had been instituted to help differentiate all the kids. Prissie carried the purple marker that would be used to record Beau's annual height. Everyone else would get a peek at their progress in pencil.

At eighteen, Tad was finally eye-to-eye with Jayce, and Neil could boast that he was taller than Grandpa — barely. Prissie had surpassed both her grandmothers and was creeping up on Momma. Beau stood straight, and Jayce took his measure. "I'd say you grew another two inches," he announced, eyeballing last year's mark.

A swift comparison was made, and based on Neil's and Tad's records, Prissie figured he would shoot up in the near future. "Can we add Koji to the wall?" she asked.

"Sure, sure," Jayce replied, waving the boy over. "Even if it's just for a while, you're part of the family!"

The young Observer's eyes were wide as he stepped up to the wall. His mark fell a couple inches shy of Prissie's current height, and with a satisfied smile, she said, "There! Now we'll know if you have a growth spurt, too!"

"Indeed," he replied with a pleased smile. "I am honored to be counted among you."

Laughter was interrupted by the dinner bell, and everyone herded back to the table. Dinner was good, cake was great, stories were funny, and gifts were gratefully received. Then Jayce raised his hands for attention. "I know this is out of the ordinary, but I planned a little something extra for the birthday boy this year!"

"What is it?" Zeke asked curiously. "A dirt bike?"

"A pony?" guessed Jude.

Their father chuckled and said, "No, but I think it's something that Beau will like."

"Where is it? Can I see?" Zeke demanded.

"It's something we can all share, but it won't be here until tomorrow." That said, Jayce folded his hands on the table and smiled smugly.

"Is that *all* you're going to tell us?" Prissie demanded.

"Yes," he replied, his eyes sparkling. "Yes, it is."

"Does anyone else know?" she inquired, for she'd noticed that her older brothers weren't asking any questions. Grandpa and Grandma were also suspiciously calm.

"Tomorrow," Jayce repeated firmly.

That night, Koji slipped into Prissie's room after everyone else was asleep. She suspected that Tamaes had told him she was still up, which made her a little grumpy. Did *everyone* have secrets from her? She hated being out of the loop! The young Observer climbed to his favorite perch on her window seat and sat with one leg pulled up to his chest, the other swinging.

"Do you know what they have planned?" she asked suspiciously.

"I believe your father wishes his plans to remain a surprise," Koji replied matter-of-factly.

"You *do* know what he has in mind!"

"In part," he said. She made an impatient gesture, anxious to hear what he knew, but Koji simply shook his head. "I will not tell you what I know, so do not ask."

Prissie flopped down and pulled her quilt up to her chin. "Is it something good?"

Koji smiled.

"So it *will* be something good!"

"Indeed."

Prissie sighed and wriggled down into her mattress. The weather had taken a bitter turn, and her room was decidedly chilly. "Aren't you cold?" she asked.

Koji looked down at his bare toes and replied, "No. The cold does not bother me."

They sat together in comfortable silence for a little while, but finally, Prissie complained, "I'm never going to get to sleep."

"I will not either."

"That hardly counts! You *don't* sleep!"

The young Observer continued to peer through the multicolored panes of glass at the stars, a smile on his face. Pushing his hair behind his ear, Koji began to hum softly. Small snatches of a tune teased at her memory until she finally placed the song. Kester's lullaby. The gentle melody filled her mind, weaving with images of harp strings and stained glass wings that carried her off to sleep.

Prissie slept late, and when she woke, she was momentarily disoriented by the level of noise coming from downstairs. Usually, Saturday mornings smelled like coffee and sounded like cartoons, but the unmistakable clatter of full-scale meal preparations filtered up from the kitchen. Whatever had been planned for today was already beginning.

Tucking her feet into slippers, Prissie hurried down the back stairs to see what was going on. "Good morning, Priscilla," her mother greeted when she peeped into the kitchen. With a glance at the clock, which showed it was coming up on eleven, she added, "Barely."

"What's going on?"

"We're expecting company," Momma replied with a secretive smile.

"On a Saturday?"

Her mother said, "Now that it's November, we won't see much business, but if customers do drop in, it won't be a problem. We'll be out in the barn anyhow."

"In the barn?" Prissie echoed blankly.

Grandma Nell bustled through with Beau and Koji close on her heels, each carrying a pan of corn bread. "This should do it! More than enough to go around!" she said to her daughter-in-law. Catching sight of her granddaughter, she beamed. "There you are, sweetie!"

Eying the baking, Prissie scuffled over to the stove and peeped under the lid of a pot simmering on the back burner, releasing the spicy-rich smell of homemade chili. Momma said, "We'll be doing chili five ways, and I could use an extra pair of hands. Why don't you hurry and get dressed. I suggest you wear something nice," she added with a wink.

From the upstairs bathroom window, Prissie caught sight of her older brothers hauling saw horses and picnic tables into the apple barn, and not long after that, she saw Beau and Koji carrying a stack of Grandma's checkered tablecloths down there as well.

In the kitchen once more, she demanded, "Who's coming over?"

"You'll find out soon enough," Naomi replied. "Now grate that cheese for me. I'll finish the onions."

"What about Dad?" Prissie asked. "Doesn't he have to work until two?"

"Our guests know that it'll be a late lunch. Nobody minded."

Twenty minutes later, two vehicles rolled up the driveway and pulled to a stop in front of the barn. As car doors slammed and greetings were called, Prissie hurried over to the window for a peek. She didn't recognize either the silver hatchback or the bright red minivan. All doors were open, and a group of people had crowded around to unload something. Her brothers were toting black cases and coils that looked like extension cords. "What's going on out there?" Then a shock of red hair bounced into view, and she exclaimed, "Is that *Baird*?"

"Yes, it is!" her mother cheerfully replied. "And he brought friends!"

"Who are they?"

"His band," Momma said. "Your father arranged it as a special treat for Beau so he could learn more about running a sound board. Baird's band is going to rehearse here, and your brother gets to fiddle with all those knobs and levers and things."

Prissie looked at Grandma Nell. "You knew they were coming?"

"Of course, sweetie. I had to do the cooking, didn't I? And your grandpa also knew, since the barn needed to be ready."

"Am I the *only* one who didn't know?" Prissie grumbled.

Her grandmother chuckled. "I think your parents wanted *you* to enjoy the surprise as much as Beau."

Prissie spotted Kester carrying an enormous instrument case toward the barn, and slowly she retreated back to the table, taking a muffin as a very late breakfast. She didn't like surprises. Today's plans had not been submitted for her approval, and while she had to admit they were *good* plans, she wasn't sure if she was excited or not. Caught up in trying to sort out her mixed-up feelings, she totally missed the arrival of yet another car.

With a short rap on the kitchen door, Milo let himself in. "Hey, ladies! I'm useless in the barn with all those cords and wires. Can I lend a hand here?"

"Oh, good. A man!" Grandma Nell exclaimed, waving him over. "Sit there."

Milo slid into a chair, and she placed a few jars in front of him. "Here, you go. Could you open these for me? Prissie can fill serving dishes." Grandma Nell bustled back to the cupboard and returned with large bowls. "I'll just go set up the coffee pot in the barn and say hello to our guests. Naomi, will you bring the silverware?"

After the women left, Milo said, "Hey, Miss Priscilla."

"Hi, Milo," she replied with a half-hearted smile.

"Something wrong?"

"Nooo," she replied vaguely, unsure how to explain her funk. On the one hand, she was glad that Baird and Kester were back, but she was a little miffed about having to share them with so many other people. In a way, she'd come to think of these angels as *hers*. Prissie watched Milo struggle with a wide-mouthed jar. "I would have thought angels were super strong or something," she remarked with the beginnings of a smile.

"I'm a supernatural being, but that's a far cry from omnipotent."

"All-powerful?"

"That I am *not*," Milo said. With a comical expression, he attacked the lid, but finally sighed in defeat. "I can tell you how to say *pickle* in every language known to man, but that won't get us any closer to your grandmother's gherkins." Prissie giggled, and his blue eyes sparkled. Then he quirked a brow at a spot across the table. "A little help here?"

In a twinkling, Taweel was revealed, sitting with his chin propped on his hand, his fingers half-hiding his amusement. Waving the jar before the Guardian, Milo said, "It would take a miracle for me to open this. Be my miracle?"

With a soft grunt, the warrior held out his hand, and the Messenger turned over the jar.

"Hello, Taweel," Prissie said, earning a nod. A yellow-haired yahavim popped into view by climbing over Taweel's head, crawling through the wild mess of black hair. "Omri!" she exclaimed in delight.

The little manna-maker grew brighter as he flew down to the table, and Milo said, "Now, *there's* a smile. Maybe the two of you should stick together today."

Meeting the little angel's gaze for a moment, Prissie asked, "We two?" The suggestion startled her, and she peeped out of the corner of her eye at Taweel. "Won't he want to stay with you?"

Violet eyes flicked to her face, then settled on his small companion. "Omri will go where he is needed most."

Prissie brimmed with hope as she faced the tiny angel. "Would you like to come with me for a while?"

Omri launched into the air and darted in a circle around her head, before settling onto her shoulder. She turned her head slightly to look into his upturned face, and small hands patted her cheek as he hummed in her ear. "I think that means yes," Milo said with a smile.

Taweel handed off the opened jar to Milo just as Grandma Nell returned. "Oh, you're a wonder-worker!" she praised, then helped Prissie finish filling the bowls with sweet peppers, hot peppers, and homemade salsa. "Why don't you two take those down to the barn and add them to the table. We'll wait to bring the hot food until Jayce is back."

"Yes, ma'am," Milo and Prissie replied together.

In the apple barn, plank tables had been lined up to create a sort of buffet, and several picnic tables were pulled together. Just beyond those, a makeshift sound booth had been established, and Baird's band fanned out to set up their gear. Grandpa Pete's space heaters were helping take the chill off, and the smell of coffee further warmed the air. Milo and Prissie left their dishes of pickles and peppers on the table under Momma's watchful eye, and then the Messenger steered her toward Baird's band.

Kester was just opening the largest of his instrument cases, and both Zeke and Jude hovered excitedly to see what it contained. A cello made its appearance, and Zeke asked, "Can ya play it?"

"I can," Kester replied.

"Can *I* play it?" the eight-year-old negotiated.

"You may make an attempt."

"Cool!"

"Is it hard?" Jude wanted to know.

"Learning to play an instrument requires patience," Kester said.

"Do you have to practice?"

"Yes."

"Do you *like* to practice, or do you *hafta* practice?" Zeke asked.

"Both."

"Lucky for you," Jude said.

"I agree."

While her little brothers plagued Kester with even more questions, Baird nudged Prissie with his elbow. "Surprised?"

"No one told me you were coming."

"This was a very hush-hush operation," he said conspiratorially. His gaze flitted briefly to her ear, and his mouth quirked. "That's a regular bluebird of happiness riding on your shoulder."

Immediately, Prissie brightened. "Taweel said it was okay."

The redhead's smile broadened. "Let me introduce you around."

Prissie mumbled, "Sure," but she was feeling pretty nervous. She didn't know any musicians, and these people seemed so confident about their instruments. It made her wish she had their talent because it must be fun to play in a group with Baird.

"Kester you know," the Worshiper said with a nod to his apprentice. "So ladies first. This is Mickie."

The young woman seated on a box drum offered a warm, "Hey."

"Hello," Prissie said. She vaguely remembered the percussionist, whose hair was woven into at least a hundred tiny braids that coiled against her neck and shoulders. Trying hard not to stare at the tiny gem that pierced Mickie's nose, Prissie fumbled for something else to say. "It's nice to meet you."

"I'm glad to meet you, too," the drummer replied. "After Baird bragged on this place, we jumped at the chance to see it for ourselves." With a smirk in the redhead's direction, she added, "Baird bragged on *you*, too!"

Prissie blushed. "Is that so?"

Baird took the teasing in stride and touched Prissie's elbow, leading her over to the two guys armed with guitars. "The tall one's Sheldon," he announced, gesturing to a balding man wearing a yellow sweater.

"You must be Prissie," Sheldon said, offering his hand. "Nice place you have here!"

"Thank you."

Moving right along, Baird said, "And Rick's on bass."

The wiry young man looked younger than the rest, perhaps college age. "Yo," he said with a tight little smile before shaking her hand.

With the niceties covered, Baird led her to one side, and as soon as they were out of earshot, Prissie leaned close to whisper, "Does your band know you're an angel?"

"Nope," he replied softly.

"Oh." She thought he looked a little sad.

"It'll make a nice surprise someday. I hope."

"You don't think they'll be mad?"

"They'll probably think it's funny. Or they'll refuse to believe me."

Searching for a safer topic, Prissie asked, "Why did Kester bring a cello?"

Baird grinned and waved at the barn rafters. "Because there's plenty of room here for large scale music!"

"It's a barn, not a concert hall," she said.

"A rustic cathedral! We'll run through our Sunday morning set, but we were planning to give *Messiah* a go, too. Kester's going to fill in the symphonic gaps with that oversized fiddle. After all that, if you're not ready to kick us out, we'll take requests!"

"It sounds fun." Glancing at her almost twin, she added, "Beau's going to be in his glory."

"Him and me both!" the Worshiper assured.

By the time the band was running through their first real sound check, Zeke sent up a cry. He'd spotted Jayce's van coming up the driveway. The Pomeroy boys trooped out to help because Dad always brought home whatever was left over at closing time on Saturdays. Jayce hopped out and circled around the back to unload bread, pies, rolls, cupcakes ... and one shifty-eyed apprentice.

"What's *he* doing here?" Prissie muttered.

"Carrying stuff," replied Neil with a teasing grin.

That much was obvious, for their father weighed Ransom down with half a dozen loaves, then pointed him toward the front door. Prissie couldn't get over how *wrong* it was for these two parts of her life to collide. Ransom belonged at school, but somehow, he'd invaded the family bakery, and now her home. "I can't believe he's at my house!" she moaned.

"Hustle up and help!" called Jayce, lifting a large, white bakery box.

Milo patted Prissie's shoulder on his way past and claimed the box, saying, "Good afternoon, Jayce! Thanks for inviting me!" As he ferried it up the front walk, he met Ransom coming and going.

"Hey, Mr. Mailman."

"Hey, Ransom," the Messenger replied with an easy smile. "You really *can* call me Milo."

"Right," he agreed, then cast a wary look in Prissie's direction.

She knew better than to be rude to a guest, especially with her father standing right there, so when Jayce handed off a box of muffins, she managed a polite nod to her classmate before escaping into the house. Prissie had a sneaking suspicion that her dad would consider *this* the perfect chance for her to apologize. "Why me?" she muttered dismally.

A tug on her hair yanked her attention away from her worries, and she glanced down in surprise at the little angel who swung from the end of her braid. In all the confusion, she'd forgotten about her passenger. Prissie's expression immediately softened, and she murmured, "Today was supposed to be *fun*, right, Omri?" With a flicker of wings, he darted up and swooped around her head a couple times before settling on top of her head. Straightening her back, she marched into the house with her head held high. "I won't let him ruin my day."

Lunch was served, and the apple barn hardly seemed big enough to contain Baird's enthusiasm, which was contagious. As it happened, Prissie found it much easier to enjoy herself than anticipated. It was incredibly hard to frown when tiny hands kept reaching down to pat the furrow that formed between her brows.

After the meal ended, Neil stepped up to play host, asking Ransom if he'd like a tour of the farm. As they walked out of the barn together, Prissie could hear her older brother quizzing him on Joey Mueller's progress. His teammate had been benched for the rest of the season because of a broken collar bone. Naturally, Jude tagged along, but he kept popping back into the apple barn to keep her posted. "He's never been here before, even for apples!" he exclaimed.

"Maybe he doesn't like apples," she suggested.

The six-year-old's eyes widened at the very thought. "That'd be *crazy*! Ransom said he wasn't here for field trips either."

"He's from somewhere else, I think. And only just joined my class a couple years ago. The orchard is more of an elementary field trip." Both Zeke and Jude had spent a half day touring their own backyard with their classmates earlier that fall.

"Where'd he come from?" Jude inquired.

"How would *I* know?"

The boy ran off, intent on finding the answer for himself. Grandma Nell and Momma returned from the kitchen with folding chairs and blankets and settled in to enjoy the rehearsal. Prissie drifted off to one side, a little further back from everyone else, because she wanted to play with Omri while she had the chance. His antics and Baird's songs lifted her spirits.

She had just decided that nothing, not even Ransom, could spoil the amazingness of befriending a yahavim when her classmate returned with her brothers. While Neil went to get a closer look at Mickie's box drum, Ransom hung back and drifted over to Prissie. To her dismay, he sat on the next bale over and said, "This place is pretty cool."

"Yes, it is." Fidgeting uncomfortably, she looked around for someone to rescue her, but Milo and Koji had joined Tad and Zeke in the balcony section of the hayloft. The only person whose eye she was able to catch was her father's, and Jayce only nodded approvingly. Folding her arms over her chest with a grumpy huff, she was caught off guard by Omri, who dropped down to nestle in the crook of her arm. Prissie smiled softly at the tiny angel's sweet expression.

Ransom noticed and quirked a brow at her, and she colored slightly. That smile was meant for Omri, not him! Silence stretched awkwardly between them until he remarked, "The music's not bad."

"They're a Christian group," Prissie pointed out.

"Yeah. The lyrics kind of gave that away."

Swallowing hard, she glanced over and mumbled, "About the other day. I'm sorry if I was rude."

"If?" he challenged.

Squirming under his direct gaze, she grudgingly said, "I might have been out of line."

"You think?"

"I'm *trying* to apologize!"

Ransom only shook his head and said, "Try harder."

Flustered and frustrated, Prissie snapped, "What do you want from me?"

"Mostly nothing," he replied. "But if you're feeling generous, maybe half a chance."

12

THE GROUP PROJECT

"I want another way in," the dark figure growled.

Dinge and Murque exchanged nervous glances, and the latter cautiously inquired, "In *where*, my lord?"

"Haven't you been paying attention?" he asked silkily.

"M-more or less," the demon replied in ingratiating tones.

"Lots of places you're wanting to get into lately," said Dinge. "If you catch my meaning."

Their superior sneered. "The girl is hemmed in on every side, but I can still reach her through those around her."

Murque's eyes took on an evil gleam. "The father's a trusting fool."

Dinge leered and added, "The brother's at a difficult age."

"Perhaps," the Fallen mused aloud. "Look for an opening. There's *always* an opening."

When the regular football season ended, the West Edinton Warriors moved on to the playoffs, and without a Friday night game on the docket, Prissie was able to make plans for a different kind of fun. The social studies assignment was due next week, right before Thanksgiving break, so she invited April for a sleepover to give their group the chance to work on it.

It was by far the best project Prissie had ever been a part of, mostly because for once, she didn't feel the need to do everything. April had bookmarked half a dozen search engines, and she wasn't afraid to use them. Koji remembered everything he read, so he was able to bring up useful tidbits from the stacks of library books he'd read on their assignment. For her part, Prissie was good at giving the teachers what they wanted. Once the report was finished, she'd be the one to present it. They each carried their own weight, and it was coming together quickly.

"Want to take a break?" Prissie asked. They'd been working steadily since right after dinner, and she was ready for a change of pace. "We could make popcorn."

"Yes!" April quickly agreed. "Homework always gives me a case of the nibbles."

They found Neil at the kitchen table, munching his way through an apple while he read. Prissie did a double take. "Studying?" she asked incredulously.

"Kinda, yeah."

"What class?" inquired April, plopping down across the table from him. She never minded being called nosy because it was a reporter's job to be curious. Prissie thought April might have made a decent Observer, except that her curiosity was a lot more in-your-face.

"Not a class," Neil corrected, flipping over the book to show her the cover.

"That's some pretty technical extracurricular reading," April remarked.

"This is the manual first responders have to learn," he explained. "Derrick Matthews loaned it to me."

"So you're interested in first aid?"

"Kinda," he repeated. "It's a good place to start."

"If that's your starting point, where are you headed?" April pried.

"I'm going to go into medicine."

Prissie's head whipped around, but her friend didn't bat an eye at this pronouncement. "What kind? Are you talking neurosurgeon … pediatrician … veterinarian?"

"Nope. I'm going to drive ambulances."

"Since when?" Prissie asked.

"Since *now*," Neil replied with a careless grin.

In spite of a late night, both April and Prissie were awake early on Saturday morning. Soft sounds from the kitchen lured them down the back stairs where they found Grandma Nell already at work. Saturday breakfast was often her treat, and with both Neil's play-off game that afternoon and April over, she was going the extra mile. The coffeepot was on, and she was just sliding some kind of cheesy potato bake into the oven.

"Blueberry pancakes?" Prissie asked, eyeing the ingredients her grandmother had set out.

"And sausages," Grandma Nell confirmed. "Help yourself to juice."

The girls padded over to the table with their glasses and joined Tad and Koji, who were polishing off cinnamon toast.

"You're up early," April said cheerfully.

"No more than usual," Tad replied.

April pointed out, "It's not a school day."

"Tell that to the pigs and chickens," the oldest Pomeroy boy replied with a small smile.

"I'm an early riser, too, but that's because it's the only way I can keep up with my dailies before school."

Tad asked, "What're dailies?"

April pulled out her cell phone and tapped the screen a few times before showing him the morning's headlines. "I keep up with several blogs, a couple of forums, some web comics, all the major news feeds, and that doesn't even begin to cover my emails, personal messages, tweets ..." Tad's expression showed April he wasn't plugged in, and Prissie wasn't much better. So she smoothly changed the subject, asking, "What kinds of chores do you have to do every day?"

"Koji and I will head into the back forty to take care of the pigs, and then I'll give Judicious a hand with the chickens," Tad replied. "The other usual stuff can wait until after Neil's game."

"Oh! I remember when your grandpa used to give us rides around the orchard behind his tractor," April said. "Do you remember that?"

"Sure," Prissie said with a smile. When it came to impressing little girls, her Grandpa Pete was a real pushover.

Tad glanced between the girls. "If you bundle up, I'll hitch the trailer to the quad. It's not the same as Grandpa's hay wagon, but we should have time for a little tour."

"You probably have an hour and a half before breakfast is ready," said Grandma Nell, giving the four of them an encouraging smile. "There's nothing like morning air to give you a healthy appetite!"

April's eyes took on a shine, and she glanced at Prissie. "Let's?" she begged.

"Sure! Prissie readily agreed. Her friend was obviously very excited, and it *would* be fun. Prissie didn't mind because, more than any of the others, April had stuck by her.

When they reached the machine shed a few minutes later, Tad had the quad ready to go. Its trailer was square with low sides, and Tad had tossed a couple of old blankets in the bottom, not that they'd do much good. Prissie knew from experience that they were in for a bumpy ride. Still, it was a nice gesture.

April clambered aboard. "Thanks so much!"

"We're heading out that way anyhow. I don't mind the extra company." Tad swung his leg over the four-wheeler's wide seat.

Prissie stepped over the side and settled down next to April, and Koji climbed in with them. The young angel seemed to have gone back into silent Observer mode, for he tucked his knees to his chest and simply listened as the girls swapped memories of the games of hide-and-seek they'd played out here when they were younger.

Their breath showed on the morning air, and frost glazed the grass that hadn't been touched by the sun. All but the most stubborn leaves had dropped from the apple trees, and here and there, Prissie could see odd pieces of shriveled fruit clinging to a branch. Even over the exhaust from the quad's rumbling motor, she could smell the sweetness of fallen fruit, the apple scent that defined home for all the Pomeroys.

Just as they reached the pig shed, which had an odor all its own, Prissie noticed that Koji's mood had changed, so when April hurried to the fence to admire their porkers, she nudged him and whispered, "Are you okay?"

His gaze darted upward, and he quietly admitted, "There are a lot of things going on right now."

"Things?" she asked worriedly.

"Fear not," he said with a reassuring smile. "There are many protecting us."

When Koji finished with his responsibilities to the pigs, Tad urged everyone into the trailer so their tour could continue. "We'll take the scenic route back to the house," he said, putting the quad into gear and driving toward the far end of their land.

Prissie glanced around curiously, wondering what Koji was seeing, and she noticed that Tad was checking out the vicinity with just as much care. The eighteen-year-old sat tall and systematically looked over the trees, keeping an eye out for signs of pests, disease, and damage. If he was anything like Grandpa Pete, he was probably also deciding which branches he would prune next time he came through.

When they reached the top of the last hill, the quad sputtered and stalled. "Huh, that's odd," Tad muttered as he hopped down. "Gimme a sec to check it over."

While he popped open the covering on the engine and began to tinker, April climbed out of the trailer and stretched. "What a view! I didn't realize you were this close to the fairgrounds!" She pointed down the gently sloping hill to the outbuildings that lay between the Pomeroy's land and Sunderland State Park.

Prissie joined her friend, replying, "Yes, we're next-door neighbors."

"How far are we from your house?" April asked curiously.

"From here, it's probably almost two miles," Tad replied, not looking up from his tinkering.

While he rattled off boundaries, Koji edged closer to Prissie, and his fingers silently found hers.

Meanwhile, April said, "I guess I didn't realize your place was that big."

"The orchard and farm have been in the family for a lot of years," Tad explained. "When adjoining properties went up for sale, we bought them. This section is part of the original orchard, and the newer parts are along the highway. There's enough wiggle room for both me and Judicious to stay busy."

April admired the acres of fruit trees. "You have it all figured out!"

"It's not so hard with a family business," Tad said.

Prissie only listened to Tad and April with half an ear. "Is something wrong?" she whispered. Koji shook his head, then nodded toward the base of the hill. She followed his gaze in time to see a figure step through the trees from a neighboring row and walk their way. "Who's that?" she asked a little too loudly.

Tad straightened from his work and frowned. "We're not close to much of anything out here. I should see if he needs help."

The teen started forward, but the oncoming hiker waved him back and called out, "Wait there, please! I'll come to you!"

Prissie stared hard at the man working his way uphill. He wore a nondescript denim jacket and carried a simple hiking stick, but even from a distance she recognized his hair. Thick black braids hung on either side of his face. "Padgett?" she gasped.

"You know him?" Tad asked curiously.

"He's ... I met him on our last field trip."

"He is one of the rangers at Sunderland State Park," supplied Koji helpfully.

"Oh, that makes sense," Tad murmured, stepping forward with hand extended.

Padgett accepted the greeting. "Good morning. I was admiring your trees and thought to see the view from this slope. I apologize for trespassing on your land."

"No harm done," the oldest Pomeroy boy replied amiably.

"Hello again, miss," the Caretaker said, a smile lurking in his dark eyes. "Koji," he added with a nod.

"Padgett, this is my brother, Tad, and my friend, April. Aren't you a long way from the park?"

"Not so far," the ranger replied, glancing back toward state land. "My ramble brought me over more boundaries than I realized. Are you having trouble?"

"Oh, nothing serious," Tad said. "Even if I can't get the quad running, it's a nice day for a walk."

"I can attest to that." Padgett nodded at the four-wheeler. "I would offer to help, but I know little or nothing about mechanical things."

"I'm pretty good with this stuff," Tad assured. "Something probably jiggled loose."

"Show me?" the ranger asked.

"Well, sure," the teen agreed, returning to the open case

to poke at the motor. "It's usually something small, so I was checking everything over."

"I see."

April joined them while Tad performed minor surgery. "Do you really know what you're doing?" she asked.

"Sure. Part of the job. Let's see if that did the trick. Start her up, Prissie?" She hopped onto the seat and hit the starter, and the engine turned with a cough and a rumble.

"Nice!" April exclaimed.

Tad nodded in satisfaction and closed everything up, then cast a critical glance at the angle of the sun. "We should probably skip the scenic route and head straight back to the house. Knowing Grandma Nell, they'll hold breakfast for us."

The Caretaker moved to stand between them and the boundary. "Yes, that would be best."

"Would you like a ride?" Tad offered.

"Thank you, no," Padgett replied with a scant smile. "I'll find my way back to where I belong."

"If you say so," the teen said. "It was nice to meet you, Padgett."

"Likewise, Tad," the Caretaker replied, nodding to each of them in turn. "Koji. April. And Prissie, it was good to see you again, miss."

"You, too," she murmured, wishing she knew what was going on.

"Have a pleasant day," Padgett said, then strode down the hill at a steady pace.

Tad turned the quad around, and once everyone piled back into the trailer. He made a beeline for home. It wasn't until they were hurrying up the front walk that Prissie had the chance to whisper to Koji, "What was that all about?"

"The boundary is a place of unrest," the young Observer replied seriously. "Padgett redirected us."

"Why?"

"The path we were on led into danger."

Over breakfast, April was in what her friends called her interview groove. Conversation at the table seemed to revolve around her, but not because she was doing all the talking. Rather, she was asking all the questions.

For a while, she quizzed Tad on his college plans and discussed the pros and cons of the various universities that offered agricultural degrees. Prissie was amazed that April managed to draw the eighteen-year-old out enough to talk about *anything*, since he wasn't much of a conversationalist. Then, she turned around and dragged Grandpa into the discussion by asking him if he thought it was more important to know how to take apart an engine than it was to earn a degree.

Fleetingly, Prissie wondered about the attention April was paying to her big big-brother, but just as quickly, her friend turned to Jude, wanting to know the current retail value of farm fresh eggs. The next minute, she switched gears and asked Neil about the upcoming football game and the statistics of the other team's quarterback. From there, she talked to Grandma Nell about the difficulties of raising blueberries in their region.

At school, April mostly talked about celebrity gossip and fashion, but Prissie supposed that's because those were the things that Margery and Jennifer were most interested in. April seemed to know a little bit about everything. In comparison, Prissie felt a little ... dull.

Later, when they were in Prissie's room, changing for the game, April asked, "Why do you always wear skirts and dresses?"

"I don't," she said, feeling a bit defensive. "I have work pants and a pair of overalls, but those are for around the farm."

"Why don't you wear jeans to the game?" her friend suggested. "They'd be warmer."

"There's no way," Prissie replied. "It just wouldn't be *me*."

April nodded thoughtfully, and said, "It must be nice to know yourself so well."

Prissie blinked. Most people called her stubborn, stuck in her ways, and even stuck up. "I guess I hadn't thought of it that way before."

"Some people can't seem to make up their mind about who they want to be," April explained. "But you're very sure of yourself. I admire that."

With a tentative smile, Prissie asked, "What do *you* like, April?"

"Me?" she asked, surprised.

"Yes. What kinds of things are you interested in?"

April tapped her chin, and her eyes took on a mischievous twinkle. "When it comes right down to it, I guess I'd have to say *people*!"

Prissie giggled. She couldn't help it. It made her even happier when April joined in.

The stadium where the play-off games were being held was much bigger than the one at Prissie's school. Jayce and Grandpa Pete escorted Neil to the team's locker room while

Momma and Grandma Nell herded the rest of the family along the concourse toward the restrooms. "Is it okay if we start looking for seats?" Prissie asked.

"Go ahead, sweetheart," her mother replied. "We'll catch up to you in a few minutes."

April, Koji, and Prissie hurried through the tunnel that opened onto the football field. Four games were scheduled today, so there were people from eight different schools in the stands. Whole sections had been claimed by the various schools, and they were already filling with crowds, proudly wearing their school colors. Prissie cast sidelong glances at a bunch of boys who'd painted their faces orange and white. A little further along, they had to edge around marching band members with fluffy gold plumes on their helmets.

Finally, they reached the West Edinton section and its sea of red. Prissie was keeping her eyes peeled for good seats close to the front. "I'm going to say hey to the other girls," April announced. "Do you want to come?"

"Not this time. But do you want me to save you a seat?"

"Do that!" April said, giving a little wave before hurrying off to where the cheerleaders had gathered.

Prissie breathed a sigh of relief. It was hard to know what to expect where her friends were concerned. Just then, a woman's voice caught her attention, loud and clear in spite of the surrounding noise. "WooHoo! Prissie!"

Koji spotted her first and pointed to a short woman with bobbed mahogany red hair who was furiously waving a Warrior's pennant at them. "How's my grand-girl?" she asked with a happy little bounce.

"Grammie?"

"Hey, Fussbudget!" hailed the tall, silver-haired man by

her side. He aimed the imposing zoom lens of his camera their way and snapped a quick photo.

"Grandpa!" Prissie exclaimed. "I didn't think you were coming until Thanksgiving!"

"We wanted to see Neil's game, so we decided to sneak in a week early!" he replied with a wide smile. "Surprised?"

"Yes!"

"These are your grandparents?" Koji inquired curiously.

Prissie nodded dazedly before making her way into the stands to hug and be hugged. Then, she politely offered introductions. "Grandpa, Grammie, this is Koji. Koji, these are Momma's parents, Carl and Esme Olsen."

13

THE STONE STAIRS

Rain slapped against shingles, cold and heavy in the night. Heedless of the wind and wet, Tamaes lay upon the roof, lost in dreams while his mentor stood guard. Taweel endured the downpour without any sign of discomfort, gazing into the storm with watchful eyes.

Omri darted from Taweel's shoulder to the relative shelter of the nearby dormer and settled on its ledge, giving his wings a flick to rid them of raindrops. He pressed his face to a pane of blue glass, then tiptoed further down the sill to peer through a golden one, brightening when he caught sight of the room's occupant. With a hopeful hum, the little angel pleaded with Taweel, but the big Guardian shook his head. "We are not here to visit."

The yahavim sighed and pressed his tiny nose to the glass.

With a faint smile, Taweel turned his eyes back to the sky. "Do not be discouraged. She may need you yet."

Grandpa and Grammie Olsen were nomads. If you asked Grandpa Carl, he'd say he was a globe-trotting shutterbug, but Momma assured her kids that he was just a retired businessman with an advanced case of wanderlust. Her parents had sold their home a few years ago and now lived in a big, shiny RV. When they weren't turning up to visit their far-flung brood, they were exploring the highways and byways of the country.

"We added five more states over the summer," Grandpa Olsen bragged, giving Jude a boost so he could better see the back of the RV that was now parked beside the barn. An outline map of the continental states was more than half filled in by brightly colored magnets.

"Which ones?" the boy asked curiously.

Koji watched intently as Grandpa proudly pointed to the new additions. "I'll show you my pictures later. I have some amazing ones!"

"Sure!" Jude agreed with a sunny smile. "So how come you're trying to go to all these places?"

"Because we're part gypsy!" Grandpa Carl confided.

Beau snorted and Prissie rolled her eyes. With her wild hair and zany plans, you'd think that Grammie Esme was someone to keep a close eye on, but the Pomeroys had learned it was Grandpa Carl you needed to watch out for. He might look mild-mannered, but was a hoodwinker and balderdasher of the first order. All of the kids had been taken in by his tall tales at one time or another.

"Gypsies?" Jude marveled. "That's cool!"

"Don't I know it!" his grandfather agreed. "You can *tell* it runs in the family! Just look at your aunt Ida! Now *there's* a girl after my own heart!"

"Wow! That's right!" the six-year-old exclaimed.

Prissie gave Grandpa a stern look, but the man only winked. Unless someone clued him in, it might be a while before Jude realized that Ida and the Olsens weren't actually related.

"How long are you staying?" Beau asked.

"Oh, we'll stick around through Thanksgiving, for sure. After that, it's hard to say. Your grammie's a flighty woman, and she might just take it into her head to follow the birds south for the winter."

"What kind of birds?" asked Jude.

"Snowbirds, mostly," Grandpa Carl replied. "Though she has a real fondness for yellow-bellied flapdoodles. Do they migrate through here?"

"I dunno," the boy said.

"How about we keep our eyes peeled for some while you give me the grand tour?"

"Okay!" Jude agreed. "What do they look like?"

"Well, from what I've read, the yellow-bellied flapdoodle is famous for two things," Grandpa Carl confided as he set the boy back down. "Their bellies are yellow, and they do a whole lot of flapping!"

"Are they big or little?" Jude quizzed.

"A little of both!"

The six-year-old led the charge to the apple barn, where all good tours began, and Prissie hung back to walk with Koji.

The young Observer peeped at her out of the corner of his eye and whispered, "There is no such bird."

"Momma says you should take everything Grandpa says with a grain of salt."

The boy nodded. "Seasoned with salt and full of grace."

With a small smile, Prissie confided, "Grammie says Grandpa is full of stuff and nonsense."

"Indeed." After further consideration, he added, "I am grateful for the opportunity to meet more of your family. I wish to see how their lives fit against yours."

"Grandpa and Grammie aren't much for fitting in," she warned.

"But they draw in those around them."

"And drive them a little crazy," Prissie countered. "If you think our house was noisy before, just wait."

"For what?"

She just shook her head and said, "You'll see. You always do."

Loafing Around always experienced a small boom during the week of Thanksgiving. Last minute orders for pies kept Auntie Lou busy, and Jayce sweet-talked his daughter into lending a hand after school. Prissie was glad to be asked, but less than thrilled to have Ransom bumming a ride with her and Koji to the bakery. Somehow, her classmate managed to be less annoying than usual, so she was able to focus on helping Auntie Lou create her signature pinwheel pattern on top of twenty-six pecan pies.

Once those were in the oven, Lou took off to take care of a quick errand, and Prissie begged her dad for the chance to run across the way with Koji to visit The Curiosity Shop. Jayce turned them loose, and Ransom watched them go with a thoughtful expression. "Did you adopt that kid?"

"Who, Koji?" Jayce replied, sounding surprised. "Nope. He's an exchange student, on loan to us for the school year."

"Huh." After a few moments, Ransom casually said, "They're close, and I mean joined-at-the-hip close. Like he idolizes her."

"No, I don't think so," Jayce countered as he rough-chopped some cranberries for the bread he was making. "More than once, I've seen him rebuke her for her attitude or behavior."

"Rebuke?"

"Whoops, sorry. Christian jargon slips in," Jayce said sheepishly. "He told her off. In fact, he scolded her for how she acted toward you on Halloween. He was very polite about it, but Prissie looked like a whipped puppy."

"So, *she* idolizes *him*?"

Jayce reached for a bag of walnuts and tossed it from one hand to the other while he considered the teen's words. Finally, he shook his head, saying, "I don't think that's it either. Naomi mentioned it back when Koji first joined the family because we sort of expected Prissie to put up a fuss about taking in *another* boy, but right from the beginning, those two acted like they'd always been friends."

"Just friends, huh?"

"Nothing *just* about it," Jayce retorted. Using a knife to slit open the end of the bag, he shook out a pile of nuts and resumed chopping. "I'd say they've hit upon that rare kind of friendship that can last a lifetime."

Ransom's eyes narrowed in concentration. "She acts

totally different with him than anyone else. I wish I could figure out *why*."

"Jealous?" her father asked with a teasing grin.

"Nah. I have friends," he replied easily. "Me and Marcus are tight, but those two are something else."

"On the surface, I suppose they're an unlikely pair," Jayce conceded. "But my girl trusts that boy completely. It's beautiful to see around the house, but I'll admit it worries me a little."

"How come?"

Jayce sighed and asked, "What happens when the school year ends? We've all grown attached to Koji, and I'd keep him if I could. But I'm assuming the boy's family will want him back."

"Makes sense."

"I know how foolish it is to borrow trouble from tomorrow, but I can't help but look ahead. It'll break Prissie's heart when the time comes to say goodbye." Her father shook his head. "Who'll be there for her when Koji leaves?"

Ransom gave his boss a crooked smile. "She'll have *you*, sir!"

"No brownnosing in my kitchen, young man!" Jayce warned, tossing a towel at him. "It would have been more chivalrous to volunteer for the task yourself!"

Laughing outright, Ransom replied, "Not on your life!"

"This way," Koji said happily.

"You don't need to hold my hand," Prissie complained, though there was no one around to see except the excitable flock of yahavim. The little manna-makers had turned up as soon as they entered the glade beyond the blue door.

The young Observer only shook his head. "Yes, I do."

"Why?" she asked, but she forgot to wonder when their destination came into view. A white door set into a white stone arch stood by itself in the middle of the forest. The masonry looked as if it had been there for quite some time. Moss and lichen had taken hold. "Has this always been here?"

"No."

In the center of the painted door, there was a carving of what looked like another door — or perhaps it was more like a gate — flanked by two imposing pillars. Like the blue door's handle, its knob seemed to be made of crystal, but instead of the opalescent glow, this one was crazed by metallic threads of gold. The sphere shone like a small sun and felt warm to her tentative touch. "Where are you taking me?"

"Up." When Koji pushed open the door, they faced a wide set of stairs that curved up and away. As they crossed the threshold, Prissie realized the stairs wound along the inside wall of a high, circular structure that wasn't visible from the outside. "Today is a good day to visit Shimron."

"This is your mentor's tower?"

"Indeed."

Gazing upwards, Prissie felt cold. "It's high."

Koji fit his fingers between hers and squeezed tightly. "I will be with you."

The stairs climbed upward in a lazy spiral. Prissie hugged walls made of the same chalky white stone as the arch marking the entrance, for there were no railings between them and what was sure to become a dizzying drop. Above and below there was only light, which seemed to flow right through the center of the tower like a stream of dazzling particles. Every so often, an indistinct burst of color zipped by, rising or falling, and when a flash of green soared past, Prissie finally asked, "What was that?"

"Who," Koji corrected. "That was Jedrick. He checks on Shimron regularly."

"He doesn't have to use the stairs?"

"He has wings."

"Oh," she replied, resisting the urge to look over the edge. By now, they had to be far above the forest glade.

Finally, they passed through a second stone arch, and to Prissie's relief, nothing about the chamber they entered felt high up. Two other arches were set into the walls of the circular room, but there were no windows. On the one hand, the room felt very empty — bare floors, sparse furnishings, and an airy spaciousness that probably had to do with the apparent lack of a proper ceiling. All Prissie could see overhead were fragments of rainbows that rippled to and fro, as if they were reflecting off a pool of water. On the other hand, Shimron's tower felt incredibly crowded, for there were books everywhere.

Neat shelves lined the curving wall, evenly spaced as they marched upward. Prissie couldn't help but notice that every single volume was exactly the same height, but they were different colors, and some volumes were thicker than others. As she gazed at those on the nearest shelf, she found that the spines were embellished by different designs. One bore a tree, another a sheaf of wheat. One looked as if it was trimmed with ribbon, another with pebbles. A buckle, harp, flowers, raindrops, nuts, grass — no two books were exactly the same, yet they all seemed to belong together.

With a gentle tug, Koji led her to the center of the room, where a large table stood. It slanted like a drafter's table, and along the top edge, an array of old-fashioned pens and brushes sprouted from a collection of mismatched jars. Some were made from glazed pottery, others glass, metal, or stone. There was even a jumble of stubby pencils heaped in an enormous seashell.

Behind all the clutter sat an old man who bent over a large sheet of thick parchment. As they drew closer, Prissie could see that a large section of the page had been covered in strange letters. The paper was expensive-looking, and the rich, creamy color was like the man's raiment. In fact, as she compared them, she realized that the paper and the fabric had the very same inherent glow.

Koji patiently waited while the white-haired man worked with a set of small brushes. He was adding color to a panel alongside the text, just like in a medieval illuminated manuscript. With a start, Prissie realized that his illustration looked like her bedroom window at home.

Eventually, the old gentleman lifted his gaze and smiled pleasantly. "Koji, you brought your friend." His voice was as soft as the fluttering of pages in an old book.

"Indeed," his apprentice replied eagerly. "Prissie, this is Shimron."

Shimron's snowy hair stood up around his head in short waves. His faded blue eyes were bright and attentive, and his ears were as elegantly tipped as Koji's had been before Abner had applied the boy's human disguise. "It's nice to meet you, sir," Prissie said.

"Miss Pomeroy, you may call me Shimron."

Koji brimmed with happiness, but she felt a little awkward with two Observers watching her so attentively. Casting about for a distraction, she asked, "Is this a library?"

"Of sorts," Shimron said. "This is an archive."

Prissie wondered if each of the books covered a year, or a month, or a week. Maybe even one day was busy enough to fill the pages of those thick tomes. Then something else occurred to her. "Did you write all of these?"

"Most," Shimron replied with a serene smile.

Pointing to the illustration on the desk before him, she dared to inquire, "Are you writing about me?"

"Not directly, no," he said. "Human lives are not my concern at the present time. It is given to me to record that which takes place within Jedrick's Flight."

"But isn't that *my* window?"

"I am pleased you recognize it!"

"It's *obviously* mine," she said. "You're a very good artist!"

"Yes, he is," Koji agreed.

"This *is* your room, child," Shimron replied. Tapping the unfinished painting, he casually said, "My young apprentice is quite fond of this spot, and he described it in glowing terms. Whether it is the seat or the view or the company he keeps while there, only he can tell."

Koji met her gaze with a shy smile. "They are all good reasons."

"Some better than others," the old Observer replied lightly.

Prissie found herself smiling, too. It was obvious that these two got along very well, even though Koji hadn't been apprenticed to Shimron for very long. "So you're writing about Koji?"

"Just so," Shimron agreed.

"Have you always been a part of Jedrick's Flight?" she asked curiously.

"No, no, no," he said with a dry chuckle. "I am much too old for that to be possible. However, I have been under Jedrick's watch-care for nearly two centuries."

"That's a long time!"

"I suppose," Shimron replied thoughtfully. "From your perspective, our lives have been intertwined for generations. The stories fill many volumes."

"May I see them?" she inquired. "Is that allowed?"

"That which is written stands as a testament to the wisdom and faithfulness of God," Shimron replied earnestly. "Though I doubt you can unravel our language, the illustrations tell their own tale. Koji, I will trust you to use discretion when choosing selections to read?"

"Yes, Shimron!"

"If questions arise, I will be right here," the old Observer assured before taking up his brushes once more.

Koji led Prissie to a second, smaller desk and urged her to sit on the bench before it. There weren't nearly as many writing implements on the ledge, and no brushes. "Don't you paint, too?" she asked.

"Not yet," he replied solemnly. "I need more practice. Wait a moment."

He padded over to one of the nearby shelves and selected two books, one much fatter than the other. He joined her on the seat, crowding close as he set the larger volume between them. Prissie found the cold gray cover and the chain pattern on the spine a little ominous, but as soon as Koji lifted the cover, the colorful illustrations distracted her. On the first page, there was a detailed depiction of a sword with a vivid blue gem set into its hilt. "This looks familiar," she murmured, wishing she could read the strange lettering.

"It is Jedrick's sword."

"That's right!" she exclaimed. As her friend slowly turned the pages, she caught sight of more familiar things — the blue door, apple blossoms, a harp, a row of onions, and a nest filled with duck eggs. Other pages had pictures that meant nothing special to her, but as they went along, she noticed that there were no people, just ordinary everyday items, plants, and animals. It was fun to try to match the various illustrations with the angel whose story it belonged to.

In the last half of the book, Prissie spied another familiar scene. "A Ferris wheel?" she gasped. "Is this from the county fair?"

"Yes," Koji replied, skimming the passage that accompanied it. "This is one of Baird's."

"Does it say anything about how silly I acted?" she asked worriedly.

He slowly shook his head. "The view from the top inspired this entry."

"Oh. Well, good."

"I would not call it good," Koji replied softly. With a sigh, he reached for the other book. It was green, with the silhouette of a single fern frond on its cover. "I have not read this one before, but I have wanted to."

"What's it about?"

"This is also a record of Jedrick's Flight, but it is from several years ago."

The illuminated panels were in a different style than those in the book they'd just set aside. The lines were sketchier somehow, and the color wasn't painted on. Soft shades and shadows had been applied and smudged in a way that reminded Prissie of chalk.

On a page decorated with twin fawns, several short lines of lettering were printed, and as Koji's eyes swept over them, a smile lit his entire countenance — literally. Prissie squinted at the sudden radiance and asked, "What? What is it?"

"This is about *you*," he shared, his voice little more than a whisper.

What words shall I use
To express the joy
Of those who await
the working of grace
within a child's heart?
Lullaby prayers,
Whispers of glory,
Cascade from wingtips
Hushed in their waiting
Now lifted in praise.
Angels surround you,
Serving in silence,
Guarding what's precious.
Joy falls like raindrops
From heaven blue eyes.

"The working of grace?" she echoed uncertainly.

"Salvation," Koji explained. "Yours!"

"*Ours*," she corrected, gently touching the two spotted fawns that graced the page. She remembered the day very well, if only because the anniversary was marked every December. She and Beau had both been five at the time, and Prissie had decided that being *almost* twins wasn't enough. Tad had tried to tell her that it was impossible to become *real* twins because they couldn't change their birthdays, and she'd gone running to Momma.

Once Naomi had sorted out the reason for her daughter's tears, she'd offered a brilliant solution. While it was true they wouldn't ever have the same birthday, they could have the same *spiritual* birthday and share it forever. That night, she and Jayce explained everything to the two of them, using simple terms, and with childlike faith, the siblings had prayed together. With much pomp and circumstance, the date on the calendar was circled twice to mark the beginning of two new lives. "We're spiritual twins, Beau and I," Prissie quietly explained.

Pointing to the account on the adjacent page, Koji announced, "This says that Milo brought the good news here, and he was so excited, he could not find words."

"Did Shimron say all that?" Prissie asked in awe.

"No," he said softly. "This is Ephron's record."

14

THE CROWDED KITCHEN

Does Koji seem different to you?" Milo asked as he played with the members of Abner's flock.

"Yes, he's changed," Harken readily agreed. "It's understandable, considering the role he's taken on in recent weeks. Are you concerned?"

"A little," the mailman admitted. "Koji's still so young, and his dreams sound so dark."

"We should thank God that we have any point of contact with Ephron."

"Yeah, I know." Milo ran his hand over the top of his head before saying, "When they find each other, it's as if Ephron's sadness rubs off on Koji."

Harken nodded gravely. "If that's so, then it may *also* be true that Koji's joy gives Ephron strength."

Blue eyes took on a thoughtful expression. "Maybe that's why?"

"Why *what*?" his mentor asked.

"I was just thinking that it's a good thing Koji has the Pomeroys right now," Milo said. "Perhaps the reason God allowed him to meet Miss Priscilla was so that her family could care for him in ways we cannot?"

"Who can say?" Harken replied, though he soon began to smile. "I'd like to think so, though. Friendships grow stronger when two people discover that they can rely on each other."

"He's grown very attached."

"That's one way of putting it," the shopkeeper said with a deep chuckle.

"Oh?" challenged Milo. "And how would you put it?"

To answer, Harken said, "The *strongest* friendships are forged when two people realize that they *love* each other."

Thanksgiving at the Pomeroy's wasn't so much a *day* as it was a three-day buildup to the main event. Grandma Nell and Momma had the preparations down to a science, but with school out for the week, the big farm kitchen was more chaotic than usual. Neil was in permanent lurk mode, snitching pie crust cookies off the cooling racks and munching on apple peels.

"Can't you do *anything* useful?" Prissie complained.

"I *am*!" the sixteen-year-old retorted. "I'm head sampler, chief pot-checker, and this year's poster child!" Clad in one of Grandma Nell's gaudiest aprons, he draped an arm around Grammie Esme's shoulders and cheesed for the camera.

Grandpa Carl backed him up by snapping several shots, then went back to photographing rows of pecan tartlets.

The Olsens had always worked hard to keep their scattered family connected. Over the years, Grandpa and Grammie had carried piles of scrapbooks wherever they went, but recently, they'd switched to virtual albums. Now, there was a family blog that allowed Naomi to stay caught up with her brothers and sister. According to Jayce, it was an improvement on the epic-length slide shows that used to kick off every one of his in-laws' visits.

"You could lend Koji a hand," Prissie said, pointing to the mountain of potatoes that still needed peeling. The young angel watched intently as Neil twirled around, then reached over to snatch a pecan tart out from under Grandma Nell's nose.

"Oh, you," Grammie Esme scolded fondly.

"Yes, me!" Neil agreed. While he nibbled, the teen cast a sidelong look at Momma, who gave him a small smile. With a put-upon sigh, he ambled over to one of the wide kitchen drawers and fished out a vegetable peeler.

Grandpa Carl asked, "Is there another in there with my name on it?"

With Grammie Esme around, kitchen chitchat became chatter because she could talk a mile a minute, often about cousins that Prissie mostly knew from Grandpa Carl's photographs. They always said that just because their kids had spread to the four corners of the continent didn't mean they couldn't be close. Between the stories and snapshots, they helped their children and grandchildren stay in touch.

A rap sounded on the kitchen door. "Special delivery!"

"Come on in, Milo!" Momma called.

"Smells good all the way down to the mailbox!" he exclaimed as he strolled into the kitchen, a package under his arm. "This one's for a Mrs. Nellie Pomeroy."

"Oh!" Grandma Esme exclaimed. "Prissie's mailman? How nice!"

The girl stiffened in her seat, a blush creeping into her cheeks as she determinedly kept her eyes on the celery she was dicing. Koji nudged her with his elbow, and when Prissie glanced his way, he quietly pointed out, "Milo is *my* mailman as well."

She smiled at what was obviously meant as some kind of odd angelic joke. "But you never get any mail."

He frowned thoughtfully. "That is true."

Neil beckoned from the table. "We saved you a spot, Milo! Grab a peeler and lend a hand!"

"Does the apron come with the job?" inquired the mailman.

"That can be arranged," Grandma Nell said, a gleam in her eyes.

When Milo finally dropped into a seat across the table from Prissie and Koji, he was wearing a ruffled apron with *Kiss the Cook* stitched across the front. She was mortified on his behalf, but the Messenger calmly reached for a potato. "It's been a while since your grandmother put me on KP duty."

"I'm always here," Grandma Nell said in scolding tones. "Which means *you're* the one who's been scarce lately."

He grinned sheepishly and murmured thanks as she placed a glass of cold milk and a plate of iced molasses cookies at his elbow. "I suppose I *have* been busier than usual."

"Rehearsals?" guessed the woman.

"There's been a lot of singing," Milo admitted.

Prissie jumped in and asked, "Who's the package from?"

"It's from Ida, of course."

Grandpa Carl perked up and inquired, "Will she be home for the holidays?"

"We hope so, but things are still up in the air," Grandma Nell replied.

Milo asked, "How long will you be staying this time around, Mr. Olsen?"

"Oh, I think we'll stick around for a bit. It's been a few years since we attended the annual concert, and what with Tad and Neil joining in this year ... well!" Patting his camera, Carl said, "Wouldn't miss it!"

That evening, Prissie tiptoed down to the kitchen to make herself a cup of cocoa and found her mother standing alone, contemplating the baked goods that lined the counter. "What are you doing, Momma?" Prissie asked.

Naomi glanced away from the long double row of pumpkin pies. "Hmm? Oh," she replied vaguely. "I was just thinking about crusts."

"Crusts," Prissie echoed, giving her mother a you're-talking-crazy look.

Naomi simply smiled and asked, "Which one of these is better?"

As her mother pointed to the cooled pies, Prissie looked them over. There were half a dozen, but since three different people had worked on them, they all looked different. One pair had high, fluted edges, each scallop perfectly formed. On two others, the edges had been trimmed neatly to fit the tin and pressed with a fork, forming tiny ridges. The last two had been lined with little stars cut from extra pastry with a cookie cutter.

"I like this one best," Prissie said, pointing to the fluted ones that were obviously Grandma Nell's handiwork. Grandma Esme's stars were really cute, and Momma's fork-crimping was nice, but scalloped pies were Prissie's ideal.

Momma nodded and asked, "Will that pie taste better than the others?"

"No."

"Then why do you suppose you like one better?"

Prissie sighed, not sure what answer her mother was hoping for. "Well, I like Grandma Nell's pies because they look more like a pie *should*. It's prettier this way!"

"I think we all like what we're used to." Pointing to the fork-crimped crusts, she said, "This is what I grew up with, so these look more homey to me. That doesn't mean you're right and I'm wrong. It just means there's often more than one way to do things."

"I *know*," Prissie replied, unsure why she suddenly felt defensive.

"Would it still be your favorite crust if it was a mud pie instead of pumpkin?"

"You mean chocolate?"

"No, I mean *mud*. Dirt."

Prissie's nose wrinkled. "Don't be silly."

Momma nodded again, saying, "There might be many ways to do things, but there's still right and wrong. There's a truth that doesn't bend, and if you don't learn that, you'll be vulnerable to those who tell pretty lies."

"Why are you telling *me*?" she asked moodily.

"Hmm? Oh, I don't know. That's just what was on my mind when you came in." Shaking off her lost-in-thought look, she smiled and asked, "Was there something you wanted?"

"Cocoa."

Lowering her voice conspiratorially, she asked, "May I join you?"

Prissie brightened and reached for two mugs.

Morning smelled like roasting turkey, and Prissie took a deep breath before she ever opened her eyes. The only day that smelled better than Thanksgiving was Christmas, which was right around the corner. She smiled to herself as a familiar excitement began to build, because the holiday season was her absolute favorite time of year. There was a light tap on her bedroom door, and she quietly called, "Yes?"

Koji poked in his head and asked, "You are awake?"

"Obviously."

"I am glad."

Prissie sat up in bed. "An appropriate attitude to greet the day?"

"Indeed!"

Pulling her blankets up to her chin, she yawned, stretched, and asked, "Did you need something?"

Slipping into the room, Koji replied, "Not in particular. I am merely eager for this holy day to begin."

Brows furrowed, Prissie asked, "Who told you Thanksgiving was a *holy* day?"

"Is that not the meaning of holiday?"

"We don't go to church or anything. Honestly, today is mostly for family, food, and football."

Koji tipped his head to one side as he took in her words. “Those are pleasant pastimes.”

“Well, yes,” she agreed. “After all the preparations, it’s nice to finally get to taste all the good food we’ve been fixing.”

He sat on the floor near the foot of her bed and wrapped his arms around his knees. “You do not plan to show thanks on a day of thanks?”

“Momma says that gratitude is an everyday thing, not a one-day thing. It would be silly to only give thanks once a year.”

“That is true,” Koji said. “Will you give thanks on this day?”

“Yes.” He looked at her with an expectant expression, and she asked, “You mean *now*?”

“It would be an appropriate way to greet the day.”

With a long-suffering sigh, Prissie wracked her mind, trying to think of something to say. She glanced around the room for inspiration, but came up empty. Finally, she hunched her shoulders and slowly said, “I guess … *you*. I’m glad I met you.”

Koji smiled. “You were foremost in my mind as well. Thank you, Prissie.”

When everyone gathered in the kitchen to admire the feast that had been laid out, Grandpa Pete said he was pretty sure he heard the table groaning. Following their family tradition, once all the dishes had been passed and people started to eat, Momma called for attention. “I want everyone to tell me one thing they’re thankful for.”

“Aww!” protested Zeke. “Do we gotta?”

Neil rolled his eyes. "You should know by now that Momma's gonna ask. We've had a whole year to prepare for this moment!"

Jayce raised his hands for attention. "Let's not be stingy, now! Our family has plenty of things to be grateful for!"

Momma spoke up. "And the big stuff that applies to everyone is off limits — house, family, friends, health, harvest, and so on. Choose something small, because it's often the *little* things in life that give us the most pleasure." Turning to her husband, she smiled. "What are you grateful for this year?"

Their father rubbed his chin thoughtfully, then declared, "Potatoes!"

Prissie shook her head. "I don't think favorite foods should count as something we're thankful for."

Jayce nabbed a warm potato roll out of the breadbasket and gently tossed it at her. She squeaked in alarm, but Tad caught it and calmly reached for the butter. Her father said, "I'll have you know that much of my livelihood is founded on the humble spud!"

"He's got a point," Neil said, slipping his hand into the breadbasket and winding up for a pitch.

Momma firmly declared, "*No* more food flinging."

As they worked their way around the table, everyone tried to outdo one another in choosing the most obscure item for which to be thankful. The list, which their mother decided to write down for posterity, included highlighters, prescription sunglasses, halogen lights, and bobby pins. Jude earned a laugh for saying he was thankful for the color yellow, and the family summarily rejected marshmallows, funnel cakes, and pizza before reluctantly accepting Neil's gratitude for oven mitts.

Prissie added mailboxes to the growing list. When Koji's turn came, he offered thanks for window seats, but there was something in his expression that made Prissie think something was bothering him. "What's wrong?" she asked quietly.

"Later?" he begged.

"Sure."

When the feast had ended and the kitchen was put to rights, the family scattered, and Prissie joined Koji under a blanket out on the porch swing. Tansy's rumbling purr filled the silence that hung between them, but finally, she prodded, "What are you thinking so hard about?"

"I am confused," he admitted.

"About what?"

His dark eyes gazed mournfully into hers as he confessed, "The thing that I am *most* thankful for is Ephron's capture."

Prissie frowned. "Usually, people are thankful for *good* things."

"Indeed," he agreed. "I have many reasons to give thanks — for my apprenticeship, my teammates, my place in your family, and for *you*. Ephron's capture opened a door for me. Without it, I would not be here."

She couldn't deny that, and it *was* perplexing. "The enemy can't be treating him well."

"No," Koji replied gravely. "Ephron is suffering greatly."

"And he's alone," Prissie whispered, remembering how frightening it had been in the darkness near The Deep.

The young Observer hummed and said, "He is lost, but he is not alone. God is never far from those who are His, and I can reach him in dreams."

"You *talk* to him?" she asked in surprise.

"Yes."

"Well, then why can't anyone *find* him?"

"I do not know. Shimron says that a thing can be impossible until the time is right. We must wait until the time is right, and then Ephron will be returned."

"Do you know that for sure?"

"I have hope."

With a sigh, she looked off toward the barn roof. "I wish I could help with the search."

Koji leaned closer. "Make your request known to God."

"You want me to pray for Ephron?" Prissie asked.

He nodded seriously. "In this, you can do what I cannot."

"You can't pray?"

"Prayer is a gift given to mankind." An expression of concentration overtook the Observer's features as he tried to explain. "Between you and me, the communication is reversed. Your voice reaches heaven, and heaven's voice reaches me."

"God talks to you," she recalled. "You can hear Him audibly."

"Yes," Koji confirmed.

"What's it like?" she whispered.

"It is like God."

Her brows drew together. "Can't you compare it to something?"

The young angel scooted a little closer to her. "*Nothing* compares, Prissie."

"Oh," she sighed, feeling a little left out. "That must be wonderful."

"Wonderful and terrible, all in one."

"So God hears me, and you hear God, but I can't hear God, and you can't pray."

"That is correct."

"How odd."

Koji tipped his head to one side. "I prefer to think of it as symmetrical."

15

THE AWKWARD APOLOGY

Koji was singing a song about cider and swords, hedges and harvest, when Marcus dropped through bare branches on golden wings. The apprentice Protector took up a post on the roof of the pig shed and watched his teammate upend slop buckets into a trough. "Man, they'll eat *anything*."

The young Observer smiled, and his song changed to include pigs, pearls, and prodigals. When Tad moved around to the other side of the pen, Koji quietly asked, "Have you been Sent?"

"Nope. Jedrick has me patrolling so I can stretch my wings for a while."

Nodding, Koji gazed curiously at the Protector, sure there was something more. Marcus snorted softly and jumped from the roof to the fence, hopping lightly from one post to the next until he reached the boy. Using his wings for balance, he crouched down and asked, "What's Prissie got against Ransom?"

"I cannot say," Koji replied seriously.

Marcus scowled. "Her attitude is messing with his head."

Tucking his chin to his chest, Koji softly said, "I have hope."

"What have you noticed, Observer?"

"Prissie has been thoughtless, but Ransom thinks things through," Koji explained. "Once he sorts out the mess in his head, perhaps he will hear the cry of his heart."

With a sigh, Marcus muttered, "Amen and amen."

On Saturday morning, Jude was unusually quiet. Tad was the first to notice, and he crouched in front of the listless boy. "Momma, I think you better take a look at Judicious."

Grammie Esme peered over her glasses at the youngster and declared, "He's a mite peaky, Naomi."

"Green around the gills," added Grandpa Carl with a solemn wink.

Jude offered a half-hearted smile at the attempts to cheer him up, but a thermometer quickly confirmed his fever.

Tsk-ing in concern, Grammie turned to her daughter. "You'd best quarantine the boy, dear. Elsewise, your whole brood will come down with chicken pox. Or worse!"

"They've already *had* the chicken pox," Prissie's mother said calmly.

"Mumps!" suggested Grandpa Carl. "Measles! Scarlet fever!"

"Oh, I don't think so," Momma said with a smile.

Grandpa was just warming up. "Typhoid! The Black Plague!"

"*Honestly,* Carl!" Esme snapped. "Are you trying to scare the boy?"

"You know I was just joshing, right, little mister?" he asked ruefully.

" 'kay, Grandpa," the six-year-old said.

The old man's expression grew serious. "I'll run you into town for medicine if it's needed."

"Let me call Jayce," said Momma. "He can meet you at the pharmacy."

"I'll go along!" Prissie offered.

Koji stood. "Me, too."

After being dropped off at the corner, Prissie and Koji hurried to the pharmacy, but just outside the door, the young angel hesitated, then grabbed her coat sleeve. "I will wait for you out here," he announced solemnly.

"What?" she protested. "It's freezing out here!"

"I do not feel the cold as you do," he reminded in an undertone. "I will stay here until your father and grandfather join us."

"Why?"

"This is where I have been Sent."

"I thought you were supposed to stay with me?" Prissie argued.

"This time, I will wait." With an encouraging smile, he said, "You will not be alone."

"Oh, fine." She marched into the pharmacy alone. On her way down the aisle, Prissie gave the case of angelic knickknacks a sidelong glance and nearly ran into someone she most definitely hadn't expected to meet. "Marcus!"

"Yo, Prissie," he replied with a smirk.

"What are you doing here?"

"Keeping a friend company," he replied, glancing over his shoulder. To her dismay, Ransom was strolling their way. With a broad wink, Marcus said, "I'll go hang out with Koji for a while. See ya."

It wasn't until her so-called nemesis stopped in front of her that it occurred to her that she didn't know if Marcus had been visible or invisible. "Hey, Prissie," Ransom said, sounding pleasantly surprised.

"You don't have to be nice," she muttered. He might have asked for half a chance, but that didn't mean she wanted him to return the favor. The guy was supposed to be angry with her, and it bugged her that he wasn't.

"I'm not being nice," he corrected. "I'm being *polite*. You should try it sometime." Prissie fumed inwardly, but Ransom kept the small talk rolling. "What are you doing in town?"

"My brother's sick."

"Which one?"

"Jude."

"The little guy, huh?"

"Yes," Prissie said and stepped past him. To her annoyance, Ransom followed her down the aisle. "What?" she snapped.

"I was kinda hoping to run into you sometime. I've got a few questions." He was clearly unintimidated by her mood.

She wanted to run from this conversation, but at the same time, she felt obligated to face it. "Fine!" she growled. Flapping her hands in an impatient gesture of surrender she muttered, "Just ... *fine*. Let's get this over with."

Ransom seemed amused, but he cut to the chase. "What don't you like about me?"

That was simple. "Everything."

"Right," he replied blandly. "Can you be more specific?"

Who in their right mind asked to have their faults listed? While she was sure Ransom had loads, she was drawing a blank. Working up a scowl, she said the first thing that came to mind. "You make fun of me!"

"Still not specific enough."

"You're always contradicting me!"

"That's because you're *wrong* a lot of the time," Ransom replied, quirking a brow. "Someone has to point out the flaws in your reasoning."

With a huff, she retorted, "And you pick on me!"

"Since when?"

Thinking back to the day they first met, she said, "You tied my braids together!"

"Oh, yeah. I remember that," he mused aloud. "Looks to me like the knot came out."

"That's hardly the point!"

"Really?" Ransom asked. "*Is* there a point to holding grudges?"

"Look, I don't like you!" Prissie said, enunciating each word clearly.

"I don't particularly like you, either."

He said it without a speck of meanness, and Prissie was completely thrown off. Part of her wanted to lash out, to hurt him so he would go away, but she remembered the bitterness of that kind of triumph. Thoroughly confused, she asked, "Then why are we even talking?"

"Partly because you're the boss's daughter, which makes

you really hard to avoid," he said. "Partly because you're *different* when you're hanging out with your conscience, and I can't figure out *why*."

"Koji?" she asked, startled.

"Yeah, where is he, anyway?" he asked curiously.

"Oh, he's around here somewhere," she said, waving vaguely toward the front of the store. Prissie was beginning to get the idea that Ransom was a little like Tad and a little like Zeke. Her biggest brother had to take things apart and put them back together before he felt like he understood them, and her younger brother was a bundle of questions, most of which began with *why*. Questions had a way of making Prissie uncomfortable, especially when she didn't know the right answer. "Is that all?"

"No. There was one other thing."

Just one. For a moment, she was relieved, but Ransom's expression hardened in a way that made her squirm.

"You don't trust 'people like me,'" he quoted. "That's what you said."

Prissie blushed in embarrassment. "I already apologized for that."

"Why?"

"Why what?"

"Why did you try to apologize? Did your dad make you?" This time, it felt as though Ransom was mocking her, but she couldn't lie. When she gave a grudging nod, he shook his head incredulously. "Unbelievable."

"He just wanted me to do the right thing," Prissie said defensively.

"Because you did a wrong thing?"

"Stop it!"

"Stop what?"

"Twisting my words around!" she hissed.

"*People like me,*" Ransom repeated. "What's so terrible about someone like me? Because I sure don't want to be like you. I'm not even sure *you* want to be like you."

"Who *else* would I be like?" she asked in exasperation. The conversation was going in circles, and she was having a hard time keeping up.

"It's been bugging the heck out of me that what your dad was *saying* didn't look anything like what you were *doing.* He finally told me it'd be best to let God speak for Himself."

"God only talks to angels," she replied flatly.

"I'm talking about a Bible. Geez."

Wait. "You read the Bible?" she asked in a hushed voice. The buzz of anger inside Prissie tapered off, which made it easier to hear what Ransom was saying.

"Yeah. Your dad gave me one," he readily admitted. "I've been working my way through it for a couple months. It's not like I'd jump into this blind."

"Oh," she replied weakly. Giving Ransom a Bible was definitely something her dad would do. But why would this guy bother reading it? Because he wanted to keep his new boss happy? She supposed it was possible, but ... Prissie glanced toward the front door. Two members of Jedrick's Flight — her best friend and Ransom's best friend — had been Sent outside so this conversation could happen. Milo had said angels were attracted to eternal things. Didn't that *mean* something? Maybe Ransom was serious. Maybe she should listen.

"So I want you to explain it to me."

Prissie's attention snapped back to her classmate. "Wh-what?"

"Christianity," Ransom prompted. "Tell me what you believe."

"Umm ..." Prissie had never felt more clumsy in her life. "I'm not sure how to explain."

"Isn't that kind of lame? I mean, if you don't know why you believe what you say you believe, how can you be sure you believe it at all?"

Prissie had tasted manna, flown with an angel, and stood in a garden bathed by heaven's own light. If *anyone* could be sure, it was her. "Look," she said seriously. "I don't know the right words, but it's really *real*. Make fun of me if you want, but I *know* that much."

Ransom studied her face. "All right. Then I'll tell you what I've figured out so far, and you tell me if I'm on the right track."

"Okay," she said. "I'll try."

He shoved his hands deep into his jacket pockets and started to rattle off the essentials. "The way it sounds to me is ... I'm doomed because of the whole sin thing. The only person who can *un*doom me is Jesus. He's willing to save me, mostly because He's awesome like that." Ransom quirked a brow at her, she nodded, and he went on. "Somehow, I'll change. Thankfully, it doesn't sound like I'll change into *you*. No offense."

The basics of salvation had been paraphrased almost beyond recognition, but Prissie was ashamed to say that he was explaining it better than she could. One thing came across loud and clear. "You're thinking about becoming a Christian?"

"I dunno. Maybe." Glancing around the nearly empty pharmacy, he said, "It makes sense when your dad explains stuff, but I wanted a second opinion."

"I could introduce you to someone who could say it all clearly," she hastily offered. "Mr. Mercer wouldn't mind ..."

"But I'm talking to *you*, Miss Priss," he cut in. "You're the one who's been making me wonder, so you're the one I want to ask."

"Oh," she repeated lamely. "There's lots of better people."

Ransom snickered and said, "Now *that's* something I never expected to hear from you."

The full weight of her father's words came back to her then, and Prissie's shoulders sagged. Her behavior really *had* become an obstacle, and it had taken her dad's prayers and the intervention of at least two angels to give her this chance to make some kind of amends. With her heart pounding, she said, "Umm, Ransom?"

"Yeah?"

Face pale and eyes steady, she whispered, "Sorry."

He smiled crookedly and replied, "Y'know, *this* time, I believe you."

16

THE WAKING DREAM

Tamaes tread lightly upon the braided rug in Prissie's bedroom. Hunkering down beside the bed, he studied his charge's flushed face. "She has a fever."

Harken's voice was warm with compassion as it echoed through the Guardian's mind. "There are some things you cannot protect her from."

"True," her Guardian said with a soft sigh.

"Come along," urged the Messenger.

Drawing his sword, Tamaes took a seat on the floor; moonlight gleamed against the bared blade as he laid it across his knees. With one last glance at Prissie, he put his back to her mattress and shut his eyes. It was time to join the dream.

The sensation reminded her of the fleeting dream she'd shared with Harken at summer's end. There wasn't the usual fuzzy, disjointed feeling that accompanied most of her dreams, and as the moment of clarity solidified, fingertips brushed the back of her hand. "Prissie, can you open your eyes?" Koji asked earnestly.

She obliged and was startled to find the young angel kneeling before her in a dark place, a candle between them. That wasn't right at all. "Is something wrong?" she whispered.

He shook his head and gave a small smile as he pushed his hair behind one ear. Suddenly, Prissie realized that Koji's disguise was gone. His black hair hung loose around his shoulders, and his ears came to points. Even his old clothes were back, the cloth of his raiment shining as if it had a life of its own. "All is well."

Glancing around, Prissie was startled to discover that while they were surrounded by darkness, it wasn't pitch black. Stars glittered coldly around them. In a moment of panic, she looked down, but to her relief, she seemed to be on solid ground. They knelt together on a smooth surface that reflected the stars and the candle on the floor between them. Its flame was warm and gentle, and she felt safe in the circle of its light.

Prissie whispered, "I don't know where we are."

"You are sleeping," he replied. "Harken let me come for you."

"Are we going somewhere?"

"Indeed." The young Observer rolled to his feet and picked up the candle. Extending his other hand, he said, "I have never done this before, but Harken promised to help. Take my hand, and do not let go."

As they walked along, Prissie stared in amazement at the stars. They seemed nearer and brighter somehow, and they twinkled with flashes of color that dazzled her eyes. "What time is it?" she wondered aloud.

"We are leaving time behind."

"For how long?"

He laughed softly, but Prissie didn't know what was so funny. Before she could issue any complaints, a deep voice beckoned from somewhere just ahead. "That's the way. You're doing very well!"

"That was Harken!"

"He is meeting us partway," Koji explained.

The Messenger strode into view, and he, too, was no longer in human guise. Harken stood tall and strong, without a trace of gray in hair that now hung in heavy coils. Gleaming raiment shone against dark skin that bore no wrinkles. "Hello, Prissie! I see Koji was able to reach you."

"This is the strangest dream I've ever had," she announced. "It's so real!"

Harken's laughter rang out as he slipped his arm around her shoulder. "That's because it *is*. I'm really here, and the others are waiting for you to arrive. This way, please."

Together, the angels guided her toward an archway from which light spilled. Abner leaned against the entrance, coolly watching their progress. Prissie offered the Caretaker a tentative smile. His lips quirked, but he addressed Koji. "Observer turned Graft turned Guardian turned Messenger? Will you be taking up a Protector's sword next? Or shall I make a Gatekeeper out of you?"

Koji ignored the jest. "Thank you for opening a way, Abner."

The silver-haired angel inclined his head. "It's the least I can do."

"Or perhaps the most," said Harken in a teasing tone.

Abner clasped his hands behind his back and nodded distractedly. "It *is* an odd courtesy, for I cannot do any more or less than I am bidden."

"Where are we?" Prissie asked curiously, trying to peek through the arch.

"*I* am here," Abner replied seriously. "*You* have been caught up, though not so high as others have been."

"So I'm not here?"

"Not in body," the Caretaker clarified.

"Only in spirit," Harken added. "Most people would call this a vision."

"And this is the garden behind the blue door," Koji said, letting go of her hand once she was safely through. "It was Baird's idea to invite you."

"What for?" she asked in surprise.

"*There* she is!" exclaimed the red-haired Worshiper as he hurried over, all smiles. "And clothed in white!"

Prissie's flannel pajamas had been changed for raiment similar to that worn by the members of Jedrick's Flight. Where the angels' clothes were of a rich, creamy hue, her simple dress was dazzlingly white, and she touched the strange fabric with an awed expression. Although there was no hint of any embellishment, she was sure it was the most beautiful thing she'd ever worn. Prissie exchanged a glance with Koji, whose eyes shone with approval.

Kester, who had followed his mentor at an easier pace, quietly pointed out, "We cannot begin if you keep Prissie on the threshold for an eternity."

"Yes, Myron," said Abner as he stepped past them. "Don't monopolize the girl."

"Whoa, whoa, whoa! None of that! Let's stick with *Baird*!"

"Myron!" called Jedrick from a short distance away. "Do you require assistance?"

From the lightness in the Protector's tone, Prissie was quite sure he was trying not to laugh. Could angels joke around? It seemed a little irreverent, but a sidelong look in Baird's direction showed that the Worshiper's eyes were dancing with mirth. "Prissie, thank you for joining us!"

"I'm pleased to be here," she replied with automatic politeness. After a moment's hesitation, she whispered, "But I'm not really sure why I'm here."

"A return of hospitality!" Baird said heartily. "We wanted to include you in our evening song."

"S-sing?" she squeaked.

"Together."

"Is that really okay?" Prissie asked, glancing at Kester.

"Most assuredly," the apprentice Worshiper said, gesturing for them to join the rest of the Flight.

Koji and Harken strolled confidently across the soft grass, but Prissie's steps lagged. Fleetingly hoping for escape, she looked over her shoulder, but the archway was gone. Only light-drenched woodland lay behind her. "How does he do that?" she whispered.

"He is a Caretaker," Kester replied, as if that answered everything.

Tamaes stepped forward. "Do not be afraid, little one."

"I'm not scared," she muttered. "I'm embarrassed."

Holding her gaze, Tamaes said, "No one who has gathered here will criticize your song."

"I'm not a good singer. Can't I just listen?" she begged.

Disappointment flickered across his features, but the Guardian nodded before saying, "I wish to introduce you to Milo."

"But I already *know* Milo."

Tamaes crouched down, and he chose his words with great care. "Prissie, what happened when you found out he was an angel?"

With a cringe of conscience, she replied, "I suppose I wasn't very nice?"

Gazing toward the other end of the glade, Tamaes said, "Milo was my first friend within this Flight, and though you were *my* charge, we watched over you together. When he became a Graft, you were the first person he sought out." With gentle words that touched her heart, the Guardian said, "I want to protect the friendship you have forged."

"I'm not sure what you're worried about. Milo and I get along okay. We made up."

Tamaes quietly asked, "And if he changed again? Would you be upset?"

Prissie caught on and her eyes widened. "Does he have blue hair or something?"

"Would it matter if he did?"

"It would be silly to dislike someone just because of their hair," she replied huffily.

Marcus chose that moment to saunter over, golden eyes bright with interest and a smirk on his face. "Glad to hear it!" He joined Tamaes in ushering Prissie amidst the slender trees.

Padgett nodded to her from his seat beside his mentor on the lush grass carpeting the glade. The pair looked like two sides of the same coin, with their long hair pooling on the ground. Abner's was a silver so luminous, it was almost lavender, and his apprentice's was black with blue highlights. Their flock of little manna-makers swirled through the air around them, looking like tiny stars, so bright was their happiness.

Marcus casually remarked, "It ripped Milo up when you were snubbing him last summer. He was a basket case for weeks."

"But that was ages ago!" With a small frown, she asked, "Do I need to apologize to him, too?"

"Nah," the young Protector said. "Tamaes already told you, kiddo. He doesn't want anything coming between you two again."

Prissie wanted to stay friends with Milo, so there wasn't a problem. Except they seemed to think there was one. And that worried her. "Is that *important* for some reason?"

"Yep. Because Milo is your mailman."

She gave him a strange look. "You're not making sense."

"I know." Patting her head, he said, "I'll remind you later. Deal?"

She swatted at his hand. "If you say so."

"Prissie," Taweel greeted. Omri perched in his usual spot on his shoulder, one small hand grasping the tiny chain ran between the Guardian's earring and ear cuff. The yahavim's wings buzzed in a friendly way, but he stuck with his favorite companion.

Just then, Baird's voice reached her ears. "You're totally gonna be fine, Goldilocks. It's not everyone who gets to make a third impression!"

"I'm *not* worried," Milo grumbled. "You're the ones making a big deal out of nothing."

Tamaes strode forward to join the angelic huddle, and Marcus gave her an unceremonious shove in the right direction. She shot him a dirty look only to discover that Koji was still close beside her. He seemed as amused by the apprentice Protector's rough manners as he was by her reaction. "What?" she whispered self-consciously. The young Observer merely took her hand and drew her the rest of the way forward.

"Prissie, *this* is Milo," Tamaes said gravely.

"Obviously," she murmured. Somewhere in the back of her mind, she'd known that Milo probably looked different when he wasn't masquerading as the local mailman. The Flight's fussing made it all too obvious that she'd hurt the Messenger by turning her back on him before. But there was no way she'd repeat that mistake. Not now.

Milo was still Milo, and he still ran his fingers through his hair when he was trying to think what to do. Only now, that hair was a mess of ash blond curls that fell well past his shoulders. He looked rather grand in his shining raiment. If he'd been wearing a blue cloak, he would have looked just like the prince in her favorite childhood storybook. With a confident nod, Prissie extended her hand and played along. "How do you do. I'm Priscilla Pomeroy."

The Messenger stepped forward, taking her hand in both of his. "Miss Priscilla," he greeted seriously.

Baird craned his neck to locate Jedrick. "Shall we begin, Captain? Everyone's gathered and the greetings have been covered!"

"Isn't there one missing?" Prissie asked, peering around the forest clearing.

"No," Koji replied patiently. "We are twelve."

"Didn't you notice we're Sent two-by-two?" asked Baird. "Mentors and apprentices come in matched sets."

"Or mismatched," teased Harken.

"I know that much," Prissie said.

"Actually," interrupted Jedrick. "Twelve names have come under my hand."

"No, no, no, my friend," Shimron said. "If we are twelve, then *eleven* names should be inscribed."

Jedrick smiled at the white-haired angel. "I do not know the plans or purposes of God, but for the moment, I have *twelve* in my keeping."

Abner stepped forward, curtly inquiring, "Why have you never mentioned this before?"

"Can I see?" eagerly asked Koji.

All of the angels drew closer as Jedrick drew his sword and presented its hilt for inspection. Koji pulled Prissie closer and showed her the blue stone embedded in the weapon's pommel. Letters in a language she didn't recognize were deeply inscribed in the jewel, and as he traced his finger over each line, he read off their names. "Abner and Padgett, Myron and Kester, Harken and Milo, Taweel and Tamaes, Shimron and I, Marcus and ... Ephron!" he exclaimed. "Ephron's name is still here!"

"We are thirteen," Jedrick agreed.

"This is unheard of," Shimron said, clearly baffled.

"But I'm glad to hear it!" exclaimed Baird. "Doesn't this mean there's hope!"

"Just so," the elderly Observer agreed.

Koji turned to Prissie with eyes alight. "See? No one is missing!"

"Oh," she mumbled with a twinge of disappointment.

Padgett unobtrusively slipped to Prissie's side and laid a hand on her shoulder. His dark eyes searched her face carefully as the apprentice Caretaker inquired, "Who did you expect to be here?"

Some eyebrows shot up, some drew together, but every eye turned to Prissie, who was fiddling with the end of one braid. Flipping it over her shoulder, she lifted her chin and replied, "Adin, of course."

And with that, everything fell apart. Light bent, and the forest tilted. A roaring filled her ears, and the dream began to swirl. Suddenly, Prissie felt as if she was falling, and with a violent start, she woke in her bedroom. The beautiful clarity of her vision was replaced by an aching head, a parched throat, and blankets that felt uncomfortably hot and heavy.

A large hand closed around hers, and she stared up into her Guardian's wide eyes. "Adin," Tamaes whispered urgently. "Where did you hear that name?"

Her bedroom door clicked, and Koji slipped inside, looking human once more and dressed in his pajamas. He padded over to the other side of the bed and gazed at her with a tense expression that frightened her. "I met him *ages* ago," she replied. "He introduced himself."

"Where did you meet him?" Tamaes asked. "When?"

She thought back and replied, "In town. This past summer. It was before Koji moved in."

"I would have seen him," her Guardian argued. "I would have known."

She shook her head. "We've talked a bunch of times."

Tamaes rocked back on his heels. "How is that possible?"

Koji sat on the edge of Prissie's mattress and took her

other hand in both of his. "How many times, Prissie? Can you remember where and when?"

"Th-the gazebo in town. At the mall. And outside the caves."

"During the field trip?" the boy prodded.

"Yes," Prissie replied. "He stopped by the bakery during Halloween. Oh, and he was here."

"*Here*?" Tamaes croaked.

"Y-yes," she admitted in a small voice, truly frightened now. "We talked on the folly bridge."

As her Guardian's hand tightened around hers, Koji quietly pointed out, "Halloween was *after* you promised not to go anywhere without me."

"I kept my promise," she hastily replied. "Adin came to the back door and invited me out, but I told him I really *shouldn't* ..."

Her sentence was cut off when Tamaes cradled her close, as if belatedly trying to snatch her out of danger. Gazing toward the ceiling, he lifted his voice in a broken song of thanks for God's abundant mercies. Koji softly hummed along, adding a descant to his teammate's solemn offering.

When they finished, Prissie stared dazedly into his scarred face and whispered, "Why are you so upset?"

"I *know* Adin, little one," Tamaes replied gravely, showing no sign of letting her go. "He is *not* one of the Faithful."

"Does that mean ... ?"

"Adin is one of the Fallen, Prissie," Koji clarified. "He is a demon."

The story continues in Book 3: The Broken Window ....

THRESHOLD SERIES

GLOSSARY

Praise the Lord, you his angels,
you mighty ones who do his bidding,
who obey his word.

– Psalm 103:20 NIV

ORDER OF ANGELS

Orders of Angels. They're variously called the hosts of heaven (Neh. 9:6), powers and principalities (Rom. 8:38), thrones and dominions (Col. 1:16), angels and authorities (1 Pet. 3:22), and ministering spirits (Heb. 1:14). Throughout the *Threshold Series* and its various companion stories, I've divided these servants of God into distinct orders. While their characteristics are inspired by the Scriptures, bear in mind that these varieties are the author's invention. Each of their proper names is spun from a Hebrew word related to the order's unique role ... and parallels those of the two kinds of angels specified in the Bible — cherubim (Ex. 25:22) and seraphim (Is. 6:2).

Protectors. In the Bible, cherubim are protectors of God's name and image. They're usually described as beings who devote themselves to blessing, praising, and adoring

Him. In my stories, Protectors fight the Fallen. Taller than humanly possible, these muscular warriors are well-equipped for battle.

Guardians. The hadarim watch over the lives of individuals. The Guardians' name is taken from *haderes,* which means "hedge of protection." In the *Threshold Series,* members of this order are famously bashful and show incredible fierceness when defending their charges.

Messengers. Malakim comes from *malak,* which means "messenger." They're responsible for communication within the ranks of heaven, and they're known for being outgoing and talkative. Language poses no barrier for Messengers. Members of this order are skilled at drawing others into dreams and visions.

Worshipers. The zamarim derive their name from *zamar,* "sing with instruments." Although all angels express themselves through song, Worshipers truly live to praise God with everything they have. One thing that sets apart this order of musically inclined angels is their wings, which are designed more for beauty than for flight.

Observers. The archivists of heaven are adahim. They get their name from *adah,* "to witness, to testify." Observers watch the intricate plans and purposes of God unfold throughout history. Writers, thinkers, artists, poets — the adahim ponder all they've seen and heard and record their thoughts in books.

Caretakers. Earth-movers and storm-bringers, the samayim were granted cataclysmic power in order to care for the created universe. There's very little a Caretaker cannot do, but at the same time, they're limited in what they're allowed to do. In the *Threshold Series*, the samayim show an affinity for nature, minister to the injured, change the physical appearances of people, and tend flocks of yahavim. Their name means "heavens."

Manna-makers. Despite their diminutive size and playful nature, all the hosts of heaven depend heavily upon the yahavim. This lowest order of angels is responsible for producing manna, the food of angels. Their name comes from *yahav*, which means "provide." They're drawn to those in need.

ANGELIC TERMS

Angelic Jargon. Several terms come up over the course of the *Threshold Series*, and while the angels take them for granted, maybe you'd like a little more explanation.

The First. In this storyline, not all angels were created at the same time. Some have been around for millennia, but others are newly formed. When an angel is described as one of the First, it means that he was alive before Time began. First Ones remember the rift that divided the Fallen from the Faithful, and they witnessed creation of the heavens and earth as described in Genesis 1.

Faithful. An angel who lives to serve God.

Fallen. An angel who has set himself against God. Fallen angels are demons.

Mentor. When an older, wiser angel is given a newbie to train, he becomes their mentor. A small, silvery cuff on the shell of the left ear indicates their rank. Mentors may train several apprentices over their lifetime, but only one at a time.

Apprentice. When angels are Sent out of heaven to serve, they always go in pairs. Sometimes, these two-angel teams involve partners on equal footing, but more often, a newer angel is apprenticed to a mentor. Some apprentices end up partnering with several different mentors before their training is considered complete.

Legion. For the purposes of this storyline, one Legion is a company of 12,000 angels.

Flight. The Faithful are organized into twelve-angel teams that are headed up by a captain. That means a Legion is comprised of 1,000 Flights.

Hedge. A group of Guardians serving together in one area is called a Hedge. The hadarim form a perimeter around individual homes, but also in crowded places — schools, apartment buildings, businesses, shopping centers, concerts, sporting events, etc. Because guardian angels come and go whenever their charges do, Hedges are in a constant state of flux.

Graft. When an angel takes on human guise and becomes a part of society, he's said to be grafted in.

Raiment. The Faithful wear raiment, clothing said to have a light and life of its own. The woven fabric is beige, faintly luminous, and resistant to spot and wrinkle. Design varies slightly depending on the needs of the wearer, and the patterns stitched on the collar and cuffs indicate flight, rank, and order.

DISCUSSION QUESTIONS

1. In the first chapter of *The Hidden Deep,* Prissie admits to herself that overlooking Koji's bizarreness is easy because she knows he's an angel. But what if he'd been a regular boy? Do you avoid people who are different? Do you consider yourself one of the different ones?
2. What makes someone trustworthy?
3. What does your name mean? Do you have a nickname? Would you like a new name? In Revelation 2:17, one of the promises God makes to the one who overcomes is, "I will also give him a white stone with a new name written on it, known only to him who receives it." If you have a Bible and you're curious, what *other* very special thing is promised in this verse?
4. Prissie's afraid of heights. Is there something that frightens you? Makes you nervous?
5. In Chapter 3, Prissie shows admirable courage in standing up to a bully. Why is that so hard to do?
6. Do you know what it's like to be lonely in a crowd?
7. Family traditions can be big or small. Grandpa Pete and Aunt Ida planned and planted a garden together. The Pomeroys always attend Neil's home games. The town's fall festival has become a family tradition. So is the annual preparation for the Christmas production of Handel's *Messiah.* Does your family do things that have become your traditions?
8. Do you enjoy dressing up in a costume? What makes a masquerade fun? What's your ideal costume?

9. Have you ever said something you wished you could take back? Is there any excuse for hurting someone with your words? Do we make excuses anyhow? Do they make you feel any better? Can anything make it better?

10. When Tad's looking for the missing thingamabob for his car, he points out that his missing thingamabob isn't any more important than the rest. "I need them *all* in the right place if this old thing is ever going to make it out of the shed." Are you part of something bigger? Who's important to you? Who are you important to?

11. Prissie's apology at the end of Chapter 11 is rejected. The next time she says she's sorry, Ransom believes her. What changed?

12. What makes Koji's friendship with Prissie so unusual?

THRESHOLD SERIES

THE BROKEN WINDOW

BOOK THREE

1

THE FIRST SNOW

In the small bedroom tucked under one of the dormers in the Pomeroy's farmhouse, a burst of silver light heralded the arrival of an angel. It was as if a door opened in the middle of the room, and when it closed, Abner stood on the braided rug. He absentmindedly poked the bridge of his nose, trying to adjust glasses he wasn't wearing at the moment. Long, silver hair swished as he turned and inspected the snug space. The ceiling sloped so dramatically that the top corner of the bedroom door was cut at an angle, and a wide seat stretched under a stained-glass window, its pattern of multicolored diamonds shining faintly in the moonlight.

"So this is where you've been holed up," Abner said. Cool, gray eyes fixed upon Tamaes. The Guardian sat in the corner, his arms folded stubbornly over his chest. "Jedrick said it might take heaven and earth to move you, so he sent me."

"This is where I am needed," protested Tamaes in a low voice.

Nodding at the girl asleep on her bed, the Caretaker said, "You cannot protect her from the inevitable."

The Guardian's gaze slid sideways. "She can hear my voice."

"Hearing and listening are two *very* different things, and there is *another* voice she must learn to heed." Crouching before Tamaes, Abner firmly said, "I'm sending you out to stretch your wings."

"And if I decline?"

"You won't, but if you *did*, I'd simply have the rest of the Hedge carry you off."

With a sigh, Tamaes begged for understanding. "She is my responsibility."

"While that's true, you're not alone," Abner reminded. "Taweel is on the roof, and Koji is down the hall. Even Omri would fly to her defense if the need were great."

"This is not the first time I have been asked to show more faith in my teammates."

"Then the lesson has yet to be learned." Standing, the silver-haired angel arranged himself on Prissie's windowseat. "I'll remain here until your return. I may not be a Guardian, but few are foolish enough to threaten a Caretaker."

"That is not true," Tamaes said, an ironic smile tugging at the long scar running down the side of his face. At Abner's quirked brow, he flatly added, "*No one* would dare."

Prissie leaned her forehead against a green diamond in the stained glass window so she could peer through a peach one. Although a little better, she still had a fever, so the cold glass felt good against her flushed face. School was out for the day, and she was watching her brothers in the snow-filled yard below. Fat, sticky flakes drifted over their whole farm, blanketing everything under several inches of white stuff. It was the first big snow of the season, and it was perfect for packing.

Grandpa Pete was clearing the driveway with one of the tractors while the boys shoveled the walks. Well, that's what they were *supposed* to be doing. Instead, they were goofing off, and Prissie had to admit, it looked like fun.

Neil's red Warriors stocking cap was pulled low over his blond hair as he threw snowballs as fast as he could make them. Since he played quarterback on their high school's football team, his aim was deadly. Tad retaliated by pitching whole shovelfuls of snow in his younger brother's direction as he worked his way along the path.

Gently tracing the edges of a blue diamond, Prissie shifted so she could watch Beau through a soft yellow pane. Until her birthday in January, Prissie and Beau were the same age — fourteen. Her almost-twin was showing Koji how to roll a huge snowball, the kind you need for building snowmen. They must have had big plans, because they called Neil over to help them push the monster boulder back across the lawn. Koji paused long enough in his play to look up at her window and wave one mittened hand. Even from a distance, Prissie could tell he was happy. She pressed her palm against her window, an answering smile creeping onto her lips.

Just then, the rumble of an engine and squeak of air breaks sounded from the direction of the road. The elementary school bus had arrived in the turnaround at the end of Orchard Lane, and if Prissie leaned a little, she could just see her other two brothers chasing one another up the driveway. Zeke was already scooping handfuls of snow, eager to join Neil's battle. Jude trotted after him, and Prissie knew that her youngest sibling would go to Tad first, then check on the chickens. But then the little boy suddenly wheeled and ran back the other way. Zeke also turned and charged after him, and a moment later, another figure came into view. Milo Leggett waded toward the house, a package tucked under his arm, and two little boys wrapped around his long legs.

At the sight of their mailman, Prissie's heart beat a little faster. Milo's blue eyes lifted to her bedroom window, and she jerked backwards, hoping the stained glass hid her from view. Prissie's fondness for the Messenger had changed shape in recent months, but that didn't mean she wanted him to see her like this. "I must be a mess," she mumbled, pushing unhappily at honey-colored hair that probably looked as limp as she felt.

The boys crowded around the mailman, who gestured broadly while he talked. Before long, Milo had her brothers laughing, and Prissie was feeling more than a little left out. It wasn't fair that she was the only one still struggling to get better.

With a sigh, she glanced down at the notebook propped on her knees. It was the nearly December, so she was making her list and checking it twice. There were several new people she wanted to give a present to this year. Christmas was Prissie's favorite holiday, and she loved the decorations and the baking, the secrets and the presents. Grandpa Pete had begun humming snatches of Handle's *Messiah* while he worked, and Zeke had already been laboring over a mile-long wish list. Prissie could hardly wait for the tree to go up in the family room or for the flood of holiday deliveries that would bring Milo to their door almost every afternoon.

At this time of the year, Prissie dearly missed Aunt Ida, who used to fill the house with carols from the piano in the corner of the family room. Her Dad's younger sister had always been her best secret-keeper during Christmastime. Aunt Ida knew how to add bits of dough to gingerbread men so that they each had their own personality and how to cut apples so they looked like bunnies. Prissie could do these things for herself now, but it wasn't quite as much fun without her bubbly aunt.

She stole another peek out the window in time to see Milo bend down to say something to Koji, who nodded seriously and hurried to the door. Glancing up over his shoulder, the mailman caught her watching and winked. Then, her brothers dragged him over to inspect their giant snowball, which Zeke promptly scaled.

By the time Koji opened her bedroom door, Prissie had worked up a good sulk. "You're not supposed to come in here without permission," she grumbled.

He studied her face and politely inquired, "Should I leave?"

"No," she said grudgingly, pulling up her quilt to hide her flaming cheeks. She was as tired of being alone as she was of being sick.

Koji stepped into the room and padded over on stocking feet. "There are messages for you!" he announced, clearly pleased to be entrusted with their delivery.

The postcard was from Aunt Ida, and Prissie smiled as she skimmed its brief note. "She and Uncle Lo are in Africa now," she said. "And she hopes we have snow."

“We do,” he answered seriously.

“Obviously.”

“There is *another* message,” Koji said.

Prissie eyed his empty hands and asked, “From whom?”

“Milo.”

“Really?” she asked, stealing another glance outside. Koji climbed onto the opposite end of the window seat and let one foot swing while he watched the activity in the yard below. When he took the time to scan the sky as well, she asked, “Is everything all right?”

“There is nothing to fear,” Koji replied. Then he relayed the Messenger’s request. “If you would not mind, Milo will come for you in dreams tonight. Jedrick has called a meeting.”

Prissie took the time to comb and braid her hair, but she didn’t go downstairs when the dinner bell rang. Naomi came to check on her, pressing a cool hand to her daughter’s forehead. “You could join us,” she invited. “If you’re up to it?”

“Is Milo staying for supper?” Prissie asked suspiciously.

“Yes.”

“I don’t want to get him sick.”

She only asked, “Are you sure?”

Prissie’s chin lifted stubbornly. “Yes.”

“Get some rest, then,” her mother encouraged. “My folks are going along to the rehearsal tonight, so once the house is quiet, I’ll bring up a tray. Sound good?”

“I guess,” Prissie sighed. “Thanks, Momma.”

Her maternal grandparents had been visiting since just before Thanksgiving. Grandpa Carl and Grammie Esme’s RV was parked next to the apple barn, and they were staying in the guest room at Grandpa Pete and Grandma Nell's house. According to Grandpa Carl, the Olsens would stick around until West Edinton's annual production of Handel's *Messiah* before following the snowbirds south for the winter.

The Christmas concert was only a couple weeks away, and excitement was building. This year, the decision had been made to mix things up a bit by doing a modern twist on the classic. Grandpa Pete, who'd been singing with the bass section for forty years, had been suspicious about the introduction of drums and electric guitars to the orchestra, but it cheered him immensely that two of his grandsons had joined the choir this year.

Prissie was actually just as excited about the upcoming concert, mostly because Milo was taking part for the first time. He'd been coaxed into it by his good friend Baird, another angel-in-disguise who led worship at a church down in Harper.

At some point, Prissie drifted off because she was roused from a fitful doze by the rattle of dishes and shuffle of feet. Lifting her head from her pillow, she squinted at the light pouring in from the hallway while Koji carefully maneuvered through the door with a tray of food. "Why didn't you go to rehearsal?" she asked in surprise.

"Your mother says this goes on your lap," the boy announced, putting off his answer. "Sit up, please."

Prissie reached across to flick on her bedside lamp, then did as she was bidden. Koji set the tray before her, then sat down on the foot of the bed. "This is the first time I have prepared food for someone. Please, eat it."

"You cooked?"

Koji's happiness came through loud and clear. "I did!"

"Did you have fun?"

"Your mother was very encouraging," he replied seriously. "I hope it will be satisfying."

Prissie dutifully picked up her fork and tasted the scrambled eggs, then took a bite of cinnamon toast. "It's good," she assured with a small smile. "Thank you."

He nodded, then addressed her initial question. "I remained behind because you are here."

"You shouldn't have to miss out just because I'm sick," Prissie said. "Rehearsals are one of the only times you get to see Harken, Baird, and Kester!"

Dark eyes gazed steadily into hers, as if he was trying to figure out what she *meant* by what she said. Finally, Koji asked, "Have you forgotten your promise?"

Nibbling at her toast, Prissie replied, "No, of course I remember." Back in October, the young angel had been given permission to secure a promise from her. She'd given her word not to wander off by herself. It was almost as if the young Observer was trying to be her second guardian angel. "I've kept my promise, too!"

"You have," he agreed. "In a covenant of this nature, we *both* have a promise to keep."

That hadn't occurred to her. "So when I promised to stay with you, you were also promising to stay with me?"

"Indeed."

Prissie poked at her dinner and murmured, "I'm sorry."

"Why?"

"Because you're stuck with me, I guess."

Koji blinked. "This is where I want to be."

"But what if you wanted to do something else?"

His eyes took on a shine as he calmly replied, "There is nothing else I wish to do."

"But if you *did*!"

"Do you still not understand?" he asked, the hint of a smile twitching at the corner of his lips.

"I guess not," she grumbled, but at the same time, she was very glad. It was completely like Koji to take a promise seriously. He'd been a faithful friend from the very beginning, a fact that warmed her heart. "But that's okay, right?"

With a smile that lived up to the description *angelic,* Koji repeated, "Indeed."

"It is late," Koji whispered. The rest of the household was completely still when he tiptoed back to her room. "You need to sleep."

"I slept all day," Prissie complained. "I'm not tired."

With a soft hum, he knelt beside her bed, and his fingers brushed across the back of her hand. "What does sickness feel like?"

"Bad."

"I can see that you are uncomfortable." He gently fitted his hand into hers and asked, "What else?"

Prissie sighed, but at least Koji's curiosity provided a distraction. Staring up at the ceiling, she replied, "When you're sick, it's like everything goes wrong. I felt weak, dizzy, achy. One minute, I was too hot, and the next, I was shivering. Now, I just feel *blah*."

"What does *blah* mean?" he asked curiously.

"Bored, restless, and very tired of being sick," she replied moodily.

"Tired, but not sleepy," he mused aloud. "You long for rest and cannot find it."

"Yes," she confirmed. "And it doesn't help knowing that everyone's waiting for me to fall asleep."

"Time is of no consequence." Koji tipped his head to one side and said, "I am permitted to offer a suggestion."

"Permitted?" she echoed, rolling onto her side to face him. It still struck her as strange that he sometimes received instructions directly from heaven ... or from his teammates.

Koji nodded. "Harken says that Marcus says that you are forgetting something he already told you."

Prissie blinked at the relayed message, then frowned. Marcus might be an angel, but he annoyed her more often than not. "I have no idea what he means," she retorted huffily.

The young Observer's eyes shifted out of focus, and then he nodded to himself. With a small smile, he said, "Harken says that Marcus says to stop dawdling and ask for what you need."

"And what's that?" she groused.

Koji gave her hand a squeeze. "I do not need sleep, so I will keep you company."

Oh. With a longsuffering sigh, she closed her eyes and tried to relax. Thoughts wandered, but she rebelled against taking advice from Marcus. Still, it would be Milo who came for her, and that was something she'd been looking forward to since that afternoon. With a much smaller sigh, she offered an awkward little prayer, asking for the sleep she needed in order to join the dream where her friends waited.

Prissie had sort of expected the dream to begin as her last one had, with starlight and candlelight, but nothing was the same. Sounds came first, a strange sort of clinking, like melting ice cubes in a glass of water, and then Milo's voice reached her. "Miss Priscilla? Open your eyes, please."

She obeyed, and immediately squinted. She was seated on the ground, but blue surrounded her, bright as the sky on a sunny day. The luminescent color overlapped itself in translucent layers, draping around the two of them in a sheltering cocoon.

Milo smiled at her in his same old way, though he no longer would have passed as their small town's mailman. His ash blond hair tumbled in a riot of curls that reached well past his shoulders, and he was dressed in raiment. The beige cloth glowed as if it had a life of its own. Glancing down, Prissie saw that she, too, wore new clothes, a simple dress as white as new snow. Turning wondering eyes on the Messenger, whose hands were folded together in a relaxed manner, she murmured, "It's different!"

"What is?"

"This isn't anything like when Koji came for me," she explained, a tinge of accusation in her tone.

"I should hope not!" he exclaimed, eyes sparkling with good humor. "That was Koji's very first attempt to reach out to someone in dreams. While he managed very well with Harken's assistance, I'm a full-fledged Messenger. This is what I *do*!"

Again, there was a distant tinkle of sound, and her attention was drawn to the bright color that hemmed them in. "This is beautiful," she quietly confided.

"Thank you," he replied just as softly.

"Where are we?"

"In the garden behind the blue door."

"I don't remember anything like this there," she murmured, tentatively reaching out to touch the melodic light. He watched her exploration without comment, which Prissie took as permission to continue. Color slipped over her fingers like nothing she'd ever encountered before — softer than silk, lighter than air. It tickled across her skin like a breeze, and slowly brought a smile to her face. Finally, she asked, "What is all this?"

Milo's eyebrows lifted slightly, and he replied, "My wings."

Snatching her hand back, she murmured, "Oooh! Excuse me!"

He held a finger to his lips in a shushing motion. "It's all right, Miss Priscilla. Ready to see the others?"

"Yes, please."

Nodding once, the Messenger gave his wings a gentle shake, then lifted them away, slowly revealing a very familiar forest glade. Yahavim zipped around like golden fireflies, but for once, she ignored the little manna-makers. Prissie had been hoping to see Milo's wings since the first moment she realized he had them, and she stared in frank admiration. Propping his chin on his hand, he wafted them playfully and asked, "Satisfied?"

Prissie toyed with the end of her braid and mumbled an indistinct affirmative. Glancing around, she spied Tamaes leaning against a nearby tree, a faint smile on his face. He was garbed as usual in armor-covered raiment, and the hilt of a sword showed over his shoulder. Sleek auburn hair partially hid the scar that ran along one side of his face, and for once, his wings weren't on full display. Instead, a vivid pattern of overlapping rings in shades of orange decorated his arms.

When Tamaes caught her eye, he strode forward to

offer one large, tanned hand, helping her to her feet. "Hello, Prissie," he greeted, searching her face with ill-concealed concern.

"I'm fine," she blurted.

He blinked, then shook his head. "You are ill."

"I'm mostly better," she argued, vaguely embarrassed to have worried her guardian angel. "I'll be better soon."

"May it be so," Tamaes said, and his gaze drifted off to one side. "Hello, Koji."

She turned in surprise to find her friend hanging back, simply observing. Milo chuckled and asked, "Is Jedrick expecting you as well?"

Koji self-consciously tucked his loose hair behind an ear that now came to a distinct point. "I was not invited, but I need to stay with Prissie."

Milo stood and straightened his tunic. "I'm sure the captain has taken Koji's responsibilities into account."

"Oh, sure," interjected a familiar voice. "Where would she be without her conscience?"

Prissie turned to see Marcus strolling toward them through the trees along with his mentor. It was slightly disorienting to see a classmate wearing armor and heavy boots with oddly woven straps, but Marcus looked right at home in his raiment.

"Her *conscience*?" inquired Jedrick.

"It is a nickname," Koji offered seriously.

From what Prissie could tell, all the warrior types in the Flight wore sleeveless tunics. Jedrick towered imposingly over the rest of them, all broad shoulders and bulging muscles. When he folded strong arms over his chest, she noticed that his fair skin was laced by an intricate pattern of green whorls. In contrast, Marcus's wings had settled into jagged markings that zigzagged in hues of cream and yellow over his warm brown skin.

Standing as tall as he could beside his mentor, Marcus also crossed his arms and smirked infuriatingly at Prissie. "Took you long enough, kiddo!" Before she could work up some indignation, Jedrick rumpled Marcus's two-tone hair, causing the younger angel to duck his head and protest, "I was only saying *hi*!" The apprentice Protector might have been able to carry off a tough guy aura at school, but next to the other warriors in his Flight, he was pretty puny.

Her soft giggle put an end to the jostling, and Jedrick suggested, "Shall we begin?"

Prissie asked, "Are we the only ones here?"

The captain explained, "These four spend the most time with you." That made sense, and when she nodded, Jedrick continued. "I cannot say if you have come to know us because you are in danger, or if you are in danger because you have come to know us. Either way, the threat is real, for Adin seems to have singled you out."

"And he's a demon?"

"He has set himself against God," Jedrick confirmed.

Prissie didn't *exactly* doubt them. Adin had been polite, handsome, and stylish ... but sometimes he said or did things that made her uneasy. Frowning in concentration, she asked Jedrick, "How can you tell? I thought demons were horrible monsters."

Marcus snorted, and with a dramatic flash of light, he unfurled his wings, spreading them wide. Getting right in her face, he made certain she was staring into his eyes, which were an impossible shade of gold. "Look at me, Prissie," he demanded in exasperation. "Is *this* how I show up to school?"

"Obviously not."

"You already know the Faithful can hide their true nature in order to fit in! It's no different for the Fallen!"

"Fine. But if he's an enemy, how do you know his name? Is he on some kind of Most Wanted list?"

For several moments, an awkward silence filled the glade. Jedrick sighed and nodded at Tamaes, who took a half-step forward.

"Adin and I were once close," Tamaes said dully. "He was like a brother to me when I was newly formed."

"What happened?" Prissie asked, aghast.

With a small shrug, Tamaes replied, "He Fell."

"That's all?"

Koji tapped her hand and solemnly answered, "That is *everything*."

Jedrick cleared his throat and fixed Prissie with a stern gaze. "The members of my Flight stand ready to back up Tamaes in his service to God. Come what may, we are with you."

Then Milo stepped forward. "I have a message for you, Miss Priscilla."

"An official one?" she asked warily.

"Yep," he amiably replied. "And it's threefold."

"Oh," she managed, her heart already racing.

Holding up a finger, Milo calmly said, "Trust."

Prissie had expected more than one word, so it took her a moment to react. "Isn't that the same message Harken gave me before?"

Raising a second finger, Milo said, "Listen."

Even more stymied, she asked, "To *what*?"

The Messenger replied, "At the moment, to *me*." A third finger joined the others, and Milo concluded, "Remember."

Truly frustrated now, Prissie begged, "Remember *what*?"

Marcus grumbled something about a complete lack of awe where divine messages were concerned, but Milo only chuckled. "I don't know, Miss Priscilla. However, I can say with absolute certainty that whatever it is, it must be important."

ROUGH & TUMBLE

While you're waiting for *The Broken Window*, you can read more about angels and the Pomeroy family on Christa's website, ChristaKinde.com. ***Rough and Tumble*** is an adventurous continuation to the Threshold Series, about a young angel named Ethan, who's sent to serve with the other Guardians of the Hedge surrounding the Pomeroy family farm. One mischievous little boy is about to turn Ethan's life upside down!

At just one hundred words, chapters are small enough to read on the fly—with daily updates and new installments.

Become a subscriber at ChristaKinde.com!

We want to hear from you. Please send your comments about this book to us in care of zreview@zondervan.com. Thank you.

ZONDERVAN.com/
AUTHORTRACKER
follow your favorite authors